D1234244

Accessing the Future

A Disability-Themed Speculative Fiction Anthology

edited by

Kathryn Allan
&
Djibril al-Ayad

Futurefire.net Publishing

Accessing the Future
First published 2015 by Futurefire.net Publishing
All stories © 2015 the authors
Cover illustration © 2015 Robin E. Kaplan

Nicolette Barischoff's "Pirate Songs," A.C. Buchanan's "Puppetry," Joyce Chng's "The Lessons of the Moon," David Jón Fuller's "In Open Air," Louise Hughes's "Losing Touch," Rachael K. Jones's "Courting the Silent Sun," Margaret Killjoy's "Invisible People," Petra Kuppers's "Playa Song," Toby MacNutt's "Morphic Resonance," Jack Hollis Marr's "into the waters i rode down," Kate O'Connor's "Better to Have Loved," Sara Patterson's "A Sense All its Own," Sarah Pinsker's "Pay Attention," Samantha Rich's "Screens," A.F. Sanchez's "Lyric," the illustrations by Fabian Alvarado, L.E. Badillo, Jane Baker, Comebab, Pandalion Death, Rachel Keslensky, Vincent Konrad and Tostoini, JoSelle Vanderhooft's preface, the editors' introduction and Derek Newman-Stille's afterword are all published here for the first time, and are © the authors, 2015.

The Vulcan symbol ⚕ used as a section marker is set in the HamburgSymbols font, a public domain font from dafonts.com.

ISBN-print: 978-0-9573975-4-5
ISBN-electronic: 978-0-9573975-5-2

Contact:
editor@futurefire.net
http://futurefire.net/

Contents

Acknowledgements

We are very grateful to our generous copy-editors and proofreaders, Regina de Búrca, Maureen Kincaid Speller and Valeria Vitale.

Our eternal thanks to the many people who supported the fundraiser on IndieGogo, which enabled this anthology to happen at all: the 309 people who showed faith in this project by pre-ordering the book or contributing money to the campaign; the extremely kind people who helped to spread the word, wrote guest posts, interviewed us or allowed us to promote the campaign on their websites or networks, or donated rewards, especially Steven Gould, Nicola Griffith, Morgan J. Locke, Lyda Morehouse, Cheryl Morgan, Nisi Shawl, Maureen Kincaid Speller, Jo Thomas and Lynda Williams.

You're all rock stars, every one of you!

Preface
JoSelle Vanderhooft

The Future Will Be Accessible

My life is a familiar piece of science fiction. You probably know at least a dozen stories just like it. Extraterrestrial gets stranded on Earth. At first they're baffled and a little bit frightened by the culture, but they quickly learn to hide or disguise themselves by mimicking the behaviors of these strange new creatures—or else. "Else" usually being an evil government agency that does Bad Things to any non-human tourists. Reese's Pieces, Big Macs, and other product placements are optional, of course.

I'm saying this with my tongue firmly affixed to the inside of my cheek, mind you. On the other hand, being an alien in an alien land is such an accurate description my life that calling it a metaphor feels like lying. I imagine this sentiment might sound familiar to other disabled SF fans and creators, particularly if they, like I do, subscribe to the social model or personal-experience model of disability. To put it another way, although disability is a neutral but ultimately subjective part of the human condition, it is often one that can be isolating, frustrating, and even dangerous at times, given that we live in a world that expects bodies and minds to perform to certain standards and seems unable to cope when they don't.

As a product of this world, science fiction can be just as abled and ableist as anything else. If we subtract stories of disabilities as superpowers, or metaphor stories like those of homesick aliens (which aren't always explicitly about disability even though they may ring true to many disabled fans), we're often left with whole worlds and human futures that don't address us—or, more worryingly, suggest or outright state that we have been cured and/or eugenicised out of existence. Given the number of pioneering SF authors and creators who were disabled—or who, with today's medical knowledge might well identify as disabled and/or neurodivergent in particular—the ableism in SF is especially baffling and awful. Given the overwhelming number of disabled scientists—Leonardo Da Vinci, Thomas Edison, Stephen Hawking, and quite possibly Alan Turing to name only a few of the most recognizable—it becomes downright insulting and erasing. Currently, feminists respond to the "fake geek girl" phenomenon and sexism in fandom by reminding men that a woman wrote the first science fiction novel in the West, and that women organized the first fan-run SF conventions. I would likewise submit that disabled people remind the abled that the modern world they take for granted would not have been possible without our minds, our bodies, our genius.

For what is much of science and technology if not the ongoing pursuit of accommodations? Our human bodies and the systems that power them—even when "typical" and "healthy" by social standards—are fragile, prone to the damage of accident, the ravages of disease, the hostility of environment, and, ultimately, death. We can only survive comfortably within a laughably minuscule set of temperatures, so we create shelters, clothing, cooling and heating systems to keep from freezing or baking to death. To speak in less dramatic terms, our bodies are also not designed to travel hundreds of miles per hour, fly, and breathe underwater or at high altitudes. Yet, we have created accommodations to do all of the above.

Likewise, much of science fiction is, at its heart, the story of the search for accessibility or what happens when something we can't access now—outer space, time travel, telepathy—is or becomes accessible to us. Captain Nemo couldn't have explored the ocean or planned his revenge without his Nautilus; the Federation could not explore strange new worlds without their starships; the Doctor and his friends could not engage in timey-wimey shenanigans without his TARDIS backed by millennia of Time Lord science and tech.

However, the ultimate question in science fiction as in our nonfiction lives remains: accessible for whom? Just as few abled people see stairs, printed books, or air-conditioning as accommodations, starships, time travel, and telepathy largely remain the playgrounds of the abled. Not so, though, in the anthology before you. The fifteen stories herein center disabled people on every page, in every keystroke, in futures disarmingly likely and uncannily unfamiliar. And just like the futures from which they hail, no two of them are interchangeable—something that abled discourse has yet to understand.

Because life itself is a constant search for accommodation in an unaccommodating universe, many of these stories feature disabled people trying to navigate environments whose designs are anything but universal. When pirates save her from a wrecked space ship, the clever but coddled heroine of "Pirate Songs" must learn to navigate a ship—and a culture—that has never heard of spina bifida. An autistic in "Lyric" uses a program to communicate with the allistic (non-autistic) people around them while reaching out to a Frankenstein's monster of a creature that the neurotypical world can't figure out what to do with. Some are also critical of assistive technology—which, like all things in life, is not without its flaws. In "Screens," where the titular devices have made the invisible world of brain chemistry visible, our protagonist grapples with the question of whether this tech has made the world a more welcoming place for invisibly disabled people, or a more intrusive one. "Better to Have Loved" even goes as far as to question what defines a disability in a future that considers grief to be disabling and thus something to be gotten rid of. Where does the line fall, it asks, between a part of the human experience society defines as abnormal and one that would cause pain, suffering, and other "undesirable" effects even in the most accommodating of cultures?

Of course, no one spends 100 percent of their time thinking about or wrestling with accommodations, and not all stories about disabled people should be about such struggles. Some, for that matter, should also celebrate the talents endowed to disabled people by our disabilities. Throughout history, after all, we have been leaders and revolutionaries, philosophers and artists, titans and shapers of the world for centuries to come. And sometimes, perhaps more importantly, we have been average, everyday people whose differences and quiet acts of defiance have made all the difference. This is the case of an ordinary soldier in "Puppetry," an army doctor with ADHD in "Pay Attention," a legally blind pilot of fighter robots in "A Sense all Its Own," and a mother who can barely move enough to leave her bed yet who changes her body—like the moon itself—to save her family in "The Lessons of the Moon."

I would be remiss to finish the preface to this astounding anthology without mentioning the other ways in which it is diverse. One continuous problem of disability activism—at least in the United States, where I'm from—is its failure to resemble and include the people it represents. As in many other movements for social change, those taken more seriously by doctors, commentators, and other authorities are frequently white, male, cisgender, heterosexual, not immigrants, and at least vaguely Christian in practice or heritage. Few of the people in *Accessing the Future* fit all or even a few of the above. Many are girls or women—and women in STEM or military fields in particular; some are of no specific gender; many are lesbian, gay, or bisexual; and many are of color. If we are ever to make any significant gains as disabled individuals, we must prioritize the stories of disabled people who are also oppressed because of sex, sexuality, gender identity, race, economic status, immigrant status, or other marginalized identities—both in fiction and in our nonfictional everyday lives. The book before you is, I think, a strong movement toward a vision of accessibility that truly typifies the motto "nothing about us without us."

A part of me would like to say, in closing, that I felt a little less alien after reading these unforgettable stories. To a degree, this is true, as the stories of people like us often have that effect. More accurately, though, I think that I am now more comfortable in my alienness for the experience. Chances are, I will never feel entirely at home in a world where my needs for accessibility are often dismissed as "special treatment," "laughable," or even "cheating." But you know what? Being an alien isn't necessarily bad. It can be a neutral thing—or even a good thing. In any case, it isn't a reason to hide away or try to become something that I simply am not.

May all our futures be so positive, so accessible.

Ft. Lauderdale, FL
March 2015

Introduction
Kathryn Allan & Djibril al-Ayad

Disability, like all assumptions of what is and is not "normal," is defined by society's expectations—it is not a person's ability or impairment but the willingness of our culture to include and accommodate all people that draws the line between disadvantage and accessibility.

In other words, disability is located, not at the site of the individual, but at the site of culture and society. When we imagine an accessible future, the question is not how should any one disabled person change to fit (or, even worse, be eliminated from) that future, but how can society adapt to that person and all people.

⚐

One of the questions that we were asked during the campaign to crowdfund this professional-rate anthology was why were we interested in editing a volume of disability-themed speculative fiction (SF). The initial answer to the question was relatively simple: we want to see more SF stories that feature people with disabilities as three-dimensional characters, as people who have strengths and flaws, who succeed and fail, dream and scheme, as they are and as they want to be (and not as flat inspirations or as nightmare villains for an able-bodied audience). In addition to this response, however, was our desire to move disability into the larger "We Need Diverse Books" conversation. As disability still largely bears the aura of "something not to talk about," there are too few mainstream conversations that address disability identity with words and insights from people with disabilities themselves. We want to open up the conversation to challenge what (especially able-bodied) people think of when "disability" is raised. Each of the fifteen stories in *Accessing the Future* deals with some aspect or aspects of what it means to identify as disabled and how the experience of being disabled impacts the ways a person moves in and interacts with the larger world. In addition, the eight illustrations (and our cover art) tell stories of their own in order to further open up the anthology to people who are better able to engage with and think about disability through pictures than through words.

When we first put out the call for submissions (CFS) we were excited by the prospect of stories that would rewrite or revisit our personal favourite genres—feminist SF and especially cyberpunk. As such, the CFS included a call for stories that might feature future assistive technologies and the different kinds of environments—even virtual—that we might inhabit in the near or far futures. As the stories began rolling in, we noticed that those narratives that spoke most saliently to disability and disabled peoples in the future went beyond the mere rejection of "technology as cure" (a common trope in SF that we explicitly sought to avoid); instead, the stories we loved the most were challenging the role of technology in making lives "easier" and thinking through the limitations of technological or pharmacological "fixes."

One of the goals of this anthology is to express the right of people with disabilities to have self-determination of their lives. While it is important for many disabled people to have independence, it is not the goal for all. Self-determination, unlike independence, underscores agency and, at the same time, recognizes that people rely on one another for care, employment, and fulfilment. We wanted to see stories that explored the different kinds of relationships that sustain us as we make our way through a world that is at times hostile and challenging. Who gets to choose the future we will shape and live in? That question needs to be one that is shared and answered by us all.

While *Accessing the Future* places disabled bodies and minds at the centre of the stories (rather than side-lining them as interesting or moral asides in tales about the able-bodied), it is also concerned with how disability interacts with other aspects of disadvantage, privilege, discrimination and bigotry, including gender, race, sexuality, nationality, class and so many more of the facets that make us each unique. It has always been pleasantly surprising, in the previous Futurefire.net anthologies as much as in this one, that so many of the best stories we receive are effortlessly intersectional. Authors who write from a position of knowledge, experience or sensitivity to these issues know not only that no single vector of discrimination works in isolation, but also that it is precisely those people who are marginalized or disenfranchised in multiple ways whose lives are made the most difficult by the discrimination and neglect of the most privileged in society.

☥

During our editorial process, we challenged each other on what made a story suitable for the this anthology. We were both attuned to the necessity of pushing the boundaries of what most people think constitutes disability and what it means to be disabled. As we read through the submissions, we were reminded of two important things: (1) the power and necessity of art to provoke; and (2) that SF is always about today. And so the stories we have gathered here are about people with disabilities in all of their complexity and diversity. There is no one way to be disabled; and there is no one way to feel or act on one's disability. The stories and images of *Accessing the Future* are not here to pacify an audience who may be uncomfortable with disability but to share disabled people's stories of disability in all their wonder and sadness, hope and rage. We wanted stories of adventure and failure (because it's the determination to act that matters); stories that scream with the passion and intensity of someone who knows what it is to suffer or face discrimination (but who refuses to be made to disappear because it would be "better" for their condition to be "cured" in the future). These are stories that refuse to go gently.

Throughout this anthology surprises await. In our call for stories, we wondered about assistive technology and imagined high-tech futures—and so Nicolette Barischoff's "Pirate Songs" gives us a story of a teenage girl who has spina bifida but is *without* her wheelchair when taken aboard a ship of space pirates (where she holds her own); and Fabian Alvarado's "Julienne the Technician" gracefully does her job with no extra tools (or arms) needed. Margaret Killjoy's "Invisible People" and Toby MacNutt's "Morphic Resonance" bring us new takes on cyberpunk. Both stories remind us that it isn't technology that sets us free but our resolution to take risks despite fear and the importance of finding like-minded allies. And while people in the future will make use of prosthetic limbs, it doesn't mean being turned into Terminators: in "To the Pitch," L.E. Badillo's grandfather with his prosthetic foot could be right at home in a Norman Rockwell painting; the augmented and prosthesis-wearing woman in Rachel Keslensky's "Need More Coffee" recalls the seemingly effortless allure of the 1950s pin-up girl; and Jane Baker's "High Handed" shows us that when we work together with creativity, we can solve problems that at first appear out of reach.

At times, the challenges we face are of the "everyday" kind and we must decide on how to face them. In "Better to Have Loved," Kate O'Connor imagines a world that has become uncomfortable with even the temporarily disabling experience of grieving the loss of someone loved. The more narrowly we define "normal" and "not normal" bodies, minds, and experiences, the more inaccessible life becomes. Louise Hughes's "Losing Touch" takes us into the far future when even what counts as human is in danger of being lost entirely to technology, while Tostoini's "Everyday Future" ambiguously features a woman who is in the process of (re)creating herself. In order to surpass barriers—whether environmental or intra-personal—the stories in this anthology underscore the need for us to come together. Petra Kupper's

"Playa Song," Comebab's "A Future Without Pain," and Vincent Conrad's "Future Coffee" all show how different kinds of people are able to talk to one another and work towards shared goals (and mutual survival against steep odds).

As it does today, technology will help us achieve our dreams, whether they are those that stem from individual ambition, like in Sara Patterson's "A Sense All its Own," whose blind protagonist wants to be the best pilot when everyone else tells her she can't, or a collective desire to explore new worlds against competing, but still very human, interests as in David Jón Fuller's "In Open Air." Of course, technology does not come with easy answers (or even instructions): in "Pay Attention," Sarah Pinker's cognitively-augmented military vet must find her way in a civilian world that is rapidly changing; and in "Screens," Samantha Rich complicates the benefits that might come with wearable tech that makes our "invisible" disabilities visible. And although the potential for continued exploitation of people with disabilities will exist in the future, it doesn't mean that we won't fight back. Both A.C. Buchanan's "Puppetry" and Rachael K. Jones' "Courting the Silent Sun" tell the stories of individuals who embrace their disability identity and turn themselves into vessels of leadership, change and hope. And the disabled protagonists in Joyce Chng's "The Lessons of the Moon," Jack Hollis Marr's "into the waters i rode down," and A.F. Sanchez's "Lyric" do not succumb to the pressures of those people who claim to have their best interests at heart—in each story, they subvert expectations of what's "normal" and carry out their own deep, conflicted understandings of what it means to live (and die) well.

Communication about and appreciation for our diverse experiences is essential for an accessible future. These are stories that recognize sometimes a person with disabilities has privilege in other areas of their identity, that neither cancel the disability nor negate the privilege. Some of these are stories in which people with disabilities are as strong and skilled as anyone else, or more so, although they're not super-powered "magical PWDs." These are stories in which choice, some-times including the choice not to have our disabilities cured (or not in the ways that are intended), is fiercely fought for and defended. In both the stories and illustrations, people with disabilities engage with the world around them on their own terms—sometimes acting with quick cleverness and at other times with heavy hearts. *Accessing the Future* is just as much about everyday trials (the bad hair days and annoying friends) as it is about grand adventures and plots of revolution in far off places.

☥

One of the reasons we chose the cover image that Robin E. Kaplan so beautifully created for the anthology is because our space woman *isn't* visibly marked as "disabled." We've as many stories about "invisible" disabilities (anxiety disorder, depression, chronic illness) and neuroatypicality (autism) as we do ones with physical impairments (and wheelchair use and prosthesis). To focus on one kind of disability would not be representative of all the kinds of bodies and minds that are in the stories. We like that the single person (with her expression of calmness and contentment), weightless in space, challenges our conceptions of what disability looks like: in a weightless environment, someone with limited mobility issues, or sight or hearing impairment, would look just as the person depicted on our cover. It's the new environment—literally, space—that has changed what counts, or what appears, as disability.

Speculative fiction offers us a peek into what is possible for our world and for our bodies (and minds). It is essential that we imagine futures where we all belong; where our differences in life experience and our knowledge of our communities and of ourselves informs a future that is diverse and adaptable to the needs of all those who will live in it. Disability (as a negative condition) will always be with us if we choose to limit or ignore people's ability to participate as equal visionaries. *Accessing the Future* is one small part of this necessary, on-going conversation. The future is what we make it. All are welcome here.

Pirate Songs

Nicolette Barischoff

The floater turned out to be one of those shiny, sky island multi-deck passenger deals that would occasionally completely lose its shit in the middle of a jump.

This one would have been alright—various backup systems humming away, fifty or sixty first-colony licensed pilots determined to discover just what went wrong—had it not jumped straight into something else. Probably a garbage scow; there were a lot of garbage scows this far out. Now, the ship just drifted, listing and rolling like a fat, pretty corpse.

The Dustpan's crew all had their faces flat against the port windows, eyeing it like a bunch of dogs with tongues out. That was the only reason Rumer had let them go salvage. You pass up a big, beautiful floater like that, you never get your men to do anything useful ever again.

We don't got the time or space to pull her apart, he'd told them. No scrapping. Get yourselves something small and shiny and get back.

For the most part, they'd listened, filling up their suit-packs with the sorts of little things you always find on a floating hotel like that; alcohol in expensive-looking bottles, VR games with an obscene number of attachments, the palm and wrist PCs that were only considered valuable out here where nobody could afford them. Bottles and needles from a well-stocked sick bay, cards, cash, the turtles out of an elaborate terrarium... Kell, the mutinous asshole, had tried to haul back two of those sultry-voiced concierge kiosks, and a broken servitor droid.

Rumer wasn't sure which of them had brought back the girl.

She looked to be about fifteen, but to Rumer Pilgrim, anybody not born and raised out of New Pelican looked young.

She didn't have to be conscious to tell you she was far from home, either Earth or first colonies... German, Canadian, American, some single-nation settlement; she was that same kind of glass-house pretty. Well fed, with pale, untouched, swany skin, and a long, long waterfall of hair that somebody brushed out for her every morning, and a pale pink mouth that looked like it was used to pouting. When her eyes did flicker open for a split-second at a time, he could see they were a pale and brittle green.

The crew crowded around that narrow infirmary bunk for a full day and a half. Diallo, a skinny kid from the pan-Africas with half a field medic's education and a permanent shit-eating grin, actually left the pilot's chair to bandage her head wound. And Kell, the lecherous one-eyed bulldog of a first mate, seemed to think he was going to wake her by flicking her nipples.

"Haven't even seen one like her in a while," he said, rubbing his scrap glass eye, a sort of endearing nervous tic once you got to know him. "Kind of forgot they made 'em like this."

"With two eyes and two whole titties?" said Diallo. "Not every woman's like your New Pelican dock-workers, Kell. Back up, man, an' stop gettin' in the light. This one's never seen anything ugly as you."

Kell grinned. "I'm sure she'll just love that child-fucker smile you got."

Rumer ignored their dick-swinging. "Who brought her?" he asked.

Diallo shrugged. "She was the only thing alive on that boat, Captain, her and that mess o' turtles."

Rumer frowned. "Bad time to have a hitchhiker, you forget that already? What're you thinking we're gonna do with her when we have to make our drop?"

"Don't ask me," said Kell. "You ask me, we shouldn't have the stuff in the first place."

"Right. But I didn't ask you, and we do have the stuff, and we're going to have to make a drop before much else happens."

"You mean before the shit's no damn good to anybody, or before big Papa Kang figures out who took it and sends a team after us? Because I can guarantee you that second thing's already happened."

"I'm thinking, Captain," said Diallo, making the sort of diplomatic silencing gesture that made Rumer like him, "she is very far from home. She might help. With carrying, with distribution. In exchange for passage, you know."

Rumer cocked his head. Nodded.

"It's useful to have someone who looks like her, where we are going, what we are doing. People trust someone who looks like that. Nice pretty white face. They'll take it from her. No need to tell her where it comes from."

"So she plays little White Mother for us, we put her down wherever she wants, she goes on home having gratefully agreed to tell nobody, and everybody's happy and still alive, is that it?"

Diallo grinned wide and white. "She won't even have a ship's name to tell her mother."

"It might work," said Rumer. "If we don't run into any transit police or any Peacekeeping Officers she feels like chatting to."

"Why would she talk to any Blueberries?" asked Diallo. "Why leave the ship at all? We are just some nice men of varying degrees of handsomeness taking her to port."

Kell laughed at that, his loud bulldog bark. "I'll agree with that! Why leave the ship at all? Hell, I'll teach her to have fun sittin' in one spot."

"You'll wait 'til she's awake, you ugly fuck," said Rumer. "If she don't immediately bite your balls off and run screaming from your very presence."

Kell laughed again, louder and longer. Rumer turned to Diallo.

"She'll get her ride, but she'll have to work. You think you can get her to work?"

Diallo paused. The girl's green eyes flickered open. And she sat up.

Or rather, she tried to sit up, squirming strangely for several minutes before going limp, and saying, in a slightly strained voice: "Could one of you please help me up?"

Nobody moved for a second. Diallo took her by the arm, and when that proved insufficient, grabbed her by the armpits, and propped her against the corner. Her feet were bare, and her legs dangled off the edge of the bunk, limp and pale. "Thank you," she said.

Diallo answered with a nod.

The girl looked around her, not exactly frightened. Not exactly. But looking a little like she'd been thrown into an icy gray lake, and was just now bringing her head up out of the water to discover which of them had done it to her. "Who... What... happened? Where is this?"

Rumer thought it best to let her have it all at once. "I am the more-or-less captain, Rumer Pilgrim, and you are currently a passenger aboard my ship, this streamlined and classically engineered cargo vessel you see before you."

"Why...?"

"Well, young lady, because your own is presently floating through deep space like a chunk of particularly metal-rich frozen shit. Now, I don't know who you are, and I don't really care to. But you've got to know that we've gone pretty well out of our way to pick you up. Now, I didn't mind doing it, and you're welcome. We'll drop you off soon as we're able, anyplace you want to be, so long as it's not a place where people are likely to get up in our business. But before that happens... what?"

The girl was shaking her head, green eyes dry. "The ship, I was just... how did...?" She blinked, touched her head bandage, and suddenly settled on a question. "Your name's Rumer Pilgrim?"

"That's right."

"That's your real name?"

Rumer frowned. "Never had another."

There was the smallest flick of a smile on that pink mouth. "So your name is actually 'Pilgrim, Pilgrim'."

"No." Rumer Pilgrim looked at her with narrower eyes than he intended. "No, and I can't say I know what you're playing at."

The girl's smile widened the littlest bit. "Nothing. Never mind."

"Young lady, if you'd rather not ride with us…"

"No, no. It's fine. Thank you… Thank you."

Rumer nodded.

She let out a somewhat shuddering breath of air. She looked around. "Sorry… can I have my chair, please? Where did you put my chair?"

Rumer blinked. Blinked again. "What chair?"

Margo had been busy hiding when the crash occurred.

She was trying to find a way to get lost and freeze to death inside the "Antarctic Exploration" levels of the ship's educational Ages of Earth VR. You never could get really lost, of course. Margo knew that. Even the game's wrong turns and avalanches and blinding snowstorms were all part of a network of programmed paths with beginnings, middles and ends.

But on the outgoing flight, a kid who'd been angling to get a ride in her chair had tried to convince her that if you wandered far away enough from all the computer-generated explorers and the Prince Charles Mountains and the penguins, ignoring the game's copious temperature warnings and the automatic chattering of your teeth, the VR would give you a slow and dramatic "death" on the spectacularly shimmering ice.

She'd read everything interesting on the ship's library terminal, and at least half-watched all the films available in the tiny holo-theater, and the VR terminals were the only other place the servitors couldn't follow her.

It had been a full two weeks of dodging the servitors. Everywhere, the servitors.

Margo had brought one droid for the return journey from Polis. Her mother had supplied the ship with the other ten. One to three of them were always hovering nearby, chirpy little orbs of plastic and metal that went into fits of attentiveness every time their sensors detected movement: "Hello. Do you need assistance? What would you like to do? Please repeat what you would like to do. If you don't know what you would like to do, I can make suggestions. The time is now 12:30. Are you hungry? If you'd like, I can access the network to tell you what is currently available in the kitchen…"

It had been her mother's idea of Margo "traveling alone." Most of the swarm even had the UN Sky logo painted on them, just in case anyone was not aware they were handling a diplomat's daughter. Every corridor she went down, every room she entered, her mother's re-appropriated machines followed, causing nearly everybody to give her and the chair an artificially wide berth.

It was exactly like she was nine years old again, the only kid in her UN-run classroom flanked by droids that were programmed to answer her questions, and pick up things she let fall, and keep her schedule, and re-purify her water, and silently alert the teacher if she, Margo, wet herself.

And so, fifteen-year-old Margo had regressed a bit, sending the servitors to run baths or make sandwiches or compile obscure information she didn't want. Luring them into closets and cupboards and password-protecting the doors. She'd even managed to send a servitor sailing into a wall of its own accord, which she hadn't done in years.

And hiding. Lots of hiding. The nice thing about servitors is that if you tell them you want to spend all remaining 10 hours of the journey harassing allosauruses in the Jurassic United States, or deliberately trying to freeze to death in early 20th century Antarctica, they don't ask you if you'd rather be doing something more constructive with your time.

It was probably being all strapped in to the VR system that saved her life. She didn't feel the crash. She didn't hear or see the crash. Her only thought as everything around her went blinding white, was that something interesting was finally happening in her game.

And when she opened her eyes next, what she saw was the factory-made steel ceiling of the dirtiest, dankest little room she'd ever been in.

⚓

She wouldn't stop talking about the chair, even after Rumer told her they hadn't picked anything like that up. "Are you sure? Are you *sure*? It has a call function, it'll come right to me." Like she thought they'd find it tucked away in the corner of the cargo bay if they just looked hard enough.

When, after about a half hour, the girl was convinced they were not hiding the damn thing from her, she seemed to think they were going back for it. Even Kell's outright laugh did not cure her of that delusion. "How long was I out?" she asked. "It didn't feel like that long. It couldn't possibly be that big a jump from here to there."

"You were out for more than a day," said Rumer. "And we don't jump, much as that might surprise you."

"What do you mean?" Such confusion in that voice, and a little bit of rancor, too. Rumer supposed that's how it was with first-colony girls. Kell saved him from having to answer.

"This ship don't jump, coochie, she's just an old dustpan ramjet. She's got no drive."

"What do you use a ship without a drive for?" the girl asked, genuinely curious.

"Oh, you're shittin' me," muttered Kell.

"Nothing has drive out here, young lady. Nobody can afford it," said Rumer Pilgrim, and then off her open stare, "Around here, we just stay close to home, and make sure that our most valued possessions don't end up somewhere where we can't get to 'em in a hurry."

The girl squirmed on the bunk, looked around for Diallo. Not finding him, she looked to the floor, gauging the distance. "I have spina bifida," she said, tightly. "That means I'm missing spine."

"Missing spine," repeated Rumer. Kell caught his eye.

"So, you can probably guess I don't really get around too well without that chair." Then, after a pause, "There are people in my life who would kind of freak out if they knew I was without it."

Kell laughed again, baldly. Jesus, the little bitch was actually making threats, or at least toying with the idea. She wasn't practiced enough at it to know to be specific.

"I am sorry about that," said Rumer. "You'll all just have to work that out, won't you, amongst yourselves. Listen, now. What did you say your name was?"

She hadn't. "Margo," she said, now.

"Just Margo?"

The girl's lips pinched together. She looked warily at Kell. "For now," she said.

Rumer couldn't help smiling a little. "Okay. Margo. Listen now, Margo. Even were I to feel such an inclination, and I don't, to track a free-floating ship through space would take days we don't have and don't want. Now, we've got our own rather time-sensitive business to see to, which you have interrupted…" Rumer put up a finger to stop her speaking, "So you'll want to keep your head down and let us finish with that, and then we'll see about dropping you at a port when we can get to one. And as I said before, you're welcome."

The brittle green eyes blinked.

"Now, where is it you'd like to be just now? Floor? I'm afraid it's the floor or the infirmary bunk, until we can find you a free hammock."

She nodded. He picked her up and sat her on the floor. She sat there with her legs oddly tucked under her, and watched the men (his sweaty, scarred and hardened crew) file out and go back to work. All except Kell, who stood there alternately scratching ass and eye. "How far out are we?" she asked suddenly.

"Far out?"

"Of major colonized space. Of UN space."

Kell barked. "Coochie, you are right smack in the middle of UN space. There's Peacekeeping Officers all over this vacuum..." Rumer passed him a look, and he shut his mouth.

Margo's brow furrowed uncertainly, and she looked at the deeply rusted gray of the ship around her, at Kell's cloudy piece of scrap glass, as though prepared to contradict. "You can just drop me at a station, then," she said, finally.

"Can I, now?"

"The officers will know who I am," she said.

Rumer watched Kell watch her drag herself from the room, legs out, across the factory steel floor. With effort, she turned herself around in the doorway. "Do I have a room?" she asked.

"Anywhere where there's no one to kick you out."

Margo nodded, the flick of a smile reappearing. "Anyone going to literally kick me?"

"If they do, you lay yourself out flat. Mess is in an hour if you want it."

The girl drew herself up, recoiling a little. "I can wait. I'll wait until a station." And she dragged herself away.

"Fuckin' hell," Kell said. "Fuckin' shit."

⚓

Margo did manage to find a long, rusted metal cupboard in a large utility closet that none of the crew was yet sleeping in. With two of the synthetic wool blankets and three very fibrous pillows, it was almost a bedroom. There was even a steel door that slid noisily open and closed, and made a locking sound when you hit the right button.

Not that the door did her much good. The men (the ones who weren't afraid of her) still went in and out like the closet was wide open. For the first couple of days, they bothered with pretext, coming in to fish around amongst the jumbles of cord, and replacement switches, and lengths of as-yet un-rusted wire. But that didn't last long.

There came a period of relative privacy after Captain Pilgrim Pilgrim picked a man to guard the door, and told the worst offenders to stop being quite so pervy, or expect double-shifts. That didn't last long either.

Now almost every one of them, including the man supposedly assigned to the door, came in at least twice a day to have a good, grinning gape at whatever she was doing. When that got boring, they'd try to get her to talk.

"You ever get freaky in that chair you miss so much? Is it good for that?"

"There's buttons on it I've never pushed."

"So it could be good for that."

"We'll never know."

"You feel anything down there?"

"I feel enough."

"You ever been with a man who's sewed back on his own arm?"

"No."

"Would you like to?"

"Not especially. Can you sew other things, or just your arm?"

Margo wasn't bothered, she decided, since being bothered never seemed to do very much. Nobody else on this ship went behind a door to strip their rank clothes off, or smell their own belches, or scratch their ass-cracks. Why should she?

At any rate, she'd learned pretty quickly to stop asking for things. The one time she'd asked about the number of servitors on board, they had laughed for what seemed like an hour. "People who use those servitors get to love them a little too much," Pilgrim Pilgrim had said. "Embrace your liberation."

"*I've* never loved them," said Margo, "I grew up with swarms of them, it drove me fucking nuts. I used to send them smashing into walls just to see if I could do it."

"I believe you," he said, in a way that told her that wasn't the right thing to say to someone like him.

And when she'd asked where the toilets were, he'd gone into another dark narrow, metal closet where he lifted up the false floor to reveal the dark, deep, seatless hole.

"How do I use that?" she'd asked, a little pale.

"How did you sit the toilet in that big, fancy cruiser before it broke?" he asked.

"It had a seat-back, and armrests, and a fall-guard. And… I usually have droids."

"Same general principle," he'd said in an absolutely unbearable voice. "Squat, let loose, and get well out the way before you flush."

(She did end up doing it, a full hour and ten minutes later, squatted on all fours with her dress up over her head, one leg on either side of the hole. She felt marvelously defiant, even as she emerged to a round of sarcastic applause from the crew.)

Margo had fully intended to keep to her closet-room as much as possible until they'd come to a UN Sky station. But whenever she asked Diallo, the grinning pilot, how close he thought the nearest one was, he would call her a little dictator and offer her some of his reconstituted soup (the sort of lumped up stuff that poor people ate before there were food labs). Also, Pilgrim Pilgrim and his one-eyed first mate seemed to be much more comfortable when she stayed put, and Margo didn't see any reason to make them comfortable.

So, she dragged herself all around that filthy, rusted-out ramjet, seeing what she could see.

They were hiding something. Margo had figured out that much. They were carrying something—in the cargo bay, maybe elsewhere too—that they didn't want found. There were a few too many halted conversations to ignore. A few too many badly suppressed glances in her direction.

Not that they were afraid of *her* finding it, necessarily. Even if they'd known who she was, she doubted it would mean anything to most of them. Most stepped right around her and carried on with their work when she crawled by, looking down to grin at her only when she called out cheerfully to keep from being stepped on.

But Kell and Captain Pilgrim had guessed something about her. The captain would straighten when he saw her, and ask her if there were any particular reason she needed to be there, wherever there happened to be. And Kell, whenever he came on her by accident, usually turned directly around and walked in the opposite direction.

"You don't let it bother you," Diallo had tried to tell her. "You must excuse a degenerate like Kell. Raised on a prison colony, the American kind. No hope of learning good manners, no experience with women. His mother was not a very successful prostitute."

Margo smirked. "How can you be raised in a prison colony?"

Diallo shrugged. "Perhaps his mother was also a less than successful terrorist. I can't claim to know."

Margo studied his smile a moment. "But there are no prison colonies anymore."

"No?"

"Not in UN space," she said, sounding like a teacher even to herself. "The Security Council ruled a long time ago that abandoning prisoners on far-world correctional colonies constitutes inhumane punishment. The ruling was just upheld again the year I was born. It's illegal."

Diallo smiled, or at least showed his teeth. "That is comforting to know. Thank you."

"It's true."

"I'm sure you're right."

"That's the whole point of UN Sky. To make sure stuff like that doesn't happen."

Diallo was silent for a moment, and then said, with irritating slowness, "As you say. It does seem to me that people will always discover a place to put away the things they do not want, so that they don't come back again. But I've never been very clever with names."

Later, while she lay in her bunk trying to think of all the things criminals would not want UN Peacekeepers to find in their cargo bay (nukes, sonics, VX gas, high-power low-precision lasers?), Margo could not help thinking about Kell's glass eye.

People without eye donors had biomechanical eyes. They had microchipped acrylic ones. At the very least, Margo had always thought, they had those plastic boxy pieces that you had to keep a cap on at night to block out images while you slept.

When you were Kell, on a faraway colony, and you knocked your eye out, what had to go wrong, what had to break down, before you fashioned your own out of whatever you could find, and carried on?

⚔

"Someone's taken an interest in us," was the first thing Diallo said when Rumer came on to the bridge.

"Peacekeepers, or the Kang family fun squad? Or both?"

"It's difficult to say. She's not marked. And she is keeping her distance."

"Blueberries," said Kell. "Gotta be. You've heard that bitch talk. She knows somebody."

Rumer ignored him. "Can you signal-cloak us?"

"I have done, of course," said Diallo. "But I cannot do it long, and eventually she finds us. Very quietly persistent."

"Keep on it 'til you shake her. She don't want us that bad, or she'd be on us already. We make our drop, even if we gotta pour it down there like manna."

Diallo nodded, and bent over his joysticks.

"About that," said Kell, rubbing his eye.

"About that," said Rumer.

"What're you thinking you're gonna do with her? Our hitchhiker, I mean?"

Rumer shrugged. "I don't know as I have a whole lot of options. We take her with us far as we can, drop her at the first opportunity, and hope she has the good sense not to talk to anybody."

"You don't mean you're still gonna take her on the drop?" Kell looked entertainingly uncomfortable. "Jesus, Rumer, she's not... she can't even... plus, you heard her, she's dyin' to talk to the police. She thinks police are like… service dogs, or somethin'.'"

"Don't shit yourself, soldier. We drop her at Black Oven before anything else happens. It's backworld enough no one's going to care why we're there, and she can go about her business, and we about ours."

"Pretty outta our way, isn't it, Black Oven?"

"Everything's out of our way. What do you suggest?"

Kell shifted a little. "Hey, I'd just like to remind you, but we got about two tons a' very perishable cargo down there, and there's some very angry Koreans want it back. This was your idea, this thing. I wanted to do something small, something normal that'd make us a little fuckin' money. You're the one who wanted to go all Wyatt Earp Robin Hood…"

"What do you suggest, Kell?"

"Well," Kell hesitated. "Well, have you thought maybe we just… maybe we just get rid a' her?"

"How the hell you want to do that?"

"I don't know, man…"

"Yeah, you do, asshole."

"Look, she woulda' been dead anyway if we hadn't picked her up, that's all I'm tryin' to say. Just, in the interest of the cargo. I'm not saying exactly we should, you know…"

"What are you saying, exactly, you fuckin' moron?"

"I'm saying, you know, maybe, we put her in one of the shuttles, with some food, if you want, and we just…" Kell mimed the dustpan's tiny shuttle drifting harmlessly away into space.

Rumer smirked, despite himself. "I thought you wanted to fuck her."

Kell recoiled like he was standing too close to a serial kiddie-diddler. "She's in a *chair*, man, don't even joke. That's some sick shit."

Rumer rolled his eyes. "Turn the temp down in cargo and head for Black Oven," he said to Diallo. "She's clever enough to catch her own ride from there, I expect."

Å

Margo wasn't going to let them continue to have their muttering, panicked, poorly-buried talks around her as though she didn't understand what they meant. From now on, she would be where they were. If they wanted to continue having conversations about their secret black hole machine, or whatever, they'd have to do it while she was in the room.

That was Margo's reasoning for finally joining them at dinner.

They had boiled the turtles, neatly diced, in four tins of reconstituted cream of tomato soup. Chin-Hae, the ship's cook, who was alternately sipping beer out of his prosthetic leg and adding it to the pot, looked up grinning when she appeared. Margo hadn't known that anyone still ate turtles. But then, until this voyage, she hadn't known there were spaceships that couldn't leave immediate space, or people who replaced their vital members with removable plastic and bottle-glass.

The mess turned out to be two long metal tables bolted to the floor. The men crowded around them on one-footed metal benches and passed stories and sloshing carafes of beer. Every one of them had scars they bragged about, and for the first time, Margo wondered whether this was because they really took any pride in them, or because they lacked the technology to remove and forget them.

Pilgrim Pilgrim looked up at her. "Come to eat, or just watch?" he asked.

"Eat."

"Waitin' on the servitors?"

"No." Though Margo realized as she said it, that she had been.

The captain tossed her down a thick wooden bowl. "Queue up and get yourself some turtle surprise, before this mess of rapists and degenerates eats it all."

Margo paused, then dragged herself to the back of the line forming in front of Chin-Hae's pot. When it was her turn, Chin-Hae winked at her, a little drunkenly, and filled her bowl to the brim, tilting in a little extra beer from the bottom of his leg.

He intended this as a kindness, she was sure, but it meant that she had to make her way to the tables pushing along a wildly sloshing bowl of oily turtle meat. The whole crew watched, apparently entertained, while she left a splash trail. Margo stopped at the benches. "You're gonna want to help me up," she said.

"Sure a' that, are you?" said Kell.

"Pretty sure," she said, evenly.

No one moved, so Margo proceeded to get up onto the bench herself. She couldn't put weight onto her legs, but if she lunged forward violently enough, the one-footed bench rocked, no matter who was sitting on it. If she did that enough times, eventually the drunkest lost his balance; the man who'd sewed his own arm back on fell straight backwards, which made everyone laugh too hard. "All right, all right..." He picked her up under the armpits and stuck her in his own seat. "Christ, you're a shit."

Diallo cut Margo a thick slice of very brown bread for her soup. Rumer Pilgrim poured her a cup from the carafe, and raised his own, almost imperceptibly. Margo flattened the smile on her lips.

Before long, Chin-Hae brought out a very motor-oil looking

whiskey, and some apples and pears in tin cups, roasted without cinnamon or sugar. "Enjoy these, gentlemen," said Pilgrim, frowning at the fruit, and Chin-Hae. "They're the only ones you're like to get out of the bunch."

"We're damn well going to have some," said Kell. "They cost us enough."

"Why?" asked Margo.

"'Scuse me?"

"Why would you pay for apples? What kind are they?"

No one answered her. "Are they rare, or something? They look like lab apples." The fruit was just exactly like the smallish, slightly underripe specimens that came out of every food lab in every corner of every galaxy in UN space.

The captain paused, then said, eyes on Kell, "That could be considered rare enough for some folks."

Margo knew a little history. "Sure, but... not anymore, though. People don't pay for stuff like that anymore."

"Stuff like what, do you suppose?"

"Like, fruit, or grains, or simple proteins. That's the whole point of food labs. You're always replicating, so there's no food shortages, and nobody has to pay."

Pilgrim nodded. "Well, that's a cracker-jack idea if I ever heard one."

"It's part of the rules of compliance for a colony's admission to the UN." That terrible, smug, teachery voice, again. Margo couldn't seem to help herself.

The captain took a swig of his whiskey. "But it only works long as everybody plays by the rules, long as nobody takes more'n they need."

Margo nodded, conceding.

"So, to your knowledge, who runs these food labs? Who maintains them? Who stops people takin' more than they need?"

"There's... private companies," said Margo. "They're vetted by the UN."

"Family companies?"

"Sometimes."

"And so what stops a real powerful company, a real powerful *family* from... gettin' creative? Say they start to decide for themselves who needs what. Say they start thinking they'd like to bring a little money back into it, or they'd like to put a limit on, I don't know, milk, for certain families with too many kids? You could keep a whole solar-system full of folks currying your sweet favor, if you went about it the right way."

"That would never be allowed to happen," said Margo.

"Why not?"

"Because it wouldn't! Because there's audits of compliance. There's officers who come and make sure you're following all the rules."

"And how well do those work out here, do you think?"

"How well do they *work*?"

"You think they work well here in our dark neck of the woods? I'm just asking."

"I don't know." Margo's voice was way too tight in her throat. "I don't know where we are."

Rumer Pilgrim nodded. "Alright. Do you think every man always does exactly the job he's supposed to, even when there's no one to watch him do it, even when he's far from home, in a place he can't stand?"

"Are you talking about Peacekeeping Officers?"

"I'm just talking about men. There's a lot of men sent to do their jobs in the very deep dark of space where nothing thrives and no sound travels. How easy you think it would be for our family—this very powerful hypothetical family we're talking of—to have a few such men in their pocket?"

"Somebody would say something," asserted Margo, more loudly than she meant to. "Somebody would alert Sky headquarters."

"They might," said the captain levelly. "If they had any idea how to go about it. And if they didn't mind a slow kind a' death. Starving's slower than just about anything, you know. Your body holds on like a muther, eating away at all your fat, and then all your muscle…"

Margo stared at him, her stomach pitching with understanding she didn't want. "What are you hiding in the cargo bay?" she blurted. "Who's looking for it?"

Pilgrim paused, opened his mouth. Margo didn't want to give him the chance to lie. "My name is Margo Glass. I'm Helena Glass's daughter. *I'm the daughter of a UN Security Council member, you stupid motherfuckers!* If somebody's breaking the law, if they're starving people, you have to tell me. Understand? *You have to tell me!*"

"Young lady," said the captain, but didn't say anything more.

"Say it!" Margo was suddenly snarling. "Say what you've got in the cargo bay!"

But of course, Margo could never really cow anyone, no matter how loud she shouted. It was easy, infuriatingly easy, for Pilgrim to pick her up, throw her into her cupboard, shut the door, and walk away.

Å

Rumer let the air out of his chest, and felt himself sag. Kell looked at his captain with a cloud in his glass eye. "You still think we can carry this girl all the way to Black Oven? Look, I can't speak for you, but I'm not prepared to die spoon-feeding a bunch of sad, sorry motherfuckers we've never even met, and I'm certainly not prepared to go to some new kind a' interstellar prison because some UN Security cunt decides we kidnapped her whelp."

Rumer couldn't find anything to say, so he said nothing.

"We need to let her float, now, Rumer. We need to stick her inside the shuttle, give her some oatmeal and quick-bread, and let her float. And then we need to drop what we're carrying quick as we can, and go back to doing somethin' we know how to do." Kell rubbed, and rubbed and rubbed the glass. "C'mon, man… I… we just can't do what you're tryin' to do. We're not built for it. Men like us don't fix the shit-holes of this world, Rumer. We're just… we're a load a' pirates."

Rumer nodded heavily. "You are right about that," he said. "I can't think of what you'd call us but a load of damn, dirty pirates."

There was a silence, during which Rumer wondered whether it would be possible to pre-program a route for the shuttle so that it would take her straight to Black Oven. That way, if her food and oxygen held out… and if nobody too bad picked her up when she got there…

That was when Diallo came in, not grinning. "We have company, Captain," he said. "They appear to have finally made a decision about us. They want to board."

It was a long, slow nightmare run to the bridge. And then Rumer looked on one of the biggest UN squadron ships he had ever seen. Still a ways off, it swallowed up the whole screen like a big, blue open-mouthed whale. "How do they keep finding us? What are they locking onto?"

"I do not know," said Diallo, "I have picked off every signal I could find."

"I think… I know."

Rumer turned. The girl sat in the doorway of the bridge. She was out of breath. Her knees were bloodied. She must have dragged herself from the stern-end utility closet to the bridge, all the way across that steel floor. "Are these them?" she asked. "Are these the kind of officers you're talking about, who are working for… for somebody?"

Rumer jerked his head. "Any particular reason why you're in here, Miss Glass?"

"I know what's going on."

"I'll bet you do. You're very clever at that. But if you wouldn't mind headin' back to your little room just now…"

"I know why the squad ship's here. I know why they found us."

Rumer stiffened, blinked. "Say what you mean, girl."

The girl swallowed. "I have... a chip."

"A *chip?*"

"I'm chipped. In case anything bad ever happens to me when I'm... it emits this low-level signal all the time, so people can find where I am."

Rumer glared at her, this pretty, pale girl he once thought too fragile to live, his eyeballs hot. "And this was something you chose not to share with us?"

"'Course not. She's got friends who'd pat her head like a good little bitch-hound if she helps land people like us in prison," said Kell. The way he looked at her even alarmed Rumer, angry as he was.

"Jesus." Rumer pressed his palms into his eyes. "Well, you've certainly fucked us, kid, if that's what you meant to do. I'd throw you straight out the airlock if I thought it would do us any good, you hear me?"

Her green eyes looked frantic for the first time since he'd known her. "No!... I mean, I'm sorry, it's just, it's not something I really think about."

"Not something you *really think about?* Is there anything you really think about?"

The girl got angry at that. "My parents made me get it when I was eight, okay? I didn't even know what it was supposed to do. It was just something that *happened* to me, like everything else in my fucking life. For God's sake, if I really wanted all of you to go down on all kinds of charges... but I don't!" She took a long overdue breath. "I don't."

"That's comforting," said Rumer. "You can tell them what perfect gentlemen we've been while they're thundering all over our cargo bay gathering up our stolen goods to return them to people we won't be able to get police protection from."

"It wasn't meant to be comforting, asshole."

Rumer let out air. "What would you have me do, girl? What is it you'd like to do?"

"I want to help," said Margo. The eyes blazed bright, now, not brittle at all. "Let me help."

⚔

It wasn't a very good plan, Margo knew. It would have been a better one if they'd roughed her up a bit first, or cut off her pinky toe like she'd suggested ("It grows all wrong, anyway. And it's not like I'm using it.") But even Kell had been too pussy to do it. She hoped the dustpan looked like a horrible enough place that it would still be believable. It was too late to reconsider.

The com-link connected on the third try, and the other ship picked up.

"You are speaking to a representative of the United Nations Peacekeeping Force. Please identify yourself."

Rumer was ready with the apple sack over his head. "I am what you might call an independent profiteer looking to do some business. If you would, please inform Secretary Glass that we have her precious little daughter, and are interested in discussing the terms under which she may be returned in one piece."

The man on the other end paused, and went pale. "One moment. Don't do anything. One moment."

"Don't take too long, now."

The man disappeared for what seemed like a very long time. Margo wiggled against her ropes so that at the very least her wrists would have rope marks on them.

The man reappeared. "We need to see her before anything can be discussed."

"You know we have her," said Rumer. "She's got a chip. We found it. Would you like to learn how?"

The man set his mouth, calmly obstinate. "If you want to move forward, put her on the com, and let me speak to her."

"Assholes," Margo muttered. "I could be dying right now." But she whipped up some shuddering breaths and let Rumer throw her against the terminal.

"Please!" she screamed. "Please it's me! Tell my mother it's me!" She didn't know the man on the com, and she hoped he knew her only by sight.

"Calm down. Calm down, now. You're going to be all right. Who are these men? What are they doing to you?"

Rumer piped in loudly. "Wrong question, G-man." Margo winced as though he'd tightened the ropes.

"I don't know who they are, they never take off the sacks," said Margo, feeling the blood pound in her ears. "They boarded our ship, and they... everyone... so they took a bunch of stuff, and they took me. They want money. That's all they want, and then they'll let me go. Tell my mom... seventy-five thousand. In credits. Tell her."

"Alright," said the man. "Alright, we'll tell her, Miss, stay calm. We're doing everything we can." The man shifted to try to get another look at Rumer, just out of frame, and then disappeared.

"We should've asked for more," muttered Kell.

"You should've roughed me up," said Margo.

"Shut up, children," said Rumer.

The com crackled in the silence, picking up no conversation on the other end.

"He's not goin' for it." Kell rubbed his eye. "We should've asked for a lot more. No one lets a piece like her go for under ninety thousand."

"Oh, they'll round it up to a nice even hundred for us when they put it to the secretary." Rumer didn't take his eyes from the screen. "They wouldn't go for this if they couldn't take something off the top."

"And this way, they'll think it was their idea," said Margo proudly.

Kell scowled at her.

The man on the com returned. "We've spoken to Secretary Glass. She'll pay. Clear your bridge. We'll send someone over shortly to make the trade."

Margo swallowed the bile in her throat. "NO!... no, you can't. If you send someone over here, they'll kill me! I don't want to die, please, don't make me die!" It surprised her how easily the whimpering came from her throat.

"Calm down, Miss. Miss? Please calm down." The man seemed more rattled by her hysterics than by the situation itself. "What does he want us to do?"

"You have to send the credits directly using the ship's AT, and then they'll send me in the shuttle. That's what he says. Just do what he says. Please!"

Then the com-link cut out, and the screen went blank.

"What happened?" asked Margo.

"Backworld machinery," said Rumer.

"Did he even hear the last thing I said?"

"Who knows?"

They were all silent, listening for sounds of being boarded, for the click-snap of metal weapons and the thunder of boots.

"I'm gonna throw up," said Margo airlessly.

"Do me a favor," said Rumer. "Save it 'til they come for me."

And then there was a disused buzzer that sounded, somewhere, a quick "ping," short and loud. Everyone turned.

"Credits," said Diallo. He aimed his grin at Margo.

Margo laughed a sob.

There were no goodbyes, exactly. Just nervous half-slaps and grumbles. Kell rubbed his eye at her an absurd number of times.

It was the captain who strapped her in.

"Well, that's just about it," said Pilgrim Pilgrim. "Gone over all the controls?"

"I'll figure it out," she said.

"You got your story straight? What you're gonna tell them?"

"I have a few stories to tell them."

"They're not gonna want to hear 'em all."

"That's my problem, not yours. Go deliver what you have to deliver, let me get off this ugly ass ship, for the love of God."

She knew she'd made Rumer laugh, though she didn't stay to listen to it. Instead, Margo darted off into the black, and prepared for what she would do when she landed. She'd have to give up the true tale soon enough, tell people there had been no kidnapping, that she was perfectly well.

First, though, she would have a servitor run a bath, and actually get in it.

"19.12.2014_A Future Without Pain" by Comebab

Previous Page:
Two women sit across a small table from each other. On the table, there are two cups of tea, a teapot, and a paper scroll that has "Traveler's Guide to Neptune" written on it. There are windows at the top of the image, where stars and planets are visible. Both women are finely dressed and are leaning in towards one another, involved in conversation. From the mouth of the woman on the left, a vine of thorns flows. As it passes through the air between them it gradually transforms into budding rose flowers, reaching the woman on the left's ear as a gentle and pleasant flow.

Pay Attention

Sarah Pinsker

In the beginning, there is noise.

"You'll get used to it, Acacia." That's what the technician tells me as I wake up from the Pilot installation to a barrage of stimuli. "It'll fade. It'll become background."

No. Try again. Different noise, different times, different soundtrack, different rhymes.

No. Try again.

My head finally clears. The scene swims into something close to focus. A high-pitched whine, and silence below it. I yawn to pop my ears. Vomit instead, without hearing the sound of my own retching.

Silence blankets chaos, but chaos is my milieu. I'm familiar with chaos. Usually it's a noisy thing: people screaming, car alarms blaring, sirens. That's where I live and work, the intersection of all of that. This is a different scene, all ghosts and echoes.

I open my eyes and realize I hadn't opened them the first time. The sky is the color of sand, gritty like sand.

"Lie still," somebody says, which isn't right.

"That's my line," I say.

"She's conscious." An upside-down face appears in my field of vision. He has two moles on his chin, which give him a second, smiling, right-side-up face, moles for eyes.

"This one's awake!" the chin-face calls to somebody else.

I try to get up, but my body doesn't oblige. A wave of nausea sweeps over me.

"Lie still," the voice repeats. I obey. Somebody is doing my job on me. My job: patching soldiers together well enough that they can be flown to bases with more advanced medical care. I lie still, on the wrong side of the equation.

I open my eyes. Try to think why they were closed. Remember a case study about a guy with anterograde amnesia from a lobectomy. "I am awake for the first time," he wrote. Crossed it out the next day. "Now I am truly awake for the first time." If I remember him, I probably don't have amnesia. It's a consolation. I remember thinking that.

Eyes closed, I gather myself in. Nest in the facts of me. Acacia Saylor: Army medic, Baltimorean, Aquarius.

Somebody far away is screaming. My job is to help. First I have to open my eyes.

"What's that embedded in her temple?" somebody asks. "Is that flashing light supposed to be there?"

"My Pilot implant," I think I say. It shouldn't be flashing. It's never flashed before.

"Some kind of implant?" Another voice guesses, as if I hadn't spoken.

"Do we need to worry about it? Can we turn it off?"

"Get the gut wound stable. We can't do anything for her head if she bleeds to death."

They aren't my unit if they don't know about my Pilot. Everyone I work with knows about my implant. I'm the Pilot evangelist.

"Don't take it," I try to say. "Don't turn it off. It helps me."

"Ssh, we've got you. You're gonna be okay," says a voice next to my ear. I'm not reassured.

Those are the fragments that stay fragmented. I manage to stitch those scraps of memory together, patch them with my own medical report. When the first car bomb went off, I had run toward the victims. The second was the one that got me, or rather the shrapnel and the blast. Concussion and a gut wound that ruptured my spleen and nearly bled me out before the transport arrived.

But why hadn't I checked for a second bomb? Or had I? That was part of the protocol. With my Pilot I could usually get the lay of the land before running in.

"You were lucky," the nurse at the hospital tells me. The first one I remember after the chin-faced medic. "Twenty-one people killed, almost a hundred injured."

She's the one who reads my charts to me at my request. I've been evacuated to Germany, and the sun shining through the window is a gentle German sun. She has to raise her voice because my ears haven't yet stopped ringing.

"Will I be able to go back?" I ask.

She gives me a confused look, and I repeat the sentence in a drill sergeant bark. Before she gets offended, I add, "Speech impediment. Shouting helps."

She knows I mean back to my deployment. "I don't know. They're sending you home first."

"What? Why?"

"You heard me say 'ruptured spleen,' right? Look at yourself. That was no laparoscopic surgery. You've got weeks of recovery ahead."

She's right, of course. I wouldn't be any good to anybody in this shape.

Something else nags at me. "You didn't mention my implant." I touch my temple, the reassuring nub of the LED.

She nods. "I haven't gotten to the implant yet, but there isn't much here about it."

"I was part of a test group."

"It says that much." She waves the tablet at me. "It says our doctors consulted with Walter Reed and Balkenhol Neural Labs and determined that your implant didn't need to be removed or deactivated despite the concussion. Continue to monitor, etcetera, etcetera."

One of the memory fragments tugs at me. I point at my head again. "The light. Is it flashing?"

"No."

I exhale, relieved.

"But it was, when you first came in. It's off now."

"Off? It can't be off. I thought you said it didn't need to be removed or deactivated. You said that!"

"We didn't do anything to it. Wait a sec." She swipes at the tablet a couple of times until she finds what she was looking for. "One of the doctors asked about the flashing, and got a response from Balkenhol Neural Labs that flashing meant it was coming to the end of its battery life.

"It says it won't do any harm staying in your head, and you can get it replaced back in the US." She looks back up at me, all smiles. "See, there's another reason to go home before going back to your deployment."

I fake a smile. As soon as she leaves, I reach for the tablet with my charts on it. Pain erupts from my abdomen, the protests of muscles torn by surgery. I grab the tablet, then fall back onto the pillow, panting. I want to read what the nurse was reading, but it asks for a password. I click it off again, then tilt it until I can see the side of my face in its reflective surface. It's a vague reflection, brown skin in black glass, but good enough to confirm: no light. She wouldn't have lied, but I still had to see it for myself.

It's been six years since I had to live in my pre-Pilot head, with its wandering attention and fizzling connections. I'm fuzzy now, but I can't tell where the concussion ends and the dead Pilot begins. The old me. I don't want her back.

⚐

"What do you think you are, a superhero?" asks the private who sits next to me on the plane back to the US. "Let them give you a medical discharge. Don't complain. Get out while you've still got two legs." He's lost both of his just below the knees.

I shake my head. Gently, since it's still a little delicate. It's loud in here, so my shouting doesn't sound out of place. "It's my job. I don't want to think about looking for another one."

"But you said you're a medic? You can work anywhere. Ambulance, ER. You can have all the excitement without the bombs."

⚐

"It won't make you a superhero," the Balkenhol Neural Lab doctor had said, back before any of this. My school principal had arranged the meeting, but she didn't explain what it was about until we were all in her office: Principal Ramos, behind her desk; Major Adderly, who introduced herself as an Army doctor, and Dr. Roffman from BNL, in folding chairs that were comically too small for both; me in the actual good armchair. I couldn't figure out why I merited this attention, or what I had done wrong, or even why I got the comfortable chair.

"So it'll help me in school?" I worked on enunciating.

"No. All it does is stimulate your attention. Lets you make use of a little more of it."

Principal Ramos cleared her throat. "Acacia, you failed chemistry twice, but you're taking it a third time. Why?"

"I want to be a doctor."

"And you've told your teachers you want to join the Army when you graduate. Why?"

"To pay for med school."

The Army doctor, Major Adderly, leaned forward in her tiny chair. "What if we said that if you volunteered for this Pilot program you would have a good chance of passing chemistry the next time around? Then after graduation, we'd work to get you qualified as an Army medic?"

"I'd ask, 'why me?'"

Dr. Roffman smiled. He had a mustache like a push-broom. "BNL needs young, healthy volunteers. The studies in other primates have been hugely successful." His mustache twitched when he talked.

I forced myself to pay attention, to concentrate on making connections they weren't speaking. "And I fit the bill because I'm old enough to sign for myself and I don't have any family to talk me out of it?"

Principal Ramos shook her head. "You fit the bill because I've seen how hard you work. I think this could genuinely help you cope better with some of your learning disabilities. I'm not in the business of selling experiments to my students, but I think you'll benefit each other tremendously. They've shown me the studies, and I don't think it's dangerous."

I didn't have anybody left at home to run it by. I knew there was probably a whole book of fine print somewhere, knew there was more to it than they were saying. At the same time, I was twenty, aging out of high school, and no closer to my goals than I had been at eighteen. If I ended up with a certificate of completion instead of a diploma I'd never be able to get into college or the military.

After school, I walked to the nursing home to tell my grandfather about the meeting. Head up, purposeful, no earbuds, just like Granddad had taught me. Know your surroundings, he had said, when he was still taking care of me instead of the other way around. I tried to be aware, but I was still surprised by a whistle from one of the corner boys. I glanced over to see if it was somebody I knew, Arin or Jay or one of the others who used to be in my class, but I didn't recognize this guy. I ignored him and picked up my pace, glancing out of the corner of my eye to make sure he didn't follow.

Granddad was already in the dining room.

"This food is why I married you," he told me, waving a spoonful of mashed potatoes.

"I'm not your wife. I'm Acacia. Your granddaughter."

"Oh! Is Acacia here? What restaurant is this?" He looked around. He had gotten way worse in the year he'd been here.

"Let's start again, Granddad. I'm going to let some scientists put something in my head. It's a good idea, right?"

"A good idea. Right, right. Where did Teenie go? Did she leave without me?" He stuck his tongue out in frustration.

I signed. I let them test me and poke me and snake the implant into my left temporoparietal junction and test me some more. Count backwards from one hundred while putting together a puzzle. Listen to a chem lecture while watching a movie, then answer questions about it. They were right that it didn't make me any smarter, but it improved my focus. The dysgraphia was still bad, but I was allowed to do most exams orally anyway, and my teachers were mostly patient with my speech. I got a C in chemistry, graduated with an actual diploma before I aged out, not a certificate. Granddad couldn't go to graduation, so I didn't bother going either.

Å

My new home is a furnished apartment near Fort Meade. Everything I own is in storage in San Antonio, but there's a couch and a bed and some random kitchenware. I could fall asleep now, after the long flight, but I'm antsy and wired. My stitches hurt. I can hear the neighbors talking through the wall.

I eat takeout chicken and read a medical journal, trying not to contemplate being jobless. My memories from before the Army are like my pre-Pilot memories: hazy. A feeling like things are just out of my grasp. Some people would argue the pre-Pilot me is the real me, original flavor. But me with my Pilot is me awake and alive. Not cured, just helped. Enhanced, maybe, but enhancement only brings out what's already there. The bettered me is the real me. Like that amnesia case. "Today I am truly awake for the first time." I know how he felt, only I'm in a better position to appreciate it.

I have no memories of the bombs that hit me, so instead my dreams piece together other incidents. Adopt other traumas as my own. There's one in which I'm both the medic and the soldier on the ground, my own bloody hands in my own bloody wound. There's one in which I'm painstakingly putting adhesive bandages over the neck of a soldier whose head has been severed. Bandage after bandage, with cartoon characters on them. "You're going to be fine," I tell him. "Lie still."

I know I should tell somebody, but the VA says it'll be weeks or months until I can get an appointment, so I keep the dreams to myself. I read a study that says dreams are our attempts to apply lessons we have learned from previous experience to new experiences. That makes a certain amount of sense.

Å

Balkenhol reaches out to me before I can get a VA appointment. They send a car the day after my flight. I'm ushered into a cramped conference room with three BNL technicians. The air conditioning is pushed up too high, and it's rattling the vents near the ceiling. I walk halfway around the room rather than taking the closest seat, so I can have my back to the wall instead of the door. I wait for introductions, but none come.

"Describe how you feel the Pilot helps you as a combat medic," one of them says, as if we were already mid-conversation. She has an air of seniority. I have the urge to call her sir.

"I can't," I say. "I've never been a medic without the Pilot. I don't know how it helps me because it's part of me."

They take notes.

"It's part of me," I say again, suddenly terrified that they're going to rip it from my head. "I can see everything. Some of the other medics get nervous because when they're bent over somebody there's a chance they're gonna get taken out. But the Pilot lets me treat my patient and stay aware of my surroundings. It's like—it's like being able to absorb multiple inputs. Watch multiple channels at once. Ask anybody I've worked with. I did great in the blood labs and on the ground. Everybody wants me on their team. Don't take this away from me. Please."

The same technician says, "The Army tells us they're very pleased with your success in the field."

"You're going to take it." Defeat tugs at me. I want to run from the room, to hop a freight train. I'd do anything to keep it, but it's theirs to take. I haven't paid for it. I can look into whether they can force me into surgery against my will, but I'm guessing I've already signed something to that effect.

I try to think of anything to delay them, and seize upon something. "The concussion."

"I'm sorry?"

I wonder if the other people in the room are just extras, and direct my plea at the only one who talks. "The implants were initially developed as part of a deep brain stimulation project, right? For epilepsy?"

"Yes."

"But it didn't work."

"No."

"And you found another use, and since then you've been testing them on healthyish volunteers like me, right? No epilepsy, no brain injuries, no disabilities based on structural defects."

"Right."

"So sooner or later, you're going to need to know what happens when an implant is put into a healthy volunteer who then gets a brain injury, even a minor one. That's me, in front of you. Right here, right now. Why would you take it out when this would tell you so much more? You probably have twenty other people you can test the other scenario on, but you can't manufacture my condition."

I keep the triumphant note from my voice, but I can already see their gears turning. I'm right.

"We'll take that back to the project director," one of the silent techs says at last, "but you misunderstand. We're not going to take it out. We simply don't have any reason to continue studying you."

That wasn't what I was expecting. They're not taking it out, but they're not turning it back on either. Though she did say she'd take it to the project director. Under the circumstances, that's the best I can hope for.

They send me back to my apartment to stew. I sit on the lumpy couch and go over a new protocol for surgical cricothyrotomy. I read out loud, following my finger. Practice the procedure in my head, let my hands go through the movements. After ten minutes, I quiz myself; again after thirty. I read the protocol again with a movie on, purposefully distracting myself, then type summaries of both what I'd read and the movie. I'm testing myself on the new knowledge, but also on my limits with the dormant Pilot. So far, it doesn't feel all that different.

I look online for a grocery store and locate one within walking distance. As I walk, I scan for snipers on the roofs and windows of apartment buildings. There are six other people in my line of sight: a couple at a bus stop, the others walking. I watch to see if anyone has a hand inside a jacket. Ingrained habits, habits that have saved my life more than once, even if they're not necessary here. Still, it's reassuring how much I can take in even without my Pilot working.

The store isn't high end, but the produce looks fresh enough, and the floors are clean. One of the speakers piping smooth jazz overhead has a whine on the high end. It makes my whole body tense, makes me yawn to pop my ears even though they're fine. There had been a sound like that after the bomb took me out, I'm pretty sure. I can't ignore it, not entirely, but I roll my shoulders back and concentrate on shopping. I fill a basket with apples, sweet potatoes, onions, cooking oil, tin foil, frozen chicken, cereal. As it gets heavier, I start to feel my stitches. In the dairy aisle, I reach for eggs, then glance to my right and drop the carton.

"Excuse me," I say to the teenage boy standing near the milk, stepping around the mess I've made. "But is that a Pilot implant?"

He looks at me uncertainly, then nods, one hand on the refrigerator door.

"How do you have one?" And where did you get it? And when? And why? I stick to one question, but he's still eyeing me.

"Look," I say. "I have one too. I'm just curious where you got yours?" And how. And why. I start turning my head so he can see mine, then remember that it's off, and finish with an awkward gesture in its general direction.

"At the Neural Implantation Center in Bethesda. BNL. I thought that was the only place in the area."

"I'm not local—Army."

He smiles then. "Oh, cool. My dad is Air Force."

I smile back and echo him. "Cool. So are you part of another test group?"

"I don't know what you mean. I got it from my parents."

"Cool," I say again. "What kind of disabilities do you have, if you don't mind my asking?"

He's put off. "Why do you think I've got problems? It was a Christmas present, that's all. It lets me play video games while I listen to lessons. Lots of kids have them at my school."

"Cool," I say for the third time, knowing I sound stupid. I move off with what I hope is a friendly wave.

I don't have a phone, so I have to wait until I get back to the apartment to look up what he's talking about. Balkenhol has opened a Neural Implantation Center. Pilots for the masses, or at least the masses that can afford them. I watch a video, then search for articles. My tablet reads them to me while I make dinner, taking my anger out on the sweet potatoes, dicing them into hash.

How can they think this is a good idea? The technology isn't fully tested yet. Or maybe it is, and I've just missed all the news while I was deployed. It looks like they're becoming a fad in private schools. The price tag is steep, as much as a good used car.

A separate page, buried several clicks deep, explains that the battery lasts about five years, and the only way to replace it is to replace the whole unit, though the leads stay in place. There's no price listed for the battery replacement procedure, but I'm guessing it's not cheap. You're theirs by the time you need it; you'll pay anything. Or maybe they haven't priced it yet since most of their commercial clients are only in their first year of implantation. I want to call Balkenhol, but I don't want to draw attention to myself if they're still deciding whether to turn mine back on.

I'm not sure why I'm so furious. Is it the for-profit bit? The fact that they used me as a guinea pig and now they're satisfied enough with how it works to market it for mass consumption? That they want to leave mine off when they're stuffing them into the heads of anybody who can pay? I see how delicately everything is balanced. If I had been five years younger, if I couldn't have signed for myself, the Pilot wouldn't be for me. It would be for some rich kid with the same diagnoses I had and parents who could afford to upgrade his brain. Or anybody with money, with no diagnoses at all, who wanted an edge in school or business. I was cheap labor, some poor lab rat who'd gotten lucky for a while.

I check my bank balance, which is depressingly low. The automatic withdrawals for Granddad's nursing home eat most of my paycheck.

There isn't anything I could go without to pay for the procedure, and I don't have anything worth selling other than the Pilot.

New dreams that night: I'm again the victim lying on the ground, again the medic. This time I have oven mitts for hands. My brain is fuzzy, sluggish. I want to do my work but I can't. I want to live, but I know I'm dying. There are sirens, car alarms, calls to prayer. Above it all, a droning voice telling me I'm not supposed to even be here, and I should report to the lab at once. I stuff my organs back into my body and walk off a fake street and into the lab, where I'm put on a gurney and rolled into a cabinet.

What am I if I'm not a medic? The Army is the only thing I've known, but it was supposed to be a temporary thing in any case. I only had another year to go. The discharge paperwork still hasn't come through, but I don't have any duties or even ID for the base here. It's over. I just don't know what comes next.

The local fire companies turn me down when I try to volunteer, say maybe when I'm fully healed. I'm fit enough, soldier fit, other than my healing gut. Paranoia says I'm being sabotaged, but I know my voice is the problem. I don't sound fast enough to keep up unless I shout. Two extremes, neither particularly good for civilian life. In high school, I had a speaking device to do the hard work for me in class, but I was never allowed to take it home, and I could never afford one now.

I try another tack, writing to local hospitals and ambulance companies, attaching my certs, offering myself as a triage expert. I warn them about my speech impediment, and I try to be as eloquent as I can on the page, so they remember that when they hear me speak.

Only one responds, and I offer to do a ridealong, a working interview. It doesn't go well. It's a slow shift. The EMTs exchange glances when I try to make conversation. They can't wait to get rid of me. I don't care what they think; all I want is a chance to show them what I can do, but nothing comes. I shouldn't wish for emergencies. I sit in the back and dig my nails into my palms, listening to the radio and the tires and the traffic around us and the voice in my head that says there must be something I can do.

I dream I'm in a cage when the lab around me starts to burn. I try to tell people to leave, to let me out so I can help, but they all act like they can't understand me.

I buy a phone and an app that lets me listen to the emergency radio frequencies. Maybe I can make it to some crisis first and impress the EMTs as a good Samaritan. It makes me feel like I'm doing something useful. I wander my new neighborhood picking up trash, waiting to be in the right place at the right time.

Balkenhol doesn't call, and I'm not about to remind them I'm out here. I wish I had the contract, so I could see if they have any obligation to maintain the Pilot, but if I still have a copy, it's in my storage unit in San Antonio. There's only one person unaffiliated with the lab or the Army who might know.

I take a train up to Baltimore, flag a cab, direct the driver on a "this is your life" tour. He drives me to the high school. I've paid him enough to stick around and take me to Granddad's nursing home next, but he takes off the second I close the door. I don't blame him: I don't know why I'm here either.

There are supposed to be guards at the metal detectors by the door, but the machines are off and nobody stops me. I wonder which statement they're trying to make: that everyone is too apathetic to bother causing trouble, or that things have gotten so bad here there's no point in pretending. The halls smell like the flu. There's graffiti on the lockers. It's been five years. Was it always this bad, and I was too focused on getting out to notice? Entirely possible.

I look for Pilots on the kids that I pass, but I don't see the telltale lights. Nobody here can afford them, I'm guessing.

The receptionist ushers me into Principal Ramos's office. I'd only ever been in there once before, the day she introduced me to the doctors. Her office is still slightly nicer than everything else around it, though shabbier than I remember. Solid furniture, a bit dinged up. An ancient Turkish rug, worn in front of all the chairs. These are things I wouldn't have noticed as a kid. A persistent fly throws itself against the top pane of the window behind her.

"Acacia, lovely to see you." Her voice is warm, though she doesn't get up from her desk. She directs me to the same worn armchair I had sat in my last time here. "Are you still in the Army?"

She isn't anyone to me. We only met the once. The vice principals were the ones who brought me in every year to tell me which classes I had failed, how long I had left before they'd be able to stop bothering with me. The only reason Ramos still recognizes me is because she sold me as a lab rat.

"Why did you do it?" I ask, slow and steady.

She tenses, but doesn't betray herself. I imagine a lot of students must have confronted her over the years. "Why did I do what?"

"Why did you pick me?"

"Acacia, I can honestly say nobody ever tried harder to graduate than you did. I thought with a little more help than we could afford to give you, you could succeed. And you were going to go into the medical field, to help people. Have you done what you wanted to do?"

I nod. "Did they pay you?"

"Yes. They paid for a whole new chem lab."

That isn't what I expected. I had pictured her in a Lexus or a new apartment. "It feels like they tested on poor kids and now they're going to sell it to rich kids and nobody like me will get a chance again."

She meets my gaze. "That's probably true."

"So was it worth it?"

"I'll admit I had hoped they might offer more help for students like you. But we needed those supplies. And it helped you, right?"

There are more things I could probably say, but I'm losing steam. "Yes, ma'am. Thank you. One last thing. Do you remember the terms of the agreement?"

She frowns. I follow her out of her office, across the reception area and into a file room. My file is thick. All those extra years, extra services, successes and failures. She leafs through it, then pulls out a thin folder and waves it in the air. Runs it through an ancient copier that sounds like an airplane taking off, hands it to me. The copy has thick lines running lengthwise down the page, but it's readable. I see what I'm looking for: they have no obligation to maintain it once they're done observing me. I'm on my own. I used to know that, but I must have forgotten.

Principal Ramos is watching me, waiting to see my reaction.

"Thanks," I say. "And, um, if you ever need a new nurse…"

She smiles. "We haven't got the budget for a nurse anymore, but I have an opening for a guard at the front door. I could put in a good word for you."

"I'd appreciate that." It's something.

Without the cab, I'm stuck walking to the nursing home, just like in high school. The neighborhood is as bad as it ever was: no better, no worse. I put in one of my earbuds, leaving the other ear to pay attention to my surroundings. The reassuring static of the emergency channel fills my head. My boot heels grind broken glass into even smaller pieces. Kids bike lazy circles on the corners, waiting for word from the dealers who employ them. As it ever was.

What will it be like being back in my old neighborhood? Is it a defeat? I don't think so. I can be a good door guard, for now. A job is a job. I can save up for the Pilot battery, and go back to school on the GI bill once my paperwork comes in. Wasn't that what I wanted in the first place, back before I'd ever heard of the Pilot? To be able to take care of people like my grandfather? If I thought I could make it through school then, pre-Pilot, surely I could do it now with the discipline I've learned. If discipline is enough.

When the sirens start, I close my eyes to catch their direction, then pick up my pace. The dispatch comes through my phone. It's for a collapsing building; I actually hear it fall when I'm a block off, a muffled whump. I remind myself where I am, that I don't need to scan for snipers.

The building is an old rowhouse repurposed as apartments. The whole front has caved in. At least two people out front in the rubble, probably more inside. Assess the situation, the first rule. We can't go inside while it's unstable, but maybe we can help the people out front.

I can tell the EMTs are thinking the same thing. They're talking it out as they swing from the ambulances, attention focused on the victims. Which means I'm the only one who notices when the adjacent building shimmies.

"Don't move!" I shout, my voice ringing clear at that volume, Army-weight behind it. They stop. We're out of the way when the wall buckles, and then that building gapes open too. My ears are ringing, and dust billows and obscures everything, but the EMTs aren't under it, and now they look at me for the okay and I nod, my attention split between where I want to be and the potential threats posed by the other rowhouses, almost as if my Pilot were still working. I realize: the Pilot helps me, and I want it back, but it's not all of me.

In the distance, more sirens. For the first time since getting back, everything feels like it's settling into place. Chaos is my milieu, noisy and messy and home.

I bend over the first victim I reach. "Lie still."

I am awake for the first time.

Invisible People

Margaret Killjoy

The last light of the sun came down through the broken windows, all pretty and shit, catching on that big jagged shard of glass and then pouring out into the room over my bed. Over Marcellus. He snored in that way he always did, endearing and soft.

I hurried to dress in the last of the daylight, but once I was done, I lingered. I paced, I ran my fingers through my beard, I watched the twilit horizon and counted the silhouette bones of the buildings Portland calls its skyline.

Anything but go to work.

It had been a lot easier, stealing from rich people, back before the anxiety had hit. I miss those days, when my biggest problems were external. It's easier to steer clear of cops than it is to get away from whole chunks of my brain.

I can't get on the net, either. I mean, I can still get in… the people in the office next door haven't updated their wifi encryption since 2019. I just can't bring myself to sign on. Not even the Darknet. It may not be corporate, but it's still the net. There's just too much data in the feed. Too much shit to worry about. Every day, someone's sick. Some friend of a friend's got cancer or your ex-boyfriend—the one you haven't seen since high school—is in for surgery. Someone you met at a party six months ago got caught doing something and needs bail. The awful shit tragedies of two thousand "friends" pile up worse than the latest mass shooting or another pandemic scare. And those are bad enough. I can't get on the net. I won't.

But I've got to eat.

The room went dark and I stumbled my way through the warehouse. Five paces out of the room, I turned the corner. A window let in enough street light and, there, past the accumulated junk of fifteen squatters, I could see the door at the bottom of the stairs. I pressed my body into the bar and I was outside. The squat's chemical smell was gone, leaving only that sickly shit stink that comes in off the Willamette, dampened a bit by the endless winter rain.

I pulled out a phone—who still uses handheld phones?—and I told it to call Ramirez.

"I'm sorry," my phone said. "I couldn't understand your request."

Fucking thing still didn't like my accent.

"Ramirez," I told it. "There're only six numbers in my phone. Only one of them starts with R. Fucking call Ramirez, Siri."

"Processing."

It said it was processing but I think it just said that to be nice. I'm glad my phone is nice to me.

"I'm sorry," it said. "I couldn't understand your request."

"Call R-A-M-I-R-E-Z."

No processing delay. It rang and she answered.

"What do you want, Vasyl?"

I could never read her tone of voice. Maybe I'd caught her at a bad time. Maybe she was still mad at me about May Day. Maybe she was tired. People who aren't me seem to just kind of pick up information like that when they talk to people. I don't think they even second-guess themselves. It seems like magic to me.

"I'm looking for work," I said.

"Of course you are," she replied.

There's some irony to that. Work was the last thing I wanted. But I was walking east, away from the water and the dead bastions of industry. I was walking towards work.

"I'll meet you," she told me, and hung up.

A random helicopter went overhead and my eyes grew wide and wild. There was a dumpster, I could throw the phone in there. Not secure enough. It was two blocks to the river, I could sprint, probably get the worst evidence into the water before I surrendered. But no searchlight lit me up from the dark heavens and the sounds of the rotors faded from the world before the adrenaline cleared my system.

I picked up the pace.

I got to the corner of Grand and Belmont, went under an awning. I took out my phone, called no one, and put it to my ear, started pacing. Fake phone call—you need a reason why you're just standing around on a street corner or you'll deal with cops. Cops and I didn't get along, and I had the warrants to prove it.

Ramirez's car rolled up, black and glossy in the rain, picking up the dull blue of the streetlights. I climbed in the passenger door. No Ramirez. No driver at all. Typical. It probably wasn't a slight; it was just efficiency. I closed the door and the car took off up Grand, heading north up past Rosa Parks, then wove into a neighborhood and stopped in front of a house I'd never seen before.

Kids were playing on the block, chasing a glowie, laughing as the ball darted between them with a mind of its own. They laughed harder when one kid tackled the thing on the pavement and another three dog-piled up.

Most of the houses on the street were burned out, and not one of them had a light on in the window. Those kids weren't from the block, or else they were squatters. Either way, they seemed happy enough.

The house in front of me was blacked out, I realized. The windows were too dark to just be unlit. It was three stories, painted the color of sand, and had an overgrown garden full of lavender and those creepy fucking passionflowers with their alien little stamen or whatever-the-fuck those antennae things are. The whole place was a paint-peeled reminder of the rise and fall of the Portland middle class.

A camera over the door saw my scowling mug and decided to let me in.

"You've got face-reg on your fucking door?" I called, when the door closed behind me.

"Good to see you too," I heard her say.

The house was an empty shell, a dusty showroom. Ramirez was sitting lotus in the dining room, her yoga mat spread out on the hardwood floor.

In the corner, discreet against the moulding, was a matte black box no bigger than my fist. Hair-thin cabling ran out its top and into the ground of a three-prong outlet nearby. If it worked right, that little wire kept the modem from overheating its core and spitting fire-hot bullshit all over the room.

It didn't even have an indicator light. The best tech doesn't anymore. The best tech doesn't want you to even know it's there.

"Sit down," she said, indicating the room as a whole. She made eye contact. Or maybe it's better just to say she looked my direction. I couldn't see her eyes behind those Readpro FOV contacts and their bright blue glow. And she probably hadn't bothered to look past the screen that filled her vision.

I sat.

"What kind of work?" she asked.

"Anything," I said. Then I thought it over. "Anything that's not on Lightnet or Darknet. Anything I can do direct."

"You're still not over it?" she asked.

I could have hit her.

"No," I told her instead. "I'm still not over it."

"Maybe you should see somebody," she told me. "If your anxiety's so bad it's keeping you offline, maybe you should do something about it."

A million answers poured into my head unheeded. I took a few breaths, then picked the only one that hurt to say: "I am."

Even squatters needed therapy, and mine came from a woman named Helga. She'd worked as a cognitive therapist for three decades before she got laid off and her husband took her savings on a one-way trip to Florida. Motherfucker had got his comeuppance, though, in one of those nightmare storms, and her cash and his corpse had washed out to sea. She moved into a squat a few months later, and we all did what we could to help one another out. Me, I fixed things. Helga, she fixed people.

"Well," Ramirez said, from her tech-zen holier-than-thou fucking yoga mat on the floor of a stolen house, "let's get to work."

She meant well. She was probably even my friend. But people don't open up in person anymore. Were we really friends if I never read her status updates? If our profiles weren't linked?

I took out my laptop. It was encrypted to nine hells with layered volumes, but I think what kept it safe is that no one even used the fucking things anymore. No one under thirty remembered how they worked and sure as hell no one of any age spent their time trying to figure out how to break into them—the damn thing still had a CD drive. I couldn't just move my eyes across the screen to shift its focus, I had to drag a little icon of an arrow around the screen and I had to press buttons on the keyboard. It was tactile. It did non-tactile things, but I could still touch it. I could close it. I could look away from it.

"There's an exec in Rackman Ltd who's been leaving a trail of meta that leads right offshore," Ramirez told me.

Ramirez was a fixer, not a hacker. She kept track of information, things like who needed robbing and where they kept their shit. But she couldn't get in the proverbial door.

"How much?" I asked.

She answered. Not an insubstantial sum.

It was a simple job. Break into Jonathan Albrecht's files and then his offshore bank account. Take out two percent. Any more than that and he might decide hiring a hit squad was worth the financial and legal liabilities. If we were lucky, we'd find some blackmail while we were in there, wire it up on a deadman switch so if I stopped breathing, his wife would find out about his affair or, if nothing else, the IRS would find out about his tax dodge. And I'd walk away with $5k for a night's work. Simple.

Took me all night.

Ramirez did yoga for awhile, murmuring instructions to her contact lens computer while in downward dog and a thousand other poses. She said the names aloud—revolved triangle, pigeon, camel—and presumably got some kind of biofeedback telling her if she was doing them right. The rest of her jabbering was pure business though—checking up on clients and projects and whatever the hell it was she did besides find me yuppies to rob.

I live in a world where some people feel it's more efficient if they multitask their relaxation with their work.

Ramirez was a squatter because it was cool. She was a criminal because it was fun. Honestly, with her skills and drive and education and upbringing—but minus her criminal record, perhaps—she could have *been* the mark we were about to rob. She could have had his job and his life and his underlings and his investments. But as she told me once, stealing felt a lot more honest when it was illegal.

I was still going hard at Albrecht's vapor drive when she checked in with me at 2am. Simple jobs aren't always simple. Ramirez stretched out on the yoga mat and fell asleep.

By 3am I'd gotten his biometrics from the pizza delivery system and was leveraging them against his drive's encryption. The privacy arms race is amusing. Lock things up with your biometrics, sure. It's a bad idea, but you'll do it anyway. Make it so your thumbprint opens your phone. But then one day you want to get into your phone when it's in the other room, and all you've got's your friend's computer. So keep your thumbprint online somewhere. What do you lock *that* up with? Another thirty-character passcode? Or maybe your retinal scan? Great. Now where do you keep *that*? For a hacker, it's a logic puzzle—once you get one clue, you leverage it against the rest.

By 4am I had everything I needed to convince his bank I was him. I set his account to make a series of payments to thirty different bank accounts, each transaction pre-approved. Random timed intervals between the transactions kept them from tripping the bank's security. Work isn't so bad.

It was 4:30am when the battering ram slammed against the front door, a bass thud that dropped me into my body from where I'd been lost in the screen.

"Pigs!" Ramirez shouted, going from sleeping to standing as fast as I'd managed to look up from my computer.

We'd lose it all if Albrecht—which is to say, I—didn't authorize the bizarre series of transactions at the end. I hate it the fucking worst when I want to fucking panic but I can't. I wanted to cut and run, but if I cut I lost it all and if I ran, well, there wasn't really anywhere to go.

"Time left?" Ramirez asked.

"Twelve minutes thirty-four," I said.

The ram hit the door again, and the frame cracked but didn't buckle. Ramirez must have done more for security than the face-reg camera.

Fuck, the camera.

"What's the face-reg hooked up to?" I asked.

"Kind of busy right now," she answered. She was typing away on the bare kitchen counter, pressing keys on an illusory keyboard only she could see.

"Is it fucking hooked up to Lightnet?" I asked.

"Yeah it's fucking hooked up to Lightnet. You think I got a face-reg database in my pocket?"

The battering ram slammed again, and this time I heard cussing from other side. They'd move to breaching rounds soon, and me without my gas mask.

"You know I'm tagged!" I shouted. 11:36 left.

"There're here for *you?*" she answered, still typing away.

"There're from the bank," I said. "Not the bank we're robbing, the bank that owns the house. I'm tagged for B&E."

A shotgun racked outside and I lost it, triggered into memory.

It was May Day, five years back, and we were all lined up, arm-in-arm—undocumented migrants and squatters' rights activists, all of us riffraff who just refused to disappear or die. I felt powerful, more powerful than I'd ever felt in my life. I felt more powerful in that company than I'd ever been while digging through the personal files of the most powerful men in the world, because that day I was part of something greater than myself.

The police weren't having it, and they did their best to corral us. But there we were, in unvanquishable number, flooding the downtown streets of Portland, disrupting the easy flow of capital. At least that day, the invisible were visible.

But the police attacked a few hundred of us at the base of the Burnside bridge.

I know what their plan had been, at least from up high, at least officially. I leaked it a few days later. They were supposed to leave us an exit, disperse us with gas and force as necessary.

But they didn't leave us an exit. The news crews dutifully departed rather than face arrest, and the cops came in with bludgeons and pepperspray. They'd tried a few new toys out on us that day, dazzlers and sticky guns and a goddam make-you-puke cannon, but at the end of it all, nothing beats the raw force of sticks and airborne poison.

And we had our arms linked together, us brave people, and we were nonviolent back then, most of us. A lot can change in five years. People can learn a lot about the nature of power.

Ramirez had been next to me, our elbows locked. On my other side, a woman I'd never met. Fifty years old I'd say. We stared the police down.

A cop came out from the police wall in front of us, took three steps towards me, looked me in the eyes, and raised the barrel of a shotgun, racking it. And I let go. I unlocked my arms and turned my face in fear.

They took the old woman off in handcuffs, and they took me off in handcuffs, and I've forgotten that cop's face but I'll never forget the barrel of his gun. And maybe I'm lucky Ramirez still works with me, still trusts me at all. I know I don't trust myself.

The shotgun blast brought me back to the present day, but the door held. Ramirez had done her homework.

Ten minutes, forty-three seconds left on the clock. I went into child pose. I'd never needed child pose as a child. Panic came over me in waves like fever, burning everything from my brain except the thought "I am not okay."

"I'm sorry about the camera," Ramirez said, in the bizarre quiet. Whatever she'd been doing, she'd done it, and we didn't have much to do but wait to see what the fates had in store.

"It happens," I said.

We waited out the clock in silence. I needed to quit, I decided, during short bouts of lucidity. No more hacking and no more breaking and entering. If I got out of there, I'd never be back. I'd just keep my head down.

I wasn't okay.

Better to just eat trash—trash was free. Sure, there were too many squatters around Southeast Portland, so I'd have to leave town. Go somewhere where I couldn't have a community. Maybe Marcellus would come with me. He said he loved me, and he might even mean it, and that might even be enough.

I'd never be okay.

Or the forest. The fires were worse every year, but I wasn't afraid of death and I wasn't afraid of fire. I was afraid of police and I was afraid of cages. Trapped in a barricaded house with bank cops outside, I kept myself as calm as I could by thinking about pleasant things, like burning alive in a forest fire.

I wasn't okay.

The clock ran out. The transactions were complete, and Albrecht signed off on them. Ramirez had it split up between the two of us in seconds. It did nothing to change my situation.

The cops shot at the windows next, their rounds leaving cracks in the first layer of bulletproof plexi. More cursing. Ramirez was sweating—literally sweating. I thought I'd experienced every symptom of fear, but I was wrong. I didn't sweat. That was a pleasant thought in the morass of my brain.

Then I heard the air-raid siren. A hand-cranked thing, coming closer. And the cops outside started cussing in earnest.

"Darknet?" I asked. It took me a long time to formulate words.

Ramirez nodded. "I put out the call as soon as I saw them."

I uncurled my left arm from its place around my knees and set the door camera up on my screen. There were lights outside—squatters gathered at the closest street corner. The cops turned their backs to us, pistols and tasers drawn.

There'd be too many of us out there for them to start shooting. That was the idea, at least. And every squatter on the street was wearing a camera broadcasting to Darknet. And for every camera there was someone at home who would rather be asleep, hitting the big fat censor button on a console or tablet or field-of-vision device every time something on screen might incriminate anyone but the police. Was it fair? Hardly. But the other side had been doing it for decades.

Just knowing they were out there, the burning waves of fear lost the worst of their power over me. But they remained.

I heard the crack of a grenade launcher and saw a muzzle flash, lasting so much longer on my screen thanks to the wonders of a low frames-per-second camera. The police were shooting teargas, I'd guess.

Ramirez was looking at me, saying something, but it was just white noise to me. All I could hear was the ruckus outside and the cold sound of my slow-beating heart. I really shouldn't have gone to work. I should have stayed in bed. I wasn't okay.

"We gotta go!" Ramirez was shouting. She didn't need to shout—words that promised a chance of escape cut through every frequency.

She had her yoga mat rolled up under her arm, the modem in her hand, and her teeth gritted. Whatever she saw on the Darknet, it must have been more promising than the haze I saw on my screen. I slammed the laptop shut.

She threw open the door and dove into a cloud of pink smoke—cover, provided by our side.

I ran, choking my way into a maelstrom of shouts and smoke and pepperspray. The cop silhouettes were the ones bulky with gear and belts and guns. My friends' silhouettes were the thin ones and the fat ones unencumbered by armor or by much weaponry. They were the ones that kept on the move, playing mouse to the police's cat.

The police were outnumbered but unafraid, backed by an empire's worth of legitimacy. They had jails and judges and healthcare and rich patrons and immunity. We had whatever we could make or steal or whatever minimum wage could buy.

Ferocity was enough that night. A cop grabbed at Ramirez as she sprinted past—they always go for the smallest target—but backed off when a heavyset woman stepped closer with a ski mask and a bat.

No one got hurt, no one got arrested. Thirty squatters—most of them strangers, some of them kids—had turned out for the alarm and the cops beat a retreat once we were past their line.

Invisible people take care of one another.

If the bank would budget for it, the cops would be back during the day, combing the house for the clues they weren't going to find. Worst case, Ramirez was going to get tagged the same as me as a person of note and she'd have be more careful around cameras in hot neighborhoods. But more likely than anything else, the bank would drop it. We won, and they weren't going to want to draw attention to that. We won, but I didn't feel much like a winner.

I was on edge the whole ride back to my neighborhood. Every time I saw another car on the street, I got a little spike of adrenaline. In the dark, every set of headlights was Schrödinger's cop car.

Ramirez rode with me back to my neighborhood and I had her drop me off a few blocks from home. I wouldn't let her self-driving car take me closer. I don't trust the things. One day, I'm going to get into some friend's car and the car itself is gonna just drive us both to jail. I know better than most people that machines will take orders from anyone with good enough code.

"Thanks for the work," I told her when I got out in the soft twilight of morning.

She laughed. Not the condescending, haughty laughter I keep thinking she'll belt out, but a childish giggle that reminded me why I trusted her. "We'd make so much money together," she said.

"I'll call you when I'm starving," I told her. And she drove off.

It wasn't her fault. She lived like she'd never been hurt, like she'd never been broken, so I kept her at arm's length. Her strength reminded me of my weakness.

There's something I tell myself, a kind of mantra I mutter on long nights when the far-off sirens keep me wired or when I'm walking home through the fog and trying desperately not to jump at my own shadow as I pass from the light of one streetlight to another and my own silhouette suddenly appears in front of me. And that mantra is: beauty lies on the far side of fear.

Everything I've done in my life that I'm proud of has terrified me. I'd earned enough that night to keep a whole warehouse of people eating well for the next three months, and that wasn't nothing. It might just be worth it.

Marcellus was lying on his back and snoring in earnest when I crept back into the room. He'd wrapped himself up in the comforter and I had to pry him free to get my naked body into the bed with him. But he murmured in joy when my hand found his chest, and I held him tight and cried with relief and fear in equal parts.

I was home, I had Marcellus. But my house was stolen and my partner was a felon, so both were things that the state could take away.

"How was it?" he asked, half-awake.

"It was work," I said.

"Fucking work," he mumbled. His eyes closed and he snored in that way he always did, endearing and soft.

"Julienne the Technician" by Fabian Alvarado

Previous Page:

A woman who has no arms is positioned in front of an open mechanical panel. In the lower right corner, there is a circular window that looks out on to a planet. The woman appears to be floating in zero gravity. There is writing on the wall behind her that has an arrow pointing left and the partially obscured words, "Gate B2—." The woman has long hair tied in a ponytail and is wearing a hard hat with an insignia on it, a harness around her upper body (which is attached to a clip on her left side, holding her in place), a jumpsuit that ends at her ankles, and toe-fitted socks on her feet. Between the toes of her right foot, she holds a small computer board. A cut piece of wiring hangs down around her left leg, held in place with her left toes. She is looking down with concentration as she works.

The Lessons of the Moon

Joyce Chng

1. Sea of Rains
Waxing, waning, dark moon, crescent, full—
like rain that comes and drench
the desert of my being
water
the bare sand, caress the skin, grow seeds.

2. Sea of Crises
Blame the fullness for the insanity that comes
like the crack of lighting or the giggle
of a child at the sight of buffoons
balloons
staying afloat at the sky,
subject to the whim of the wind.

3. Sea of Tranquility
I hope to remain calm—
consistent, sure as the tides
and as violent as rip currents that pull me
apart,
tear me inside out,
outside in.

4. Landing
Landing, hoping to land,
that's all I want, all I desire—
Landing.
I have been storm-tossed, thrown away, pulled apart:
terra firma, solid ground.
Land now, just land.

☾

I am staring out of the window, at the colors that sweep across the sky, the pinks and the oranges and the red and the rare streak of purple. They cover me, the patches on my chest going up and down. I am awash with colors, swimming in them. I am alive.

My IV drip feeds me, giving me the salt and glucose. My mouth craves the feel and texture of food. Oranges. Apples. A fat juicy medium-rare steak so red that the blood blends with the caramelized onion sauce. Glasses of wine, water and fruit smoothies. Quivering red jellies gleaming like pure ruby, tasting of fine plum and grape liquor. Food, glorious food. Hard to eat when your taste-buds hate you and your intestines reject food straight away.

They are saying that I am changing. Like the moon. I am so low in energy now, the dark moon, that I can only lie on my bed and stare at the colors. Sometimes, I am in my waxing phase, energy coming back—and when I am full, I can do so many things. I write. I dance. I cook. I move. My garden of green and red chili, of rosemary and mint. Then I crash and I am back to square one. My limbs feel like weights. My joints ache and my pain synapses are on fire. I am brought back to earth. I am changing. Into what form, I am not sure.

I am not changing into a phoenix, for sure. The thing running in me isn't some mythical bird due for re-birth. The thing inside me is some insidious beast, sometimes tame, sometimes vicious. All I can do is to chain it down.

Now I am earthbound.

They want me in a Pod, so that I can live further and enjoy more years. I am not sure I want to fly a Pod and fight bad aliens in space, where physics still work and there is no sound. If my body fails, the surgeon tries to reassure me, be patient, this disease needs patience, I will have a new body and I will be a warrior. A good cause. I am fighting for something noble.

Am I?

How many warriors are there out fighting? Are they stationed next to the moon? Can I be the moon instead?

I want to be the moon?

When I die, eventually, I want to be buried in the Sea of Tranquility, or have my ashes scattered. Pods get destroyed at the end. I do not think Pod warriors retire. I want to be scattered like stars. Turn into diamonds. Better than just being destroyed in a burst of mangled steel and voiceless pain.

Å

My little girl comes to see me during visiting hours. She has just turned five. But somehow, she knows what I am going through. She looks at me with huge dark eyes. I don't know how I look. I don't want to know. I refuse having a mirror in the room. The nurses laugh and say I look beautiful. I think they are just pulling my leg and lying through their immaculate teeth. The kind of polite laughter able-bodied and healthy people use, the tone they take with me. "Hang on in there", "You will be fine", "You should pull your bootstraps", nonsense

nonsense more nonsense. Where are you when I am in pain? Where are you when I need help?

My little girl is unafraid, daring. She is always like that. She will pick the coat's button daisies growing outside our house and braid them into tiny bracelets. Coat's button daisies have smiley faces and grow wild everywhere. Endemic. Pest. Resilient. I think they are more resilient than me. I love them. When I sleep, the bracelets are beside me. There is sap and sweetness in my nose. When I wake, the nurses have removed them away. Thrown them into the bin. For fear of contamination, they explain. This is a germ-free environment.

There will always be new bracelets.

They remind that I am resilient. I hang on.

I am hanging on.

"Remember the dandelions?" My little girl would whisper next to my ear. "Remember the dandelions, will you? Please? There are no dandelions in space."

I remember them. They are not really dandelions, but they have similar blowballs. I used to pick her up after day care, plucking the flowers and blowing at the cotton-like puff. She loved the seeds floating in the air. I told her about the pappus that act like parachutes, drifting in the wind. She loves these memories.

"Yes," I reply and my voice rattles in my lungs. My pain synapses snap and bite. My body is rebelling against me.

"You will be in a Pod," she would say later. "You will be like the pappus. You will fly away. I will miss you."

"Yes," I say and I think about the moon. Always the moon.

⚹

Waxing, waning, dark moon, crescent, full—
like rain that comes and drench
the desert of my being
water
the bare sand, caress the skin, grow seeds.

⚹

The Pod is big, like a silver egg with wings and turrets built in. A mobile missile, piloted and inhabited by a brain. My brains. Someone else's brains. Brains, without bodies. A mess of synapses and nerve, stuck in a machine.

I see the Pod in images they show me, just to convince me how fabulous it is. I am on a noble mission. To fight for the Earth in an egg. To fight for humanity against big bad aliens who want to conquer us and our planet.

To fight for my family.

"I want my ashes scattered in the Sea of Tranquility," I state calmly to the attending surgeon. "I want my dust to mingle with the moon dust."

Smiling, he scribbles something down on his writing pad. How quaint. He wants to humor me. We fly through space to fight aliens and he is writing on paper. Like me, some parts of him have not changed. We remain changed and unchanged. Like the moon.

Some people are afraid of change.

I am changing.

I should not be afraid of change.

⚊

So, when they fit me into the Pod, I am ready. My little girl cries and kisses my cheek wetly. Her arms hang onto me. She refuses to let go. "Mama, mama!"

"Make bracelets for me," I whisper. "Wo ai ni." I love you. "Go to your mummy." I mean my wife. She will miss me too. I miss her butterfly kisses. "Wo ai ni," I repeat. "Listen to your mummy." My little girl smiles through her tears.

My wife stands beside my little girl, her eyes dry. She has accepted. She is still accepting. She is tired. She is now free. She kneels down and holds my hand, rests her cheek against mine. I have known her for fourteen years. She is beautiful. She will always be beautiful. She has been there when my synapses flare up and I burn inside out. She has been there when I collapse in my chair and feel like shit. She has fed me herbal soups and told me stories about her family. I have pulled her back. She is earthbound, because of me. Now she is free. I have given back her wings.

She begins to cry now, her tears streaming down her face. My heart clenches painfully and I cry too. My little girl is quickly coaxed away from the bed by one of the nurses. I hear her sobbing outside the room. "Mama, mama, MAMA!"

"Shh, don't," I soothe my wife, patting her hand with my fingers. My fingers look bony, my skin so dry, so thin. "Please don't cry."

"Remember me," she sobs. "When you are with the stars."

"I will," I whisper.

I am going to be free.

I am going to fly.

The doctors and technicians shoo my wife away. I see her behind the glass, blurred, separated from me. Like she is under water. My little girl is not there. Is she spared from this unkindness?

Then, the metal synapses and cords snap into me. I feel a brief pain, like fire in my nerves, in my joints. When I finally open my eyes, I am in the Pod. My human flesh body is gone.

I am going to fly.

⚐

I learn and unlearn to love my new body. The Pod. It is all metal, motherboard and circuits that form my new blood vessels. My new synapses. There is no body, no flesh, no breasts, no pubis. Nothing. I am artificial. Metal and wire and cord all over.

In the Pod I feel no pain.

I flex my fingers and the missile pods cycle.
I turn my head
and the Pod changes direction.

But where is my body? Why am I still linked to it? Am I cursed with an eternal body? Is my brain my body too? What am I? Who am I?

⚐

Explosions in space so dark the stars are diamond-eye-piercing bright, but they are dying or dead stars. We only see the light, much much later. My Pod, my body, moves through nothing. I can only hear the sounds of my Pod. The alien ship chases me, like a comet tail, like a very hungry bristling sea urchin with long black spikes. Comet. Falling star. Bad luck. I spin, dodge and spin again. I feel dizzy. My body is steel. I should not be feeling dizzy. I shouldn't be. I am healthy. I am healthy. Colors light up. Beeps and shrieks of the Pod echoing in and through me. My body is screaming at me. Evasive manoeuvres! Turn, turn, turn! Flee! I am the Pod. I am invincible.

Flee, flee, flee! All my instincts are shrieking. Flee!

A sharp pain lances down my spine. I have been shot!

But I have no spine.
I have no actual body.
My body is metal and wire.
I am linked. I am me. I am the Pod.
I am no warrior.
I am going down, down, down.

The moon looms before me. A new moon, unknown, nameless.

I think of home, of my wife, of my little girl, of her little flower bracelets.

⚐

I am going to land.
terra firma, solid ground.
land now, just land.

☖

I hope to remain calm—
consistent, sure as the tides
and as violent as rip currents that pull me
apart,
tear me inside out,
outside in.

☖

I have landed.
My moon.

My home.

Screens

Samantha Rich

We had to take our screens off for gym class. It always left us feeling weird and numb, or muffled; how much could you get from facial expression and body language? Barely anything. So many cues for communication were lost when you couldn't see how someone's nervous system was responding in real time. It was like trying to speak underwater.

My mom got so mad any time she thought about it. "Gym class is practically when you need your monitors the most, Ellie!" she would say, her own screen lighting up silver-gold with the rush of indignant adrenaline. "How is the teacher supposed to know if someone is hurt without it? It's pure negligence."

"Screens are expensive," my sister Kate always pointed out, like this argument was ever going to change. "They don't want them to get broken and have parents asking the school to pay for replacements."

"Then they shouldn't do high-impact activities," Mom would snap. "What's more important, dodge ball or adequately monitoring children's health?"

For now the school was still prioritizing dodge ball, so we took our screens off for gym.

Putting them back on afterward was always a relief. They came back online and lit up like bright flowers scattered around the locker room. We could really see each other again; Megan Phillips' ADHD showed up as intermittent flashes of green as her neurons fired, Jenna Abrams showed a low constant orangey glow of pain from the shoulder she'd messed leading the volleyball team to state, Liz Rogers had a gray-washed tinge of fatigue over everything.

My screen showed mostly neutral, with some shivering gold around the edges whenever I remembered my upcoming pre-calc test. "Calm your yellows," my friend Becca told me, bumping me with her shoulder. "It's going to be fine."

I did my best, but having your neurology out on display didn't make it controllable. I almost envied Sandhya Walker, who had for-real anxiety, the disorder kind; she kept Xanax in her purse and whenever she took one we all watched her screen fade from a field of shivering gold to blank neutrality, while the lines eased from her forehead and the edges of her mouth relaxed. Lucky. It was just like watching Jenna's screen when she took a painkiller, or Liz's when she drank coffee. We could all watch them feel better.

Of course, screens also meant that after pre-calc everyone was broadcasting who had come prepared and who got blown out of the water. Jeff Horman's screen was dark blue with red pulses, to nobody's surprise; he was never prepared but somehow still always disappointed. A screen like that screamed an undiagnosed learning disability, my mom always said, and then got indignant about the school not intervening.

"They have the data right in front of them! They should do something!" she would say, and Kate and I would look for the nearest exit, because once Mom went off Dad was going to jump in and we'd heard the argument fifty billion times.

"There is still such a thing as a right to privacy, Helen," Dad would say, shaking his head. "Just because your biometrics can be put out there for everybody to see doesn't mean there's an inherent right to—"

And she would tell him to stop living in the dark ages, and he would say that kids these days didn't learn how to communicate with others at all, that we would be a *crippled generation*, and she would tell him to watch the slurs. Fifty billion times. Kate and I were over it.

Our dad was in a different world about this stuff. The Visibility Movement had won everything a few years before I was born, and Kate didn't come along for another two years after that. The protests, the speeches, all of it was history to us, not reality like it was for our parents. The first screens came out when I was four and Kate was two; they were basically always part of our worlds. Dad's ranting about privacy never made sense to us. How could biometrics be private? Everyone deserved to have their story known, and the best way to do that was to make it visual. Visibility was the key to maintaining respect in a diverse population.

The first time I ever thought that Dad might have a point was the week after that math test, when Ms. Ellison handed back the results. Jeff got a D, of course, but he expected that as much as anybody else. His screen was blue and red, but he laughed and shrugged it off. Dan Pelgin slipped him a buzz patch hand-to-hand under the desk, and Jeff's screen flashed bright orange joy. We all looked away. He was fine.

It wasn't Jeff that made everything weird. It was Stella Marshall.

Stella and I had been good friends in elementary school, and then she'd been really popular in seventh grade—one of the queen bees, really. Something had changed, though, gradually enough that nobody really noticed, and at some point she'd slipped down from the pinnacle to not even the bottom, but outside of the world at all. Nobody picked on Stella, because picking on her would require that anybody acknowledge she existed.

Ms. Ellison called out names one by one and we made out way to the front of the classroom, taking back out tests and glancing at the grade, a corresponding burst of satisfaction or disappointment going across our screens. Those sitting at the desks tracked those colors closely, if they weren't busy with buzz patches or sneaking in a few minutes of SMS while Ms. Ellison was distracted. Kids who cared about grades cared about each other's colors.

I cared about grades a lot, so I was watching when Stella took her paper from Ms. Ellison's hand.

Stella's screen was usually a muddy mix of dark blues and grays, brown around the edges. She didn't seem to feel much, as far as anyone could tell; of course, maybe that was because none of us were looking.

When she took her paper, a bright line crossed her screen, a genuine, visible burst of happiness blooming up and out like a flower. The other kids who were watching seemed indifferent—Stella was smart, everyone knew that, her brains were as invisible as the rest of her—but I kept watching. The happy-flower was nice to see, even though her face stayed resolutely blank.

"Hey, Stella," I said when she sat down again. "What did you get?"

She glanced up, then looked down again, putting her paper away in her binder. Pretending not to hear me. That was kind of shitty, but I wasn't going to push her; what would be the point of that?

Becca saw the flash of embarrassment cross my face and my screen. "She probably wrecked the curve again," she said, rolling her eyes. "She's such a nerd, she always ruins it for the rest of us."

Stella's face was blank, but her screen flickered in a rush of colors, embarrassment and anger and low, dull, throbbing shades of pain. I didn't know where those were coming from—Becca hadn't even touched her—but they were undeniably there.

I opened my mouth to say something; I don't know what, just something to distract Becca and take her attention off Stella, but before I managed to get anything out, Becca sneered and said, "Oh, are you going to cry about it? There's no point getting all pissed off that nobody likes you. If you weren't so fucking boring and gray all the time, maybe somebody would."

Everybody was watching now, the whole class, eyes going to Stella's screen to see if Becca's words had hit home. What Stella said in response was way less important than knowing how she really felt, if Becca had really managed to hurt her.

"Fucking gray," Becca said. "Your screen is a fucking diagnostic readout of major depression, you know. Everybody can see it. Why don't you do something about it? They have meds for people like you, you know."

Stella wrapped her left arm across her body, covering most of the screen with her sleeve. "Don't fucking look at me," she shouted, her voice cracking. "God, why can't you just back the fuck off, all of you?"

"Stella," Ms. Ellison said, "language—"

But nobody really heard her, because Stella was ripping her leads out. The wires that connected the screens to our bodies were hair-thin and delicate, to be as minimally invasive as possible, but they were still *wires* and getting them caught on something hurt a lot. I couldn't imagine the pain of ripping them out the way Stella was doing, wrapping them in her fist and just *yanking*. Blood spots blossomed on her skin and somebody on the far side of the room shrieked.

"Stella!" Ms. Ellison shouted. "That is not appropriate!"

"Fuck you," Stella said, but her voice was low now, still angry but with no defiance. "I'm done with this."

"You're going to be written up!" Ms. Ellison called as Stella walked out of the room. "Go to the nurse's office right away! You can't bleed here!"

Whispers and nervous laughter rushed around the room, the loudest laughter from Becca. I could see the flickers of gold-edged worry across her screen, so I knew she didn't feel as cool as she was acting, but nobody else seemed to notice.

☩

Everybody forgot about it within a day, of course. Stella went back to being invisible. I seemed to be the only one who noticed that she didn't wear her screen anymore.

It was weird to see someone without a screen, just blank space across their chests. She pinned the screen openings in her shirts closed and wore scarves. I couldn't read her at all. Her face, her body language, they were both a mystery without the biometrics onscreen as a starting point.

It threw the teachers off a little, I could tell. Their eyes would scan the classrooms, looking for the telltale colors of distraction or someone actually enjoying themselves, which meant they weren't paying attention, and when they got to Stella they'd just kind of stop. Then they would look away again, and things would go on.

I knew I should just shrug it off and forget about it like everybody else, but it kept coming back to me, a nagging distraction. I thought about it one night when I was supposed to be writing my essay for

Civics on the Visibility Movement. Since I had written some version of that same essay every year since fifth grade, it wasn't hard to let my attention wander.

I made myself drag up the video of Sana Tayadi's speech before Congress again. The peak moment of Visibility, just three days before the legislation was passed.

Tayadi was held in a moment of time, forever before the podium, balanced against her mobility frame as she spoke. Her hands had a constant tremor that broke through the neurological controllers of the day. The screen set up on the podium before her—tiny and crude compared to the ones of today, and not yet portable—showed the impulses of epileptic seizures firing in her brain and being diffused by the controllers. Her voice was clear and had the edge of anger that had caught my attention the first time I heard it as a kid, and left me never able to ignore it no matter how many times it was recycled through school and the evening news.

We will make the invisible disabilities visible. You will not be able to pretend we don't exist. We will be here. We have always been here. But you will see us, each and every one of us. All of these lifetimes you have been telling us to speak up, to make ourselves heard if we want to be counted. No more. We will be seen, we will be known. The burden will be on you to believe your own eyes. Not on us.

Tayadi's speech was a watershed moment. It was amazing. Everybody agreed; it was right there in my assigned reading. What else could I possibly have to say about it?

"Hey, kiddo." My dad leaned over my shoulder, squinting at the screen. "Again? Didn't you write about this last year?"

"Every year." I tapped the screen to pause it. "It was a big deal, though, you know? The major civil rights victory of our time. Your time. I guess it was before my time."

He pursed his lips and stepped back a little. "I wouldn't call it a cut and dry victory, Ellie."

"Why don't you like it?" I'd been hearing him and Mom fight about this for years, but I had never asked him. "Why are you against visibility?"

"I'm not against visibility at all."

"You're against screens." I waved my hand at the tablet. "You don't think this was a victory."

"It was absolutely a victory. But not a cut and dry one. It's more complicated than that."

"What's complicated? Explain it to me."

He sighed, rubbing the bridge of his nose. "Do you remember your grandmother?"

She died when I was four. I had vague impressions at most, but I couldn't tell him that. "Yeah, of course."

"She had multiple sclerosis. Do you remember that?"

"Kind of." I remembered the words more than anything, hearing my parents say them. I didn't really learn what it meant until Visibility Enhancement in fifth grade.

"Well, your grandmother was a very private person. She would never have wanted anyone to know how much pain she was in on a given day, much less every random stranger who walked by."

"But why not? If people know how you feel, they can make accommodations. They can help."

"They can also be intrusive and judgmental." He folded his arms across his chest, still looking at the paused video. "When people can see things, they have a tendency to think that's all there is, and they stop listening. Stop letting you speak for yourself."

"Well, you don't have to speak. It's right there."

"There's something right there. But not everything. There are... unquantifiables. Things we only find out if we talk to each other like people, instead of thinking seeing is knowing, all the time." He sighed and turned away. "But maybe you're right, Ellie. Maybe I'm just out of touch and you and your mom and the school are right."

I felt like I'd done something really wrong, though I didn't have any idea what. "When is dinner?"

"Twenty minutes or so. I'll let you know when it gets closer." His footsteps faded down the hall and I sat there, looking from the video to my half-started essay. Probably no one would notice if I turned in last year's essay all over again. If Dad was right, they would see what they wanted to see and think it was all there was.

I knew that wasn't how he meant it. I sighed, tapped the screen to start the video again, and started typing.

⚐

The next day at school, my dad's words were still following me around. They got louder at lunch when I saw Stella sitting by herself in the far corner, face blank, still without a screen.

I walked over and sat down next to her without knowing what I was going to say, or if I was going to say anything. She looked up, her face tightening. I stared at the scabs below her collarbone where her leads had gone in. Scabs and faint bruises. Our screens really showed our insides. Breaking the link left marks. I could never do it.

She stared at me, her eyes unreadable, her lips parted just a little. I could see her teeth. I cleared my throat twice before I managed to talk.

"Hey, Stella."

She didn't answer, just tilted her head a little in an unspoken *What?*

"How, um." I cleared my throat again. "How are you doing?"

The silence stretched out for a really long moment. I could feel other eyes across the room drifting toward us, and I knew my screen was starting to flare with embarrassment and discomfort.

Stella knew it, too. Her eyes narrowed and her lip curled. "Fuck off."

My screen lit up brighter and I heard the laughter start up somewhere across the room. I stood up and hurried away from her, stunned by how little I understood of what had just happened. What Dad said made me think that she would be secretly glad I asked, grateful. How was I supposed to tell if she was, deep down? How much could you hide when knowing things relied on everybody really paying attention? It wasn't fair.

"Why did you do that?" Becca asked, frowning past me at Stella. "She's not worth getting humiliated over."

"Just forget it."

Becca looked at me and her eyes widened. "Wow. You're, like, actually upset. Over *her*? Why?"

I folded my arms over my screen and shook my head. "I don't even want to talk about it. Let's go outside, come on."

She looked at me for a moment longer, frowning, but with my arms over the screen, I was invisible to her eyes.

"To the Pitch" by L.E. Badillo

Previous Page:

An old, bald man and young boy with short hair are in a residential garage that has a workbench and "everyday" tools hanging on the wall. There is also a window looking out on to a yard. The young boy is on the right side of picture. He is smiling and looking down at a soccer ball that he is kicking. On the left side of picture, the old man is sitting on a chair, making adjustments to his prosthetic right foot. There is an oil can and two ratchets on a cloth in front of him. He is holding a ratchet in his right hand and his shoe in his left hand. He is happily looking at the boy.

A Sense All its Own

Sara Patterson

Bren leaned forward, adrenalin surging as the final seconds of the battle clock ticked down.

3. 2. 1. Fight!

"Let's go, Fang!" Bren cried. Her droid, Ivory Fang, added a metallic howl to Bren's. Then they were surging across the battle zone in a blur of silver and gunmetal. Bren barely had to touch the accelerator. Her droid was just as eager for the hunt. In this way and others, Fang was a different kind of droid. Just as Bren was a different kind of pilot.

On Bren's main display, one of Fang's targeting scanners flashed a reading. Bren's fingers moved across the controls with ease, magnifying the image to her preferred extra-larger-than-average specifications. A hundred yards away, her opponent piloted his tawny raptorin behind a jutting ridge of rock. Luring Bren into the small space gave the more heavily armored raptorin an advantage. But Bren still had a trick up her sleeve.

Canid droids—normal factory-standard ones—weren't built to climb. But Fang was a hybrid, built from scratch with a more creative design. At Bren's command, Fang leapt headlong towards the cliff. Bren tapped a customized button on the controls. Small compartments on the tops of Fang's toes opened, releasing the spring-loaded claw-blades that Bren had installed. For a few seconds, Fang clung to the cliff, the motors in its joints straining with discomfort. Bren felt her droid's resistance then—just the faintest hint of a tremor. A reminder that, yes, Fang still had traces of feral programming and could, if it chose to, disobey Bren's commands. Even kill her.

"I know, Fang. Just bear with me a little longer. Soon, we'll get to face some worthy opponents, just like I promised. But now, if it's all the same to you, I'd rather not lose my first audition match to some noob and his clunker."

Her droid *harummed* in response and the controls slackened once more.

Bren pushed the accelerator, urging Fang up and over. More button pushing prepped the mounted rifle between Fang's shoulders. The raptorin pilot was holding position in a narrow gap on the other side. Judging from the number of weapons he was powering, he hadn't expected Bren to thwart his brilliant strategy by climbing directly over his cover.

Atop the ridge, Bren eased Fang forward, so that its head peered just far enough over the side to get a visual on their opponent. Only when they got there, Bren couldn't seem to find him.

That couldn't be right. Fang's sensors were picking up the raptorin's core readings directly below her. Fang was snarling. Urging her on—

Realization dawned, filling Bren with fury.

It's my damn eyes.

Alarms blared, "Incoming projectile."

Bren dodged aside, more out of instinct than skill. The sound of a rocket whizzed past—bare inches from Fang's left optical sensor, and the reinforced glass-alloy that was Bren's only protection from the battle.

She swore again. Bullets accosted her. The raptorin pilot was hoping to hit a vital point in Fang's armor. But Bren still had the cliff for cover. And now, thanks to her opponent's desperation, Bren had his location, too.

"Time to end this."

Fang gave a metallic snarl of agreement. A hatch opened above Bren's head, lowering a scope. Bren fitted it over her left eye, which was only marginally better than the other. She magnified the view with a custom lens until she could see the distinct blue glow of the raptorin's core flickering in its chest. She aimed a little to the side. Enough for her shot to immobilize the droid without breaching its core.

This was just sport, after all.

Å

Inside Dome Central, the weather simulators were working overtime. The sky-image was clear and cloudless, the temperature a comfortable 72 degrees—perfect conditions for Audition Tournament shopping.

Pilots hunting for deals on droid parts crowded the area. Bren was no exception. Fang needed repairs. She turned down a double–wide street, a metal basket of various doodads in each hand. This particular street in the Business Quarter was called "Mechanics Lane." The mechanics and their garages were organized by quality—in a convenient (and strategic) descending order.

Though still a novice pilot, Bren was not as naïve as other noobs. She was a Gipson. And Teresa Gipson, rest her soul, didn't tolerate sloppy work in *her* garage. So Bren moved on, ignoring fancy displays and their so-called "deals" for first-time auditioners.

She passed by an impressive garage with huge windows. The Victor team crest glowed in bright neon on every wall, giving the place a showroom quality. Inside were three of the four Victor brothers' droids—all glistening, perfect, and incredibly rare—being tended by at least a dozen mechanics.

Bren started to move on, not realizing the youngest Victor was outside pacing and talking on his palm pad.

"'Attacked?' What do you mean 'attacked'? Won't be here until *when*?" He turned sharply, clipping Bren in the shoulder. "Owf—hang on! Watch where you're going, you clumsy bi—" He froze.

Bren caught a distinct whiff of nervous sweat as he jerked away. "You."

"Heya, Aiden," Bren said, curling her mouth into a wicked smile. "Been a while since your last challenge. I was starting to think you'd finally given up piloting. Can't say I blame you, considering how I nailed your ass to the wall last time."

"Shut up!" Aiden yelled, then realized he still had the palm pad to his ear. "No, I didn't mean you—damn it." He made a shooing motion. "Get lost, Gipson. I don't have time to deal with you and your mongrel droid. I've got a tournament to prepare for."

Bren smiled wider. "Oh, I didn't realize you were auditioning this year. What happened? Daddy's friends at the Droid Battle Committee couldn't bend the rules and put you on a team?"

Aiden glared.

Bren knew she was being reckless. Here, in a Dome full of droid pilots and other folks in the industry, she had to be extra-mindful of how she presented herself in public—lest someone catch on that her eyes weren't quite as good as they should be. But with this one pilot, Bren couldn't help herself. Gipsons didn't let go of grudges easily, and Aiden Victor had spit in her face twice.

Not literally, though Bren was sure he wanted to right now. The first offense was three years back when the Victor brothers had paid a visit to her mom's "quaint" garage for tune-ups. A cocky Aiden, then fifteen, had slid a hand down Bren's backside and offered to pass the time "tuning up" in a different sense. Bren had bloodied his nose. Aiden's second offense came in a battle zone when he'd offered his father's money in exchange for her surrender. Bren had refused and defeated him in record time.

Aiden made an obscene gesture right in her face. "I'm going to make you regret that, Gipson. Just wait. My father has friends in registration. The next time we meet, it'll be in the tournament!" He turned.

"Great!" Bren cheered after him. "It's going to be fun *kicking your ass* in front of half of Dome Central!"

Aiden went back to his call with the underling. "Now listen here. I don't care if you had to fend off an entire fucking army of feral canids. You get your asses and my droid out here or..."

Bren moved on, walking down Mechanic's Lane until the storefronts were a bit less flashy and the merchandise a bit less expensive. Fang was parked at Old Warrant's garage—one of the few mechanics that allowed pilots to rent his space and tools, and didn't grouse when they opted to do their own repair work.

Warrant wasn't in when she got back, which was just as well. He was a suspicious old codger and not too keen on hybrids after one crushed his leg years back. Warrant actually got off lucky compared to some. He could afford surgery to replace the limb with robotic cybergear. The enhancement legally ended his piloting career. Droid fighting, after all, was a test of human skill, not of human-enhanced-with-robotics skill. But giving up piloting, he claimed, was a small price to pay to be normal again. Bren thoroughly disagreed. One more reason she was glad Warrant wasn't there.

Bren dumped her baskets and began to sort through the pile of scrap she had painstakingly salvaged out of discount bins. A necessary precaution. Her older brother, Brice, didn't exactly factor in Bren's secret piloting career as part of her expenses when he wired her monthly funds. But Bren was no scrapper, and the tedium quickly irritated her.

This is your own damn fault, you know. If you just stayed put in mom's belly like you were supposed to instead of popping out early, you would have had been born with normal eyes. You could be a pilot like everyone else and wouldn't have to sneak around building a half-feral droid with junk parts. Or lie to the only family you've got about how you've been spending your spare time.

Bren had a mental flash of Aiden Victor and his family's army of mechanics, and her mood soured even more. Come lights-out, Aiden would have a full belly and be sleeping well, knowing his droid would be in pristine condition for the battles to come. Bren would be lucky if she caught a few winks in Fang's cockpit. She couldn't afford to rent both Warrant's space and a hotel at tournament prices. Plus, thanks to the expense of fixing Fang, she'd have to go without dinner, too.

Sadly, her situation wasn't uncommon for a novice pilot. One more reason Bren ached to be on a team. Droid team pilots were given food and their own room in the team rig. Not to mention a fair cut of the winnings.

Of course, being on a team would bring up another complication—hiding her bad eyesight. Despite all the advances in society and technology, the Droid Battle Committee was still hesitant to alter its no-tolerance stance on pilots with physical limitations. Why exactly, Bren didn't know, though she theorized corporate ass-covering played a significant part. As things stood, only pilots in "peak physical condition, as determined by a legitimate medical-scan" could participate. Which, in this day and age, was a bunch of shit.

Fang's repairs weren't complicated this time—mostly prying out bullets and replacing damaged minor circuits. Nothing Fang's internal repair program couldn't handle with a few days in sleep-mode. But Bren didn't have the luxury of time during a tournament.

Hours later, weary to the bone, Bren rested against one of her droid's hind legs.

"Get some rest, Fang. You earned it."

Fang gave a soft *viruummm*. The sound Bren equated to a sigh. Then Fang's minor systems powered down and Bren heard the faint whir of Fang's core entering sleep mode.

Outside, headlights blared, lighting the space beside her for a moment. The chugging engine of a transport droid idled just outside the back entrance. Bren strained to hear.

"You can't bring that in here," Davon, one of Warrant's staff, insisted hotly. Bren caught snippets of other voices, too.

"…emergency!" argued a woman, clearly annoyed.

"…friends with the owner…" a younger man pleaded.

Davon wasn't impressed. "Well, Warrant ain't here. And he's the only one who handles droids with feral cores."

The young man again. "Already bought the taming chip… just need… can't just leave my droid like—"

"What part of NO don't you understand?"

"Now you listen here, you witless lugnut…" the woman snapped. Bren couldn't quite catch all of the rest, only that it was one hell of a telling-off. She didn't know if Davon really deserved it. After all, it wasn't his fault that Warrant insisted on handling all the taming chip replacements himself. Bren thought about stepping in and defending Davon. Then, Bren's stomach growled and she got a better idea.

Grabbing her multi-pocketed utility belt and a pair of customized, high-powered goggles, Bren met the woman and the young man just as they were about to drive away.

"Hey, hold up. So, I couldn't help overhearing your little predicament."

The woman leaned out of her hauler droid's cockpit, revealing her cybergear right arm. She had customized the gear as only a scrapper could—soldering on holders for tools and hatches for hidden compartments. She had even painted the limb purple to match the dyed tips of her hair. "Yeah, the kid fried his droid senseless and had shit timing about it. What's it to you?"

"Well, I was thinkin' I could install the chip for you. It won't take long. Ten minutes tops."

"You a mechanic?" The woman was suspicious. No surprise there—most scrappers were. Bren wasn't sure how specific she should be. Her mother dealt with scrap traders from all over—before she and Bren's father were killed—but that didn't mean she was especially well-liked among them.

"Occasionally," Bren answered, deciding to be vague for now. "My family ran a garage."

The young man, who still looked half a boy, seemed to perk up.

"How much?" the woman asked.

"I'd settle for a hot meal and a bed for the night." There was an uncertain silence. Bren shrugged. "What? I'm hungry. And I know what a taming chip cost you at tournament prices."

Another pause. The boy chewed his lip. "My team's rig is parked outside the city. I'm sure our manager won't mind if you crash on the couch." The boy glanced at the woman like her say was the deciding factor.

"Don't look at me, kid. It ain't my droid that's busted."

He looked back to Bren. "Okay, deal. But you'll have to fix my droid first, since I need it to get back."

"Fair enough."

Bren walked to the back of the woman's hauler and hiked herself up onto the flatbed where the boy's jacklin droid was lashed. A moment later, she heard clumsy movement behind her.

"Here, let me help you." The boy offered her a leg up to his droid's shoulder. "Thanks again. You're really doing me a huge favor. I'm Pitt, by the way, from team Howler."

"Bren," said Bren.

Bren and Pitt reached the jacklin's back. A power restraining collar kept the droid from attacking, but Bren knew from the warmth of the metal that it wasn't happy. Core access, if she recalled right, was at the back of the head. Still, Bren let Pitt guide her as the sky-image darkened.

"Hey, Nadine. Can we get some light up here?" he called down to his companion just as a pair of blinding spots lit up his face. "Ahhhk!"

The woman, Nadine, had slipped atop her hauler without a sound. Now her outline stood on an adjacent pile of crates fiddling with a third spotter lamp.

"Thank you," mumbled a dazed Pitt.

Bren smiled appreciatively as she blinked away purple spots.

"Nice. You wire these in yourself?"

"Yeah. To keep thieves away at night. Doesn't do much for ferals though. I've been trying to petition specs to the Battle Committee to let me install a pulse rifle to chase 'em off." She made a snorting sound and mumbled, "Waste of fuckin' time."

"That sucks," Bren agreed, slipping on her goggles and retrieving an auto-screwdriver from her belt. She unscrewed the jacklin's core hatch by feel. But she kept her head down for appearances.

"Bunch of nosy manual-quoters..." Nadine was ranting. "My security shouldn't be any of their damn business, seein' as how I'm the one braving the badlands while they sit in their cushy offices."

"I hear that. Some of the Committee's rules have been giving me trouble, too." The hatch came free, letting out a hiss of smoke. Inside a display screen wired to a circuit board flashed red warning errors.

"Must have been some battle," Bren muttered, zooming in her goggles to examine the damage.

"Yeah, kinda," said Pitt.

"Don't you have a mechanic on staff?"

"He had to stay behind to guard the rig. Local scans reported a pack of ferals roaming the area."

Nadine huffed. "See. This is exactly what I'm talkin' about."

Bren pulled out more instruments. Even with the droid's damage, her hands moved with routine ease. For all the smoke and noise of Pitt's jacklin, Bren had repaired worse. A few minutes later, she retrieved the new taming chip from Pitt.

"I wonder what makes droids go feral like that," he mused as she worked. "I mean, you would think they'd be smart enough to realize they'd have a better, safer life if they just accepted the taming program."

"Safer, maybe. Better...? How can a life be better if you don't get to choose how to live it?" Bren's fingers slipped, just a hair, and her instrument sent up a spark that singed her hand. "Damn it! Can you adjust the light a little?"

"Sure," Pitt moved to comply. "So, what? We should get rid of taming chips?"

"If the droid doesn't want to accept the program, I think that should be their choice, not ours."

Nadine spoke up. "That's a noble thought, but if we start givin' droids a choice, what makes you think they won't choose to kill us all? Ain't that what happened with the Ancients? The beasts got too smart.

Tried to take over or some such."

"I've heard that story, too," Pitt chimed in. "Back when the sky was still open, and animals were made of flesh, just like humans. There was a huge war. In the end, the Ancients had to wipe out the other species to save themselves. It's why they built the first droids. To take up the role of the animals after the world went to shit."

"I'm not saying there isn't a risk," Bren clarified, not looking up. "But maybe if we treated them with respect instead of like slaves, the droids wouldn't have a reason to turn on us." She finished the final touch-ups and slipped her instruments away. "Right. All done. Now we just need to see if your droid accepted the program. Power down the collar, and I'll reset the core manually."

Pitt hesitated. "But isn't that dangerous?"

"Only if it doesn't work."

⚊

Bren hunched behind Pitt in his droid's cockpit as they bade farewell to Nadine. Part of her envied the woman. Nadine had conquered her physical limitation with some kick-ass cybergear and was still able to do what she loved. If Bren got cybergear for her eyes, she could never legally pilot a droid again.

Bren chose piloting, hands down, which would have been fine if her brother agreed. But Brice Gipson was a mechanic to his bones. If something was broken, like say, Bren's eyes, he was obligated to fix them. He had even taken up their father's old droid, Shadowrunner, and become a pilot to earn the money for Bren's surgery. He was on a team and everything. And Brice didn't even like piloting.

When they arrived at the Howler team rig, Pitt directed Bren up one level to the lounge.

"Make yourself at home. I'll go let my manager know you'll be staying."

Unlike the droid parking space below, the rig upstairs was cozier, with painted walls, carpets and plush couches fit for human habitation. On the furthest end, delicious smells wafted from a small, partially concealed kitchen.

Bren waited, bouncing lightly on her toes, stomach growling.

"So, you comin' to the semi-finals with us tomorrow?" A young woman asked from the kitchen.

A male voice responded, too muffled by the stove vent to understand.

"Pahf," said the woman, "and you call yourself a pilot. I need someone who actually cares about the audition lineups to talk with. Where'd Pitt run off to?"

Muffled laughter and a remark that made the woman snort.

"Boyfriend? That little twerp? Yeah, right. He *wishes* he had this." She shifted in her chair, giving Bren a clear view as she spanked herself playfully.

"Wishes I had what?" Pitt asked as he entered with the most perfect timing ever.

The mumbling teammate by the stove raised his voice and answered.

"Meara's sweet, sweet booty."

Bren perked up. She knew that voice!

She pushed past Pitt into the small dining area, barely dodging the wadded-up napkin aimed, piss-poorly, at her brother Brice's head.

"Bren—?" Brice nearly dropped an entire kettle of protein stew on his foot.

"Brice, holy shit, it is you!"

Brice moved to embrace her, and Bren met his hug. He was leaner then she remembered and had grown his hair out, but there was no mistaking her big brother. He smelled of engine grease and just a hint of their father's aftershave. She buried her face in his shirt and inhaled the familiar scents of home.

Pitt cleared his throat. "Oh, you two know each other?"

Her brother replied, "Pitt, Meara, this is Brenna, my baby sister."

Bren laughed, a little more dryly then she meant to, and pulled away. "I'm not such a baby anymore, Brice."

"What are you even doing here?"

Oh, nothing much. Just fighting in the Auditions with the half-feral droid I secretly built using your design specs.

Pitt relayed the events at Warrant's without skipping any details.

"I meant, what are you doing here in Dome Central?" Brice clarified when Pitt finally finished. There was an accusatory edge in his voice. Bren wasn't surprised; her brother knew the hell-raising she was capable of better than anyone. He also knew she wasn't above lying to get out of trouble. But having such mistrust before Bren had even offered an explanation pissed her off.

"Could ask you the same thing," Bren countered, "last I heard you were going to be outland for another year."

"Plans changed." He hesitated for a second. Unlike Bren, Brice was a shitty liar. "One of my teammates was injured. My manager wanted to scout the auditions…" Bren could hear honest pain in his voice.

"That bad, huh?"

Brice made a soft "hmm" noise, then changed topics. "You never answered my question."

"I came to watch the Auditions."

Not a total lie, at least.

"By yourself?"

Bren felt the corner of her mouth twitch. "I'm here, aren't I?" She held her brother's gaze preparing to square off. Then her stomach growled. Meara snickered, and the tension dissolved. Soon, Bren and everyone on Team Howler were squished around the small table, bumping elbows and bolting down stew and hunks of carbo-loaf.

"You know, it's strange," Meara said after Bren's bowl was licked clean. "I can't help thinkin' I've seen your face before."

Bren swallowed. Meara knew her from the auditions. Her picture and license information were displayed before each match.

"Probably at one of the souvenir booths," she suggested.

"Oh, Brice, I almost forgot," Pitt mumbled between mouthfuls, "Nadine told me she'd be over later."

Meara snorted, prodding Bren's ribs. "We all know what that means!"

Bren didn't at first. She was so relieved Meara didn't blow her cover, the rig could have caved in without her noticing. Then Bren heard her brother hiss, "shut it" and realized exactly what Meara meant.

"You and Nadine…" Bren prompted, unable to resist.

Meara grinned. "…are on each other like magnets."

Bren covered her mouth in delight. "Oooo, wait until I tell the guys back home!"

"Don't you dare—" Brice began, but too late. Bren whipped out her palm pad. Brice dove for her, snatching it away before the call could go through.

"Hey! Give it back!" Bren laughed. But Brice kept her at bay with one foot and held her palm pad far out of reach behind him.

The device vibrated, then let out a particular chime, indicating a text from the Droid Battle Committee. This one likely concerned her next match.

Bren's fingers twitched, aware that Brice was holding her secret in his hands. She reached again, trying not to sound desperate. "Give it back, damn it!"

But Brice must have seen something change. He stood and opened the message, reading aloud. "Pilot Brenna Gipson. Auditions opponent selection was approved—"

Bren snatched the device away before he could finish. "Bastard! What the fucking hell makes you think you can read—"

"You're a droid pilot."

His voice was almost a whisper, so unreadable that for a split

85

second Bren wasn't sure if he wanted to hug her or slap her.

Meara broke in. "I knew I recognized you from somewhere!"

Bren didn't respond. She kept her eyes locked on Brice's, not daring to look away.

"How long?" he said softly. There was warning in his voice. If she lied, he would know.

"Since my sixteenth birthday."

"A year? An entire *year you've been doing this?"*

Pitt and Meara watched the exchange with blissful ignorance.

"So she's a pilot. What's the big deal?" Meara asked.

"The big deal?" Brice's reply sounded on the verge of frenzy. "The big deal is Bren is *blind*. I've risked my life for three years trying to fix—" he shook his head, fighting tears. "And now I find out you— Do you have any idea what I've seen—what I've had to—"

Bren started to cry, fierce angry sobs that came out more like screams. "Well, excuse me for not going along with your perfect plan, but this is *my* life and I don't want any damned cybergear surgery *because I'm going to be a pilot!* I've already proved I can!"

She felt Brice's glare before she saw it and when she looked into his eyes, it was like looking down the barrel of Fang's gun.

"Oh really? How did you get past registration? Hmm? Bribe someone on the Committee? Hack the bio-scan?"

"Fuck you, Brice!" She started to storm out but Brice caught her shoulder and shoved her into a chair.

"No. You're not running from this, Bren." He pulled out his own palm pad. Bren gaped at him.

"You're gonna snitch on me?"

"Fuck no. You think I want to see my sister in prison? I'm calling the hospital to schedule you for surgery."

Bren blanched. "No! You can't!"

"The hell I can't. You're seventeen. I'm still in charge for another year."

Meara gaped. "You're going to force her! That's fucked up, Brice."

"Yeah Brice," Pitt added. "I mean I know she did sorta break the rules, but cybergear is so… permanent."

"It's also none of your business," Brice snapped at them.

"No. It's *my* business," interrupted Bren. "Piloting is who I am. Yeah I admit I lied and cheated for it this time. I had no choice. But who's to say the law won't change?"

Brice just shook his head. "I don't care if the law changes or not, Bren. I promised Mom and Dad I'd take care of you—"

"—and you think this is what they wanted?" She looked him hard in the eye. "Who do you think taught me how to pilot in the first place?"

The room grew very still.

"No, they wouldn't..." Brice whispered.

"All those times Dad took me to run errands and you could never figure out why he always used Shadow instead of the hauler. Or when Mom taught me to repair droids even though you were better at it..."

"But your eyes—"

"Yeah they suck, so what? You know what Mom and Dad used to tell me? Piloting is a sense all on its own and if I trained hard enough, I wouldn't even need my eyes." She stood. "And guess what, Brice, they were right. Like it or not, I'm a damn good pilot."

"Bren..." Her brother's voice wavered. "I can't. I can't lose you like we lost—" His call went through. "Yes, I'd like to speak with someone in the cybernetics department about scheduling a surgery." He started to leave the room. "Three days! Is that really the earliest appointment you have?"

Bren looked to Pitt and Meara.

"Sorry," said Pitt softly. Meara punched him.

"Fuck this. Your battle was officially confirmed. I say show him what you can do!"

Not a bad idea. Bren raised her voice. "My match is in tomorrow's lineup, Brice. If you really give a damn about me you'll be there."

Her brother stiffened.

"Fine," he said, and was gone.

Meara gave Bren a lift back into the city. Angry as she was, Bren didn't want to be under the same roof as her brother, let alone ask him for a ride. Meara was even kind enough to use her cred card to check Bren into a hotel.

"You can pay me back when you win."

Bren smiled at the thought. In all the drama she had forgotten to check the match data.

"Who's my opponent?"

"Aiden Victor."

Figures.

"Going to be tough strategizing against him. Smug bastard's used a different droid for each battle. He won't even announce his droid's model until the match starts."

"He breaks weapon regs, too. I've fought him before. All flash and no skill."

"Kicked his ass, did ya! Ha! No wonder he's gunning for you," Meara punched her playfully in the shoulder. "Don't worry, Bren, unlike a certain prick back at the rig, I've actually watched you fight. I can tell you were holding back."

"Thanks, Meara. It's good to know at least one person believes in me."

Bren tried to laugh at the irony, but the sound was closer to a sob.

⚔

Just outside the battle zone starting boundary, Bren moved Ivory Fang in a wide arc, veered sharply, then leapt over a small bolder in perfect view of the cameras. Her display provoked praising comments from the announcers.

Good, she thought. *Let Brice see what Fang and I can do.*

In the back of her mind, Bren wondered how he was feeling. Was he proud seeing his design brought to life? Or did he feel guilty, knowing his specs were the whole reason Bren was even out here?

Across the battle zone, Aiden's debuting droid took a few lumbering steps towards the cameras as well. Then, with a lively prod from Aiden in the cockpit, the huge droid opened its mouth, revealing the glowing barrel of a pulse cannon, and roared.

"Oh, fuck." Bren gripped Fang's controls until her knuckles were white. She could hear the announcers mutter similar reactions through her tournament live feed.

"A dragus! No one's been able to tame—"

"Thought the Committee had them all destroyed—"

Apparently not. The proof stood right there in the battle zone, its body glittering with the Victor family logo. And Aiden had the balls to pilot that thing? Perhaps she'd underestimated the youngest Victor.

As if he had heard her thoughts, Aiden opened a communication channel and his smug face appeared on Bren's center monitor.

"I'm going to give you one last chance, Gipson. Forfeit now. Spare yourself an unnecessary thrashing." There was an odd echoing quality as he spoke—his threat coming not just from his channel, but from the tournament's feed as well.

That arrogant prick is broadcasting this live! He wants me to surrender with everyone watching!

So much for underestimating him, Bren fumed. Fang rumbled disapproval and teased the controls out of her hands. Bren didn't resist her droid's feral pull this time. The moment the battle timer hit zero, Fang aimed its rifle and fired, landing a shell smack between the dragus's optical sensors. Caught by surprise, the huge droid staggered and barely righted itself. Then it roared.

"Ref!" Aiden shrieked through both channels. "That was clearly a violation of—"

Bren flicked on her own visual, projecting a sassy grin and her middle finger for all the Domes to see. "Hey, Victor, maybe if you spent less time gloating over your new toy, you'd notice the match started!"

"Why, you—"

She switched him off mid-retort. Much as she enjoyed irritating him, Bren had sense enough to know that Aiden's dragus was probably pissed. And Aiden, being Aiden, would seek vengeance with his droid's pulse cannon.

She directed Fang into a sprint for the nearest cover. The battle zone had been prepped with a decent number of tall boulders. Bren made for the densest concentration, ducking away just as she heard the dragus's pulse cannon fire with a great *boom-virrrrrr*.

The ground shook. Fang's sensors screamed a warning and Bren slammed the controls, barely avoiding a chunk of speeding boulder that could have taken off Fang's head. Other smaller debris left dents in Fang's chassis and a crack in the windshield. Bren switched to rear sensors, just for a second, and got a hazy, dust-filled view of the crater that had, moments before, been the boulder field. Aiden had missed her. Quite badly, in fact. But that wouldn't stop his cannon from vaporizing her if she got any closer.

She enlarged Fang's land readouts and tapped a point atop a mountain of boulders. The one grace of facing a pulse cannon—it took time to recharge. Enough time for Bren to take the high ground and lodge a bullet where it counted. Fang agreed, jumping agilely along a path of ledges up the mountain.

One leap away from the top, Fang's sensory alarm blared, and it lurched to a halt.

"Unidentified droid signatures detected."

Bren zoomed out her view and stared in horror. Thirty-five angry red dots moved across the placid greens and blues of her map. A feral pack that, if provoked, would kill everyone in sensor range.

Bren patched into the emergency channel.

"We read you, Pilot Gipson. Our sensors confirm the same. Initiating evacuation protocol."

She was expected to return to the city. An announcement blared on her tournament live-feed, declaring the battle zone restricted and telling everyone to evacuate. A second later, Bren's palm pad vibrated, then chimed with an official Battle Committee text. Bren skimmed the text quickly.

"Match data was verified…"

Blah, blah…

"Pilot Brenna Gipson and Droid Ivory Fang received a damage

rating of 0% versus opponent Pilot Aiden Victor and Droid Revenge…"

Revenge? Really?

"…who received a damage rating of 0.02%… "

Victory by a potshot. So much for her epic Aiden ass-kicking. Bren tried opening a channel to Aiden, to concede to a re-match (though he didn't really deserve it), but he didn't answer. Instead she heard his voice blaring through his live-feed.

"No! This isn't over! Ferals or no ferals, I'm finishing this match!"

Then all the sounds in Bren's cockpit were overwhelmed by a BOOM-VIRRRR.

"Jump!" Bren screamed. Fang lurched for the top foothold. Only it wasn't there anymore. Rocks exploded all around. One sent a portion of Fang's left console jutting inward, showering Bren with sparks and shards of metal. Three more left networks of cracks across Fang's windshield, obscuring the spinning world outside. Then everything stopped and something hard struck Bren's head.

Far off in the distance, Bren heard a male voice sputter through static, calling her name. She opened her eyes slowly. There was pain in her side. A warm liquid dripped down her face, blurring her vision.

"Bren! Answer me!" the voice called.

"Dad?" Bren wheezed. The static skipped.

"Ferals…attacking… get out of there!"

Ferals. She blinked again. Ferals had killed her father. So who… Realization came, clearing some of the haze. That was Brice's voice.

"I'm okay, Brice," she said. "This is just a scratch. Right, Fang?"

Her droid rumbled, provoking sparks from the consoles.

"Come on. We gotta get back."

She was having trouble breathing. Only one of her arms would move right. No matter. Fang knew what she wanted; Bren only needed to nudge the controls. Fang's feral program would do the rest.

Fang rose slowly, joints shuddering. Its gait was off, Bren knew right away. Most likely one of Fang's hind limbs was damaged.

The sound of battle stirred her and made Fang pause. Bren could hear numerous canids, four or five at least. And another droid. Its deep roar was fiery and familiar.

Aiden's dragus.

Aiden! She gasped and nearly fainted from the pain. Was Aiden still inside his droid?

Surely he ejected. Aiden wasn't that stupid. Still, Bren had an uneasy feeling. There was a reason the Battle Committee ordered the dragus models destroyed. She fought to think over her throbbing head. Something about a flaw in the design. The pulse cannon shorted out certain circuitry if it was used too frequently. Like the taming chip...

Shit.

Bren had no love for Aiden, as a pilot or a person. But her parents had been taken by feral droids, and no one, not even the Victor family, deserved that pain. She fumbled for the communication switch but couldn't reach it with her good arm. She tried Fang's optic scanners next, but the display monitor was as cracked as Fang's windshield. No sensors. No radio. Not even a clear view outside.

I'm blind.

Bren had the sudden urge to vomit. She had lived with poor eyesight her entire life and never felt as crippled as she did now. She wouldn't stand for it. Fuck her crappy eyes. Piloting was a sense all on its own. And Bren was a damn good pilot.

She reached under the console to the emergency drawer that was, of course, her brother's idea. Inside, among other things, was a self-contained breather.

Bren pulled it on, feeling her chest spasm painfully from the change in pressure. Then in a compartment above her head, she pulled the lever to manually eject Fang's windshield. It popped off with a pressurized *woosh* and shattered on the rock outside. The air was hot and caustic. Bren would have twenty minutes—not even, since she had open wounds—before the poisons would start doing damage. Then she would have no choice but to activate her ejection pod. She wouldn't be much help to Aiden then, but the pod would keep her alive until a rescue team came.

The dragus wasn't hard to spot. Not even for her. It stood among a scrapyard of feral canid parts. Its core, like those of the five remaining ferals, blazed a violent red. Without Fang's sensors, Bren couldn't see Aiden inside the cockpit. But she could hear him, faintly, when she came within communication range. He was crying.

She spoke slowly into her breather, trying to concentrate past the pain in her chest, her throbbing arm, and the slow burn of poisons creeping into her blood.

"I promised you a worthy opponent, Fang. And there it is."

Aiden's dragus flattened another feral, ripping out its innards in a shower of metal bits. Then its mouth opened, exposing its cannon and the charging pulse within. It made a low *wurwurwur* noise that grew louder every second it gathered energy.

"We'll only have one chance. Directly after it fires the next pulse."

The remaining four ferals edged closer, compelled by their program to fight the powerful rival despite the inevitable bad outcome.

"Now I can't use the scope with this mask on. And your sensors are screwed up. So, we'll have to breach the core another way. Otherwise…"

Otherwise her droid would end up like those ferals, with a little bit of her thrown in.

"How 'bout it, partner? Ready to show everyone why I named you Fang?"

Fang roared. Despite its injured limb, Bren's droid started into a loping run. Bren watched the dragus splay its legs, straighten its neck and dig its talons deep into the rock. The whirring of its cannon reached a new terrible pitch. Then the air erupted with a great *BOOM,* followed by a more sonic *VIRRR!*

Two unfortunate ferals were directly in the path of the discharge; they turned into a fine, gray powder. The other two were catapulted hundreds of yards into the air in opposite directions. They hit the ground, shattering limbs and shedding other chunks as they tumbled.

Its program satisfied, the dragus vented a great hiss of steam, unlocked from its battle stance and began to turn towards Bren and Fang. But it wasn't fast enough.

"Now!" Bren commanded. Fang leapt. Bren pushed the claw-release just as it slammed into the dragus' chest. Then she hit the button beside it.

Fang opened its mouth wide, allowing two sickle-shaped saber teeth to release like switchblades. Momentum did the rest. With a snarl, Fang drove its weapons through layers of tough dragus armor.

"Deeper, Fang!" Bren urged. She could barely hear herself over the sound of grating metal and the dragus's roar. Heat poured out of the punctures, making Bren's many small injuries sting.

Too much heat. Venting too fast. The mechanic in her knew. But she couldn't pull Fang back now. Not even if she wanted to. She found herself looking up past the dragus's overheated core into the pilot cockpit. Aiden had his hands and face pressed against the reinforced alloy. And though Bren couldn't see the terror in his eyes, she hoped he saw hers. And all that her fear implied.

The final layer of the dragus's armor gave, letting Fang's weapons sink deep into the core with a pressurized *crack.* For a moment, the huge droid's power dulled—enough to give Aiden the control to eject his escape pod and send him rocketing away from the coming explosion. The dragus gave a furious cry in response. Its body sparked, twitched, then fell. Fang fell, too, its claws and fangs buried too deep to allow escape. The impact rattled through Bren's bones, making her see spots.

"Great job, Fang. You won. I knew you could," she praised

between pained breaths. "Now we need to get the hell out of here before... before..." She tugged on Fang's controls, but the droid refused to budge. The effort left Bren dizzy. She fought to try again. But this time, even her good arm wouldn't move. She stared ahead, watching but not seeing anymore as the dragus's core flickered, then began to glow brighter than any core should.

One of Fang's controls clicked without her order. And Bren heard her droid gave a soft *vrum*. So soft Bren could barely hear. The sound of goodbye.

Terrible heat poured from the puncture, melting Fang's face into the dragus's armor. But Bren didn't feel it. Reinforced alloy closed around her, along with a rush of cool clean air. The sensation stirred her enough to recognize the rumble of her escape pod's rockets speeding her away from a great plume of fire and smoke.

Awareness came slowly. Soft beeps. Antiseptic smells. A hospital.
My eyes!
Bren tried to sit, sending a spasm of pain through her chest and shoulder.

"Easy," her brother said, resting his hand on her forehead.

Bren squinted through the dim light. Nothing seemed any different. "No surgery..." she finally dared to ask.

"No surgery," he assured. "After what you did for Aiden, I couldn't bring myself to..."

"Thanks."

A nurse arrived at the door. "Excuse me, Brenna? A representative from the Droid Battle Committee is here to speak with you. "

"Send him in." said Brice. Then he patted her hand. "It's okay. We'll get through this."

The Committee rep arrived. He was stiff and official-looking and reeked of expensive cologne. He proceeded to inform Bren that, "the Droid Battle Committee simply cannot tolerate this blatant disregard of protocol from one of their—" he stopped himself before he could say 'pilots.' In any case the rules were there for a reason and she was "lucky she didn't kill someone."

Bren listened in silence—because Brice gripped her hand every time she started to protest.

"We will be contacting the authorities to take you into custody."

Brice cleared his throat. "Before you do that. There is something I think you should see." Brice reached over and hit the shade-open button on the window, then stood aside. The metal slats opened and lifted, filling the little room with light. Bren winced. Below, a mass of people and droids crowded near the hospital entrance.

"What the—?" The rep strode over. "What are all these pilots doing here?"

"Rioting," said Brice, in a tone that was almost… excited. He gripped Bren's uninjured shoulder. "They know about your eyes, Bren, and they aren't too happy the Committee wants to arrest the pilot who risked herself to save a fellow competitor's life."

"My own riot…" Bren resisted the urge to grin. "But how did they find out?"

Brice squeezed her shoulder and suddenly Bren knew. She looked up into the blurring image of her brother's face.

"What made you change your mind?"

"You," he said. He hugged her. "You were amazing out there Bren. You scared the living shit out of me… but you were amazing." Tears welled in his eyes. "Things will be different after today."

Bren looked to the rep, who was still staring out the window.

"I think maybe you're right."

Better to Have Loved

Kate O'Connor

The funeral began at ten o'clock on Wednesday morning. It was supposed to be a simple service: a short viewing and then a flower-bedecked car would take Deanna to the crematorium. Sophie had arrived half an hour early to make sure everything was ready. It had taken five minutes to adjust the flower arrangements and set out a few pictures. She had been sitting in a padded folding chair, alone, ever since.

The event director had hovered until her silence and the lack of other attendees had cut into his enthusiasm for a "Real Old-Fashioned Funeral!" Sophie tried not to blame him. People didn't want to be bothered with funerals. Until Deanna's death, Sophie would have wholeheartedly agreed that they were a complete waste of time. She still wasn't sure why she had changed her mind.

At a quarter till eleven, the door opened. She didn't look up, expecting the director to make another attempt at being friendly and consoling. The coffee in her recyclable plastic cup had long since stopped steaming. She swirled it with the little red stir stick anyway.

"Heya, Sophie." The sound of Ben's voice made her jump.

Sophie nodded a greeting. Ben's long brown hair was tied up in a scruffy ponytail and he still had his work boots on. Sophie ground her teeth. Her brother-in-law wasn't dressed for the event. Funerals were supposed to be about respect. A moment later she was ashamed of being angry. Deanna had never cared what her baby brother wore.

"So," Ben sat on the edge of the seat with two chairs between them. His eyes were red and puffy. Sophie felt even worse for having noticed the boots first. "We got the invite, obviously. Mom and Dad aren't coming. They took their tabs already. You shouldn't have sent it. It could have made a real mess if I hadn't seen it first."

"Sorry." Sophie shrugged uncomfortably. She hadn't really been thinking when she messaged Deanna's family. Like the funeral, it had just seemed like the thing to do at the time.

"No big deal." Ben looked equally uncomfortable. "Look, Soph, I know this has been hard on everybody. Let's get this funeral thing out of the way and then forget all about it. Your doctor gave you the prescription, right?"

Sophie nodded.

"Okay then. You know Dee wouldn't have wanted any of us to suffer. I'm going to go home after this and take mine. Mom and Dad did two days ago. They're normal now. Really happy." Ben sniffed and blinked rapidly.

"Okay." Sophie answered in a small voice. Ben was right. This had been a silly idea. She stirred the coffee again. Ben gave her a watery smile and took her hand. She squeezed it once and let go after an uneasy moment. They got along well enough, but they had never been close. Most of what she knew of Ben had come from Deanna's stories.

The rest of the vigil passed in oppressive silence. When the time came, the director returned with his staff, shooting Sophie a reproachful look as they wheeled the coffin out. Evidently the event hadn't met his standards. Sophie understood. Whatever a funeral was supposed to accomplish, she didn't think this one had.

♟

On the way home, Sophie drove by the pharmacy. She circled the block twice, fighting the panicked feeling that was burning off the numbness she had been living in since the call about Deanna. On the third time around, she turned the car into the lot, furious with herself for prolonging the inevitable.

Fewer than half of the spaces were filled, but she waited while an elderly man pulled out of the spot nearest the door anyway. As she walked through the sliding door, a woman gave her a curious look. Sophie ducked her head, pretending interest in an eyeliner display. She didn't want anyone to see her face. Grief was an embarrassment. There was no point to it beyond selfishness.

There was a line at the pharmacy counter. She waited anxiously, shifting from foot to foot and trying not to meet anyone's eyes. When it was her turn, she pushed her card under the scanner and tapped her PIN onto the screen. There was a momentary delay before a message flashed up: SEE ATTENDANT.

Sophie looked around uncomfortably. There was no one working the counter. She turned to go. It would be easier to just call her doctor and get the prescription sent directly to the house. Wishing she'd thought of that earlier, she turned towards the exit. Out of the corner of her eye, she saw a woman poke her head out of the office behind the counter.

"Sophia Latner?" Her voice was bored and tired. Sophie turned back around, feeling like she had been caught doing something illicit. The woman stumped slowly around the end of the counter. "My name is Irene. Right this way, please."

Sophie followed her behind a screen advertising 'Influenza vaccines: Protect yourself! Inquire HERE!'. A wheeled cart, partially stocked with gauze and little fluid-filled bottles was pushed off to one side of the small space. The woman sat down in one of the two plastic chairs. Belatedly, Sophie sat as well, clutching her purse with both hands.

"Don't worry, sweetheart. It's just standard procedure. We have to tell you all about how this one works. Legal reasons, you understand." Irene patted her clenched hands consolingly, seeming not to notice Sophie flinch at the unexpected touch. "First off, the tablets work as limbic regulators. They inhibit emotions and memories associated with the person who passed away on a very selective basis. You'll be able to move on with your life without having to spend all of your time moping and worrying."

Irene looked at her expectantly. Sophie wondered what kind of response she was waiting for. The moment stretched uncomfortably. She finally nodded once, hoping this would be over soon. She was so tired. She hadn't gotten more than a few hours of sleep at a time during the last six days.

Irene sighed, looking a little disappointed as she continued. "It's best if you get rid of anything that will strongly remind you of the person. The brain is vulnerable, especially during the first few days while the drug works. Any big emotional reminders could cause the problem to pop back up again. Re-medicating is an option if that happens, but it can cause some nasty side effects. Better to get it right the first time!

"We recommend taking the first week off of work. Most people are tired and forgetful for three or four days. You may also have a few lingering emotional twinges, but don't worry! They'll be vague if they happen and shouldn't be painful. If you get a headache or have any unusual mood swings, be sure to let your doctor know right away. Any questions?"

Sophie shook her head.

"Just print here then and you'll be all set." Irene held a portable scanner out to her. Sophie pressed her thumb to it. It beeped once and Irene tucked it away again. "I'll go get this for you. Just come back over to the counter in ten minutes and it'll be ready to go."

Sophie followed her out from behind the flimsy privacy the screen had offered. The line at the counter had dissipated. Sophie walked past a few teenagers comparing the relative merits of different hair products and then back down the next aisle. She should have been at work today. It would have been just after her lunch break. There was going to be so much to do when she got back. She hoped the time off wouldn't hurt her chances at the promotion. Her boss had hinted that he thought she might be ready to move up to the next level. She had been so pleased.

Deanna had taken her out to celebrate just last week—a pre-promotion dinner. At the time, Sophie had been angry over the frivolous expense.

Her eyes stung fiercely. She bit her lip as her vision blurred. A half-swallowed sob popped out anyway. She clenched her hands, nails digging into her palms as she looked apprehensively around, hoping no one had been close enough to hear. Now wasn't the time for stupid displays of emotion.

Scolding herself only made it worse. She ducked into the ladies' room and locked herself in a stall. The toilet seat was scattered with a few drops of unidentifiable liquid. It didn't have a lid. Sophie rolled out a wad of toilet paper and scrubbed at the seat, weeping and angry. When it was clean enough, she perched on the edge. As quickly as they had come, the tears were gone. She stayed for a few minutes, needing to be sure of herself before venturing out again. The tears didn't return. She felt cheated.

Leaving the stall, Sophie checked her reflection in the mirror. An automated cleaner wheeled by, loaded with toilet paper and disinfectant spray. The cheap lighting buzzed almost inaudibly. Her eyes were red and her mouth pinched. She splashed lukewarm water on her face, smoothed her hair, and straightened her skirt.

When she returned to the pharmacy counter, Irene was waiting. Sophie took the crinkly white bag with a feeling of profound relief. She wanted to have control of herself again. No more not sleeping and unexpected crying. No more feeling like the rest of the world was running away without her.

♟

Sophie pushed open the door to their apartment. It was tiny: one bedroom, a bathroom that could barely contain both the shower and toilet, and a joint kitchen/living area. It was a corner unit with windows on both sides overlooking the city. She loved the view. Deanna had wanted more space. She had won that argument by default. There hadn't been any other units available in their price range.

Albert lumbered out of the bedroom as she was closing the front door. Deanna's dog: a big, hairy, dirt-colored lump. He sat on Sophie's feet and panted, his decidedly doggy breath wafting upwards. She pushed his head away in disgust and he thumped his tail twice in appreciation. They never communicated well.

Albert had come with Deanna, part of the deal when Sophie married her. They had argued about him more than once. Sophie wanted children. With a ninety pound dog eating up their meager resource allotment, they had never managed to scrape together enough for both. Her promotion was supposed to fix that.

Sophie rummaged through the dog drawer, Albert following in her wake like a furry mountain. She finally found a half-chewed bone underneath a box of stale dog treats and tossed it across the room. Albert bounded gleefully after it and out of her way. Sophie headed into the bedroom to change. She needed to get the packing over with as soon as possible—for her own sanity if nothing else.

Standing by their bed, Sophie skimmed off her jacket and blouse. Both were simply cut, black and new. She didn't bother to hang them. They had been purchased for the funeral. She would get rid of them with the rest of Deanna's clothes. The skirt was one of the ones she usually wore to the office. She stepped out of it. Grimacing at the string of dog drool decorating the fabric, she kicked it towards the laundry pile.

Finally dressed comfortably in her old sweats, Sophie sat on the couch with her mediapad in her lap. More than anything, she wanted a nap. She shook her head. The sooner she got this done, the sooner she would be able to actually rest. **Deanna's Things** she typed at the top of the document. **Albert** The stupid dog had to go. She wasn't really a pet person and the last thing she wanted was a reminder of the children they wouldn't have. She stared blankly at the screen. What else qualified as important enough to trigger memories?

She set the pad aside and got up, collecting the pharmacy bag from the counter. She ripped it open and scanned the pamphlet that was tucked in beside the little orange bottle. It didn't offer any clarification: just reiterated that things carrying strong, emotional memories should be disposed of prior to taking the proscribed dosage.

Sophie put the bottle back on the counter and pushed it out of Albert's reach. Deanna had never made the effort to break him of surfing any reachable surface for goodies. She returned to the couch and picked up the pad again. **Clothes** She wasn't sure they counted as memory triggering, but they needed to go anyway. **Pictures** were obvious. The coroner had disposed of Deanna's wallet, phone, and cards on Sophie's request. They had never done the paperwork to combine their accounts and Deanna's were automatically closed when her death was confirmed. Her scant savings had been transferred to Sophie's account as per her will. Death made easy.

Sophie looked around the room and wondered if she should move out. It was their first place together. If she closed her eyes she could almost believe Deanna was there sprawled on the couch watching a movie, sitting on the counter with her morning coffee, rolling on the floor wrestling with Albert, kissing her as they left for work. Sophie sat there feeling sick. She couldn't leave. There was nowhere to go on such short notice.

Common sense reasserted itself after a few minutes. If Deanna's parents were managing without moving, there was no reason she would have to. Her churning stomach settled a little. Maybe the warning was only meant for things attached to really extreme emotions. She looked down at her hands. The little diamond on her ring winked up at her. **Wedding rings** got added to the list. Deanna's was probably still sitting on the dresser in the bedroom. She said it got in the way at work, that she had never liked wearing jewelry. They fought over that too.

Unable to sit still any longer, Sophie abandoned the list and brought an entire roll of garbage bags into the bedroom. Drawer by drawer, she pulled clothing out of the dresser and stacked it neatly on the bed. She separated the laundry into piles, then dumped all of Deanna's into the washer. As an afterthought, she gathered up all of the bedding as well. She held it to her face, breathing deeply before shoving it into the washer. It smelled like Deanna. While she waited for the cycle to finish, Sophie called the first local charity listed and arranged for a pickup that evening.

Sophie's mind drifted in defeated exhaustion as she folded and bagged clothes, wrapped mementos, piled up pictures and personal items for disposal. Several socks were missing their mates and she could only find one of Deanna's running shoes. She wandered back out into the living room. She reached a hand down between the couch cushions and came up with three socks. A painful bubble of feeling burst in her chest. Deanna always kicked them off when she was napping on the sofa.

Sophie pulled the cushions off and tossed them on the floor. Albert looked up from his dog bed, observing solemnly as she searched every nook and cranny of the furniture for any further trace of her wife. Sophie didn't think she would be able to stand it if the drug didn't work the first time—especially if it failed because she had missed something simple.

The living area didn't take long. Sophie had done the decorating when they moved in. Deanna's bachelorette furniture hadn't made the move with them. Sophie turned on the entertainment center and erased Deanna's personal settings and saved shows. She couldn't bring herself to read through the list before dumping it. The missing running shoe was buried lovingly among Albert's toys. When she picked it up, he grabbed hold of the toe and tugged it back out of her hands. Not wanting to fight for it, Sophie detoured back to the kitchen and got a handful of dog treats. While Albert was busy with those, she retrieved the shoe and tossed it into the bag with its mate.

Three more circuits of the tiny apartment convinced her that it was clean. Sophie dragged all of the carefully packed bags out to the door. The sun was setting over the city. The dim, orange-red light bathed the room in shadows. Other than the cushions on the floor and Albert dozing with his dog toys, it looked like a showroom. Sophie shivered, wondering if this was what it would feel like tomorrow when she woke up without any emotional memory of Deanna. Sterile. Alone.

A knock on the door startled her. She pushed her way through the bags and opened it. She blinked dazedly at the man and woman standing there. Both wore lurid green t-shirts advertising the organization she had called earlier. The two volunteers exchanged a look before the woman stepped forward. "Pickup for ApparelAid?"

"Yes, of course. It's all right here." Sophie pointed to the obvious pile of bags. Out of habit, she grabbed Albert's collar as he lumbered forward to greet the newcomers. He sat on her foot and looked reproachfully up at her. The aid workers wasted no time transferring the bags to the cart they had brought along.

"You need a receipt for this stuff?" the woman asked as her companion hauled the last bag out the door.

"No, thank you." Sophie shook her head, still hanging onto Albert.

The door closed behind them and silence descended once again. Sophie let go of the stiff nylon collar and pulled her bare foot out from under Albert's furry hip. It was time to eat. Three steps into the kitchen, Sophie turned around. Her stomach turned over at the idea of food.

Instead, she measured out Albert's dinner and dumped it into his bowl. Deanna was in the habit of giving him an amount that 'looked right'. When the vet told them the dog was overweight, Sophie had taken over feeding time to save resources. She left the dog inhaling his food, wondering one more time if there was anything left to do.

She flicked the light on as she walked back into the hollow-seeming living room. Deanna was gone. She checked the clock. In just seven hours, she had all but erased their life together. She sank down onto one of the couch cushions still scattered on the floor. How could it be that easy to make everything they had shared go away? Had three years of marriage really meant so little? She lay down, hiding her face in her arms. Only one thing left to do and then it wouldn't matter what their time together had meant. Sophie closed her eyes.

Deanna was smiling at her, goofy and girlish as always. Sophie felt an answering smile spread across her face as she took Deanna's hand and led her towards the waiting group. One by one, she introduced her to their friends and family as though Deanna didn't *know them. She shook hands and smiled. No one spoke. Sophie saw each vague, happy face clearly as they waited for their turn to be introduced. When they had seen everyone, Deanna turned to her with the same good-natured expression still on her face. She held out a hand to Sophie just as she had to all of the others.*

Sophie woke with her heart racing. Curling up as tight as she could against the ache in her chest, she sobbed. Deanna hadn't known her. It was just a stupid dream, but she hadn't known Sophie at all.

Doggy breath assailed her as Albert's cool, damp nose shoved its way into the crook of her arm. When he reached her face, he set about cleaning it from chin to forehead. Sophie sat up and put her arms around his furry neck, crying hard into his shoulder. Gradually, the tears dwindled. With a long sigh, Albert settled across her lap. Sophie scratched his ears, studying him for what felt like the first time.

Deanna's dog. That was how she had always thought of him. Almost like a piece of furniture. A large, smelly, unwanted piece of furniture. He looked trustingly up at her with large, dark eyes peeking through tufts of brownish fur. She had forgotten about him. She didn't know why she hadn't thought of it before. The patch of hair on his shoulder was damp from where she had cried on him.

Sophie sighed. She hadn't thought about it because he had been part of the background. If she was honest about it, she knew Deanna hadn't been ready for kids. Albert had just been an easy excuse. He licked her chin as she sniffled back a new round of tears. With a rush of remorse, she wondered if she should try keeping him—for a little bit, at least.

Shoving him gently off of her legs, Sophie retrieved the bottle and a glass of water from the kitchen. The pair of tablets clattered against the orange plastic as she sat back down next to the dog. She put the bottle and glass on the coffee table and picked up her mediapad again. She deleted the list and leaned back against the sofa. The tablets looked black through the plastic.

It occurred to Sophie that she could throw them away. She knew people had done without such things not too long ago—gone about grief the slow way, waiting for the pain to fade and trying to keep hold of the good memories. That just wasn't how it was done anymore. It took too much time and there was no point to hurting that much over something that couldn't be helped.

She stared at the bottle, one hand buried in Albert's fur. Letting go of Deanna made sense. People would expect her to be back to normal when she returned to work in a week. It was ridiculous to imagine that she would be able to pretend things were fine if she didn't take the tablets. She would sleep badly and dream too much. Work wouldn't get done. It was possible she could lose her job over it. She might never be able to fall in love again. Her parents and friends would worry, maybe even pull away. Sophie didn't want to be old-fashioned and useless like the funeral.

But if she didn't remember Deanna, nobody would. Deanna hadn't been brilliant at anything, never made a fortune, painted a masterpiece, won a championship game. Her parents and brother had already all but forgotten her. It felt disloyal to do the same. Sophie loved her. Deanna was supportive, immature, playful, lazy. She loved Sophie even when she was controlling and snappish. She thought Sophie was beautiful first thing in the morning. All of it was worth remembering.

Sophie picked up the bottle and opened it, dumping the tablets into her hand. The easy way wasn't always wrong. Mourning Deanna wouldn't benefit anyone but her and probably not even that. It was pure selfishness. A few more tears dripped off of her chin. She got up and headed for the bedroom. Albert heaved himself to his feet and followed.

Sophie detoured to the bathroom. She raised the toilet lid. Her hand trembled as she stared at the little pills. Mind nearly blank, she turned her hand over and let them fall. Heart racing in her chest, she hit the lever and watched the water go down.

With a shuddering sigh, Sophie returned to their bedroom, pretending to ignore Albert as he hopped up onto the bed. Tomorrow she would figure out how to recover, return to work, and live her life without forgetting. She didn't know if she could do it, but as selfish as it might be, Deanna was hers. Sophie wasn't going to let her go that easily.

"Needs More Coffee" by Rachel Keslensky

Previous Page:

A woman with short, messy hair held back with a headband stands against a background of stars. She is facing the viewer, in a pin-up girl type style. In her left hand, she holds a mug with steam rising from it. Her right hand is pressed against her upper chest in an expression of surprise. An exclamation mark symbol is projected from the glasses over her right eye and it hangs in front of her face. She is wearing a very short robe that is tied to one side. On her left foot, she has on a fuzzy slipper. Her right leg is a shiny prosthetic.

Morphic Resonance

Toby MacNutt

If it weren't for the damned new highspeed maglev trains, he'd never have known. Vasily was emphatically not a fan—but the old trains were being steadily replaced, like it or not. The ride was not just quicker, but smoother, for most everyone else, and as a result the cars were frequently crowded. The worst thing about them, though, was that the morphic docking spots for people floating on g-skips or using other mobile aids had a tendency to slip; something about the new trains' stronger magnetic fields interfering with the resonators.

That's what had happened: in a too-crowded train, on a too-fast section of track, the resonator gripping his g-skip had cut out. Vasily went sailing off into the bodies around him. He tried to tug his arms into position fast enough to grab a rail, but his fingers slipped off and past. They caught on the arm of a fellow passenger, instead—or should have. His hand hit the man's coat-sleeve, and slowed, but did not stop. The fabric provided no more resistance than water, and Vasily's fingers sank into it, and below, into what ought to have been the flesh of the man's arm. It wasn't till his grasping hand wrapped around a little metal post, there in place of bone, that Vasily made sense of it: a hard-light hologram, in place of a prosthetic.

In that split-second of slip and grasp, there wasn't time to wonder about it. He slipped, flailed, was caught by other passengers; the man with the projected arm didn't notice till Vasily touched its true core, and in that moment he turned and winked, before slipping further into the crowded car.

Vasily's curiosity overcame even the terror of slipping weightless into the crowd. He was intrigued, rather than shaken, and kept replaying the memory as he made his way home. Slip. Grasp. Fall. A green woollen coat-sleeve, broad round shoulder, substantial but nonexistent bicep. He could still feel the texture of the post in his fingertips, its smooth curve and tiny threads; otherwise he might think he had imagined it. And then the face of its owner, dark broad cheekbones, densely curly short dark hair, warm brown eyes, that fleeting wink. The wink that had seemed to say *welcome to our secret*—but with no fear of reprisal.

Hard-light holograms were heavily licensed technology, and had never been cleared for prosthetic use, Vasily was sure; a quick web search confirmed. There's no way that had been a sanctioned use—but where would you even get such restricted technology? And then: to wear it so flagrantly! Anyone could have knocked into his arm on that train!

The thought was still tumbling through his head the next morning. His resonators worked in sequence, pulling fabric around his floating body, implant-chrome and his skin and its art all slowly disappearing. (Who had that man been? Government? Hacker? Just a rich playboy?) His tattoos were plain ink, decoration only, no augments. All the same, he liked having them close and covered, private. The resonators let him dress much more efficiently and stylishly than he could have managed alone, these days, and their effortless, infinitely configurable fabrics still felt like the most indulgent of luxuries. (Where would you go, to get projection tech? Why would you want it, and not a functioning prosthesis?) He was in a layered frame of mind and went for outward layering, too: full-length soft stretch jersey base layers, wrap pants, loose vest, scarf, armwarmers, all in shades of ruby and chestnut. The g-skip's gentle fields settled him comfortably upright, on a little cushion of suspension and warmth. (How had he been so confident? Cheeky, even.) He checked his reflection in the wall-mirror: blue eyes shining out amidst the layers of browns, sharp cheek and jaw bones softened by the drape of fabrics and his shoulder-length curtain of auburn hair. (Who was he?) It would work. He went out.

Vasily kept his eyes open for the man with the arm that wasn't. He looked for brown, and for green, and for any strange clipping errors in reality; he jostled up against strangers far more often than was strictly necessary, rather than letting the g-skip buffer him in crowded places. He sought out mezzanines and upper windows to look out on the people below, though what he'd do if he saw the man from afar he didn't know. At public computer stations he searched for as much as he dared: shape-shifter stories from the tabloids, boilerplate tech regulations, obscure licensure loopholes, scientific publications on hard-light advances.

Heading past the washrooms at the library, his eyes flicked habitually over the doors. Morphic-enabled doorhandles to the women's and men's, first. Then, this close to the center of town, the restricted fob-tap to the androgynes' room, as alluringly enigmatic as ever—and with that he jolted a little, internally. If his winking stranger was using contraband projection technology for *one* part of his body, what *else* might be projected? How much of what Vasily had seen had been physically real? He didn't have the look of most androgynes, far too broadly masculine for that, but if he was using hard-light projecting for one out-license purpose already… it might be reshaping the rest of him, too.

This thought only fed his obsession: if there was a way to shape-shift yourself, even just a glamour, without going through the governmental demands and scrutiny involved in aesthetic licensure or authorised gender alteration, he wanted to know. He ached for it.

⚨

It was the trains that did it, once again. Vasily was on the same green-line ultrafast, but late at night; the car was nearly empty. He'd docked, buffers up and strong, and had a hand at the wall toward the nearest rail, just in case. Trains were not to be trusted.

The door between cars opened, and Vasily got a brief glimpse at the person who stepped through—tall, dark, broad shoulders, warm browns, reds—before the lights flickered out. The power had gone, somehow, though the train still moved and light still glowed from the previous and following cars. It was cut only here. And that meant the morphic point was unpowered, too, and he was sliding, again, slick as oil on water across the car...

He scrabbled in the darkness, caught only air, shrieked a little without meaning to. He hit something solid, but soft, and hands caught him.

"Hello again, Vasily Lewandowski." The hand on his right shoulder was warm, smoothly curved. The hand on his left was cool and unyielding, dense.

He twisted in the g-skip's embrace, looking for a face in the shadows. "How do you know? Who *are* you? *What* are you?!"

"You weren't subtle. Searching for information at the public library instead of at home is a good start, but the logging technology is too good. And we wondered if we might hear from you, so we were watching more than usual."

"Who's 'we'? You aren't—" he faltered "—Teeth, are you?"

"Not Teeth. Not Hands, either, no pun intended." He wriggled his prosthetic fingers, this time apparently solid, against Vasily's thin arm. "No, I am not the government's man. But you'll have to take my word for that."

"Then... what? What are you?"

"I can't tell you."

Vasily hutted, put out. "Then why all this! Why follow me, why talk to me? Why do—whatever it is you've done to the train?"

"Despite what I've done with the train, it's not entirely safe to talk here. But if you need to know more, this will reach me, securely." He pressed a little hard plastic square into Vasily's hand, and gently nudged the 'skip back towards the dockpoint. "Just press. It's a resonator, I'll know, and I'll come to you. Stay put at home, after. We'll have to flash your block."

Vasily shook his head, trying to clear it. "I don't know what you mean."

"I know! Out of time. Catch you later, kiddo."

"But—who are you? What's your name? Why does this—"

The man interrupted: "Call me Ammon."

And the lights came back on, and Vasily was safe in the dockpoint's grasp once again, and Ammon was gone.

Å

The calling-card Ammon had given him was no more than a thin dense wafer of plastics. One side was smooth, gently translucent with veins of thin wiring showing through. The other side had a nubbled edge surrounding a central square of pale blue mesh. If Ammon was to be believed, it was some kind of resonator key; it must have a matching morphic output, somewhere.

He studiously ignored it for four whole days. He wouldn't call. He didn't want to know; it was dangerous.

The card watched him from its spot on the shelf by the door. He felt as if it had eyes on him, tracking his every move. He hid it in a little box of wood-inlay. It didn't help.

He shouldn't call. A stranger with out-license tech: a preposterous proposition.

And yet.

He lasted another three days. Early that morning, home alone, he asked his resonators to fetch it down. He held it in his palm, released, turned it over and over, spinning it in the 'skip-field. Such a little thing—most folks would be able to crush it without a thought. He reached for it, trembling, brought his fingertip into contact with the mesh. It yielded immediately; his finger sank into it, deeper than the chip ought to have allowed. The translucent materials glowed gently, with a warmth like amber, and stayed ghost-lit even after he took his hand away.

He waited, stared at the little glowing cardlet. He tried not to panic; he breathed deep for a while, shaking, wondering what he'd launched, if he'd just dropped himself into trouble's maw. Government watchlists, anarchist plots, identity theft, black-market body-runners: what else? He wondered if he'd done anything at all, or just been taken for a fool.

It just glowed softly at him, silently. Nothing else happened.

Two hours later, the power went out. His heart leapt in his throat and his breathing sounded loud, so loud, as the constant passive hum of his resonators faded into the blackout. His blood thundered in his ears, almost drowning out the next sound: three quick raps on the door.

The building was usually shaped to his needs by morphic technology; with a full power cut (why hadn't the backup generators come on?), he was a fish out of water, though thankfully the g-skip carried its own charge. He fumbled at the doorknob, grip slipping. He swore briefly, bitterly, and got a better grasp. It came open.

Ammon was there, apparently two-armed once again. He wore a nondescript black jacket, messenger bag slung over his shoulder.

"Hello, Vasily. Sorry for the inconvenience. Give me a moment, and I'll explain." He edged carefully past Vasily's floating fields to the middle of the room. It was mostly bare; there was a heap of cushions and quilts in one corner, a built-in dresser-like repository for resonators and clothing materials, a few shelves for books and knick-knacks. There was the mirror on the wall, and a standing-height desk with a screen (dark now) and soft silver touchpad. Ammon crouched in the middle of the floor and opened his bag, taking out a little spindle and stand. He stroked it to life and it threw a shower of amber lights across floor, walls, and ceiling, like a star-projector. "That should give us some time. Half an hour or so, if the rest of the team do their part. We can speak without being overheard."

"What is that? What did you do to my building?" Vasily floated nearer the field projector and felt his implants hum with a gentle heat.

"This?" Ammon gestured at the spindle. "Think of it like a sort of Faraday cage, maybe, or like sound-absorption panels, whichever is more familiar to you. It just keeps any signals from being sent out of here to anyone who might want to be listening in. As to your building, and the rest of your block," he shrugged, apologetically, "I really am sorry for the inconvenience, but it's vital no one know I was here. The generator didn't kick on, by the way, because it can't tell the power is out. My team are good at their work. Now. What would you like to know?"

Where to begin? The thousand-thousand questions of the last two hours, and the week prior, bubbled up at once and Vasily struggled for words.

"Are you a body-runner?" Well. Not the most elegant beginning.

"Depends. What do you think a body-runner is?"

"Someone who does… augment stuff, on the black market?"

"Yeah, then, arguably yes. Nothing exploitative, though; we try to liberate, not to trap."

"Who's we? Are there more of you? Who are you, really?"

"Well, those are complex questions… let's do the easy one first: yes, there are more of us. We're mostly called shifters. What that means, who we are, that's the complicated part. We're only sort of an 'us'. It's loose. Like I said, we're into liberation, bodily liberation. Some of us are androgynes, some just have unusual aesthetics, some are into augmentation—adaptive or superhuman or both. It's a little different for everyone. But we help each other when we can."

Vasily paused, digesting. "Am I in danger? Because of you?"

"You? No. No one should know this has happened, unless you decide to tell them, which I'm trusting you won't."

"Why are you telling me this?"

"I saw the look in your eye—call it a gut feeling, a hunch, if you like. Fleshed out by your search strings. I thought you could use someone like us. And, hey, you passed your background check."

"My searches?! Background check? You read my stuff!"

"Of course. Basic safety precaution." They sat with that for a moment, a dense silence.

"How do you keep from being arrested, anyway? With all this out-license gear! Where does it come from?"

"The 'black market', as you so astutely surmised. We also make a lot of it. The starfield damper is one of mine. DIY helps keep us under the radar, and we're also just careful. Background checks, sensors, that kind of thing. We're taking a risk on you, actually."

"Why? I don't—why are you here? Why me?"

"A hunch. I trust my gut." Ammon smiled, and his eyes softened. "If you're not interested, I can go. No hard feelings."

"No! No. I am, I always wondered... I don't even know where to begin. I always wondered if there were... other ways. To be different."

"Yes. There are. Ways and means."

"How do I start?" Vasily tried not to sound eager; failed.

"We clean you. That's why this," he waved his right arm through the image of his left, "isn't here. We hacked my original biomech arm years ago, cleaned it, so it's probably safe, but I didn't want to risk being wrong. It's at home in its cage. All licensed tech tracks and broadcasts, and that won't do at all."

More information to digest. Vasily hadn't thought about what his implants might be telling the world; he knew morphic point usage was aggregated, but it was supposed to be anonymous. There had been a licensure agreement, of course, but he'd signed it so many years ago. "They track me."

"Constantly. And monitor how you use what you have."

"Shit." He rocked back in the air, skin crawling. "Shit, shit. Okay. But. I can get out?"

"Yes. We can scrub you; I have the tools with me. It doesn't take that long for just a cerebellar-sacral 'skip clean—that's what you have, right?" Vasily nodded. "You'll have to power down, I'm afraid, but from there it's simple. Just open and patch."

Vasily chewed his lip, as his stomach churned. With the resonators out of commission, if he powered down the g-skip he'd be utterly helpless, ground-bound and weak. Alone, with a body-runner.

Ammon could see the hesitation. "It's a lot to take in all at once, I know. I remember how afraid I was when I first handed Xerxes my arm. I can come back, someday, if you aren't ready." He spoke gently, respectfully.

Vasily shook his head. "No." He summoned up his courage, the same courage that had taken him on high-speed maglevs late at night; he asked it to grow. "I want this. I want to know. If that means—I want to try." He drifted to his jumbled nest of cushions, and lowered himself onto them. He forced himself to take a long, slow breath. "Ready when you are."

He waited a few long seconds, watching Ammon rummage in his bag, before he sent the command to power down. He was so accustomed to the constant low hum of the 'skip that its absence felt like shaking. The cushions were angled strangely, pressing into his flanks. He sagged.

Ammon had got out something little and shining—a tuning fork, it looked like—and some even tinier electronic implement with little conduits and wires exposed below a rounded handle. "I'll need to get to both your implants, at your neck and your sacrum. Can you move at all?"

"No, it's—you'll have to help me turn. And with my shirt, I guess." Ammon slipped his broad arm behind Vasily's back, working the hem of his shirt up past his shoulderblades with his fingers. Soft, deep green fabric slid up past his web of ink. Ammon's hard-light fingers couldn't grasp the delicate material, but with a combination of one warm hand, the resistance of the cushions, and Vasily's little shivers, they freed him. Vasily shook from the effort as he fell back into Ammon's shoulder. "I usually have the resonators for this... Sorry."

"Hey, I'm the one who cut their power, I should apologise. Are you ready to roll? Need a minute?"

"No, go ahead—put me down. I can rest there."

Ammon's body weight pressed against Vasily's shoulder, shifting him sideways. He wrapped his right arm—the solid one, warm and strong—around Vasily's narrow chest and shoulders, and bent them both forward from his waist, to roll Vasily onto the cushions, belly-down. A combination of lifts and nudges, tucked against Ammon's broad chest, got him settled comfortably, or at least as comfortable as he could be on solid ground, and Ammon released him. The spindle's amber starlights played over Vasily's back, glinting off the chromed surface of the exposed implants.

"Okay, Vasily. I have the frequency here to open your implants, and I'll be sending them a bit of new information, physically and digitally. We'll start with your sacrum." He touched the shining metal there, curved and blood-hot. The implant itself had no sensory capacity; Vasily couldn't feel the touch, though he could see Ammon's movement from the corner of his eye.

There was a tiny metallic *ting* as Ammon struck the tuning fork. It didn't ring audibly after that, but the pressure of the frequency could be felt, prickling in the eyes and the ears, tickling the back of the brain. Ammon set its base against the chrome of Vasily's sacrum. It was answered by the quiet hum of tiny servos, different from the ones that operated the 'skip. Vasily could feel the thrumming and tickling through his hips and up his spine. Slowly, the metal split along an invisible crack, exposing its inner circuitry and data-stores. Ammon switched the fork for the little wiry interlocutor tool, and it began its work, scouring out report routines, soldering a few key points.

"I like your tattoos," Ammon said. Vasily's back was webbed with geometric lines and curves, circled with little egg-shaped nodes. Framed in the center, in an open oval like a cameo, was an exquisite little bird, hovering mid-flight. Its body was that of a shimmering, flamboyant hummingbird, in tones of emerald and sapphire and amethyst. Its head was that of a young woman, with a pale face and blue eyes reminiscent of Vasily's own—but yet not him, not a true self-portrait. Her auburn hair drifted above her, wind-feathered, like a crest. "Is she someone you know? Family, maybe?"

He'd lied to the tattoo artist, told her the face was his sister's, as a memorial. "You could say that. She is, after a fashion..." Not family; no one real. The design truly was a memorial, though. He continued a little too briskly, a little too brightly. "The bird though, that's all myth, old as the hills. She's a gamayun." He told Ammon about the gamayun, the girl-faced bird of folklore, a creature of wisdom and beauty. "Usually she's drawn as a bigger bird, but—I have a soft spot for hummingbirds, the way they shimmer and float. They do it better than I."

The interlocutor tool had done its job. Ammon struck the tuning fork again, and closed the sacral implant. "There's one done. The next one—won't be as pleasant. It's kept a lot deeper down, and opening it won't be very nice."

"O…kay."

Ammon brushed Vasily's hair away from his neck, carefully, meticulously. He struck the fork and set it to the base of Vasily's skull, against the coin-sized disc of shining chrome visible there. It made Vasily's teeth hum, and his sinuses felt like they were ringing. Then the disc began to move: the center slid free, sliding slowly from his neck, releasing a finger-long curving spike that had nestled inside his cerebellum for years. It felt *wrong*. It didn't hurt, exactly, but it felt like someone had reached a finger up his nose and down his throat, somehow to wetly stroke his spinal column. He gagged. "Easy, easy, you're doing well, just a moment longer now," and it stopped, and Vasily could breathe properly again.

The interlocutor got to work. "You know," said Ammon, with deliberate nonchalance, "we have all kinds, among the shifters. Licensure, for adaptive or androgynous or any other augmentation purposes, is one route. But it isn't the only route."

Vasily bit his lip, and said nothing. The interlocutor finished, and the spike slid back in, with agonising slowness; it left him coughing, wracked and goosebumped. Ammon got him sitting upright, till he could breathe again, and helped him with his shirt.

"One last thing," Ammon said. "After a reset like this, the implants are designed to need a full re-charge. It's designed as a 'safety' feature, so they can discern tampering as quickly as possible, keeping you locked down till the Hands can work out how to solve you, or collect you. Doesn't work that well, though. Where do you keep your tail?"

"It's just here. See the blue blanket? Beneath." The plugless recharging cable for the 'skip was coiled up, half-hidden. Ammon fished it from the cushions, and brought out from his bag a little bit of perforated waxy paper, studded with tiny metallic circuitry. He popped the cover from the recharging surface—just held with magnets, like everything else these days—and slid the paper over the conduits before closing the unit back up.

"That's all. Now your tail won't rat on you, either."

Vasily was too exhausted to be surprised any further; if his implants could track him, why couldn't his cables as well? Maybe everything did. Of course. It made sense: dockpoints, transit, doorfobs, charging stations, augmented folks' entries to restricted housing. Of course someone would be collecting all this data. Reading it. Shaping it. Ammon joined Vasily up to the tail cable, and the g-skip hummed back into life, buoying him up from the floor. His body settled, at last his face relaxed.

Ammon pulled another calling-card from his bag. "When you're ready for the next step, you know how to be in touch."

Vasily nodded, wearily.

"Anything else you need? Questions? Power should be up as soon as I clear the block."

"How much of you is real?"

Ammon laughed, dark eyes sparkling, face creasing into well-worn laugh-lines. "Oh, all of me!"

"I meant... solid. I guess. Made of matter?"

"Ah, well, 80% at least. Hard light's just this arm, I promise. Anything else?"

"No, I just—I need time to figure out what just happened, I think."

He nodded. "It's a lot to process, I know. I remember. Do you still have my previous card?"

"Yes, on the bookshelf..."

Ammon nosed around till he found it, and crushed it swiftly between finger and thumb. It crumbled surprisingly fine. "There. Traceless. Be in touch, Vasily." He scooped up his spindle and stand, the amber lights fading from the walls, and was gone.

⚐

Vasily panicked.

He pretended he didn't, of course, but he panicked nonetheless. He didn't leave his room for two days straight, keeping the curtains drawn, the door locked tight. If anyone called, he was "just tired", and he hung up as quickly as possible. He ignored his mail. He stared hard at his implants with mirrors, worrying: was there a crack there, or just a hairline shadow? Was this the way they used to feel? What kind of fool had faith in a slip of waxed paper in his electronics?

Eventually, he had to go out, if just to the kitchen. The building lobby felt like enemy territory; the open air beyond, outside, was too enormous to contemplate. He started at little sounds, eyes flicking back and forth and up and down. He crouched in the kitchen, zipped as quickly as possible along the halls. He avoided the windows and shivered passing the doors. The coat rack looked like someone lurking, skulking. The groceries his housemates had left in the kitchen were an obvious trap. He sweated and shook.

Over the following days, though, his paranoia gently ebbed. He wasn't arrested. His implants still worked. No Teeth came for him in the night, save for in dreams, where the questions they grilled him with were nonsensical: how many feathers had he shed this year? Which star was he named after? How long had his sister been invisible? Where did the library go? The waking anxiety turned to chuckles (oh, silly me, spooked by a dream...). He couldn't shake the looming spectre of the omniscient government—after all, it certainly seemed true—but he remembered also the amber stars of silence, and the contrasts in touch between Ammon's solid and hard-light hands. They were real, too.

It took three weeks, this time, before he held the calling-card again, pressing one slender finger into its improbable mesh.

This time, the power didn't go out.

⚔

Ammon collected Vasily from his apartment, and they took a train: a slow one, ancient and buzz-shaken, running to a nondescript corner of town. He wouldn't say where they were going, just that there was someone Vasily needed to meet. They walked past run-down, crumbling concrete buildings, and Ammon stopped at one that was little more than a shell: roof gone, weeds growing out of what once were floors. Under a little bit of lingering overhang was a door, metal and scratched but intact, padlocked.

Vasily shifted in his fields, feeling conspicuous hovering in navies and purples here in this ghetto. "Where are you taking me?"

"You'll see." Ammon touched his thumb to the padlock, which shimmered open: not a true physical lock, then, but a morphic one. The door swung in and revealed a dank basement stairway, air moist and stale, walls slimy—but with a subtle dockpoint at the top of the stairs, to let a 'skipper glide down in safety. Curiouser and curiouser.

At the downstairs landing was another door, sturdier-looking than the last. Ammon knocked a simple skittering pattern, and it opened inward. The basement was cramped, low-ceilinged, all rough-stubbled concrete. Fluorescent light from a bare bulb caught its jags. The man who had opened the door looked strangely at home here underground. He was short, stout, and bristling with dark hair. It peeked out from his shirt-cuffs and dusted his knuckles; his beard and brows were bushy, and the hair on his head shaggy. He was dressed in nondescript dark colours, utilitarian fabrics. He nodded to Ammon. "This the new one?"

Ammon smiled and made introductions. "Yes. This is Vasily, no other designator of yet. Vasily, this is Kvedulf, our sensor." Kvedulf nodded to Vasily, in turn, and made a gruff hello.

Vasily tilted his head to Ammon: "Censor?"

"Sensor, like senses, sensory function, not censor like limiter or redactor—though it does kind of work like that, sometimes. If you don't check out, if you might be dangerous, you won't make it past him." He turned to address them both equally. "But I scrubbed Vasily myself and you've seen the background check, Kvedulf, so I'm sure you'll be alright, Vas."

The hairy man harrumphed, darkly.

"Kvedulf really only trusts his own senses, though. No offense meant," Ammon added. "*Despite* the outstanding quality of my work, I'll have you know, and my being such a fine judge of character."

"I thought you had the... star-thing? To be sure." Kvedulf was circling Vasily, peering, nostrils flared. The hair on his head seemed to have a life of its own, the ends floating and drifting in a little cloud around him.

"Oh, this room has an actual built-in damper mechanism, it's in the walls, but still: safety measure. This is the last bar of clearance before you can access the rest of us. Kvedulf keeps us all safe."

Vasily's skin tingled as Kvedulf probed the g-skip's fields; he tightened them in as low as he dared, to make it easier. The hairs on Kvedulf's knuckles danced as he prodded the air around Vasily. He made several more circuits, crouching below the 'skip, then beckoning him to lower down so he could swirl the air above his head as well, before he seemed satisfied. He nodded to Vasily.

"They're alright, Amm."

"See? Told you, Vasily, you're fine. Let's go meet the family."

Kvedulf stepped aside, and tapped the wall opposite the door. The jags of concrete suddenly seemed to make sense, to resolve, as an irregularly-edged, heavy door opened out, onto a low, arched brick hallway, dimly lit. Vasily followed Ammon along it, to a simple wooden door. Vasily paused before they reached it.

"Why did he call me a 'they'?"

Ammon's smile shone in the dim light. "Remember, I said we have all types? You can be—anything you need to be, here. It's your choice, and no one else will make it for you."

Vasily's heart seemed to skip a beat, several beats. "Oh."

"Anything. Man or woman, or neither, or little blended gamayun-bird, Vas, anything."

"I can't—I don't—" Vasily choked on the words. "I never dared. I only dreamed—barely dreamed—I never told anyone." And how could he? Certainly someone like him would never meet the criteria for sanctioned androgyny, or for any change like that; the mandate was mutually exclusive with adaptive licensure. He couldn't. "I don't think I can."

Ammon rested his warm hand on Vasily's shoulder, squeezed it gently. "You don't have to choose today." His smile seemed to bring a bronze glow to the russet colours of his skin. "Ready to say hello?"

Vasily nodded.

Ammon rapped out another short, skittering knock. This door opened into another low-ceilinged room, though it was larger than

Kvedulf's antechamber, and lit warmly. The bricks were hung with richly-coloured cloths, and there were couches, chairs, cushions on the floor: all filled with the most amazing array of individuals Vasily had ever seen. At first glance alone he spotted scaled heads, many-jointed legs, glittering eyes, outlandish prostheses, blended sexes. He gaped in wonder, then tried not to stare and look the yokel, then gaped again. A few folks waved, called hellos to Ammon, who cleared his throat theatrically.

"Everyone—could I have your attention? Everyone. We have a newbie!" There was some hooting, some applause. Ammon turned, said softly, "Vas. You don't have a shifter name yet, I know, but," he turned back to the crowd, spoke out clearly, "here you go, this is everyone. Everyone, please give them welcome!"

The cheer that greeted him was so full-throated and genuine it felt like it rocked him backward on the 'skip. Ammon's voice, soft though it was, rumbled warmly beneath.

"Welcome to the shifter family, little gamayun."

Losing Touch

Louise Hughes

I want to cry but the only eyes I have are not my own.

These eyes, through which I see too clearly in the dark, are Ghent's. They put my brain inside his metal, human-mimicking body and he *told* me they were mine. But mine, the ones I closed years ago and never re-opened, would need more light to see by. The cloud-access bunker is not lit for the old me.

As the computer thinks, my fractured memory retreats to two clear images.

Skating. I remember that. Blades on *my* feet, not these feet.

Waking up. I remember that too: the first time Ghent and I awoke together, my brain in his body. But my memory has replaced that lab, the first place these eyes saw, with another. I've taken all those feelings and wrapped them around a more familiar place. The lab we go to each year to be checked and polished. That first one is probably under the ice, somewhere.

Most of my other memories are last-gasp echoes. When Ghent lay down to take the sun and recharge our cells, I used to pass the time remembering so much more. Everything after and before the day we woke. The lying down, the stillness and the silence, are all insistently familiar. Our life together started like that, with a whisper and then an attempt to lift these legs that aren't quite mine. A need that grew and grew, too big to fit inside my tiny head.

I try to remember when the screaming merged into the background, but have no place to start. Ghent provided me with dates, so earnest, trying to make me feel better like he always does. The battering of the walls around my thoughts is like the endless thud, thud, thud of the engine in our chest. The engine that will keep me alive forever.

Å

"Here." Search successful. Less than a minute. Ghent tried to coax Adela out, the mind inside the brain inside his—their—head. "When I've downloaded this year's records, I can upload all this if you like. I'll delete some things, to make the space."

No. Don't do that.

"We're nearly full." 95.4%. Adela took too many pictures. All of ice or snow in different kinds of light. The point of their walking wasn't to take pictures but to find what of the human race had survived the ice. But it made her feel better to save what their eyes saw, so he allowed it.

"I'll put it into backup. And they'll be here, if we need them."

But I don't want that. Just let me see.

Å

I look down at the screen. He's turned on the display just for me, because it's not like he needs it. I hate having someone do such a simple thing for me. *I* should turn the screen on. Myself.

Let me, I say. He relinquishes control only of our hand and arm. We found the ocean last week. The ice drifted away in a hundred white lily pads. I wanted to know if swimming was something one never forgets how to do, like riding a bike.

Not it isn't. And I've never ridden a bike. Ghent reminded me when he hauled us back onto land.

The ocean. I lived near the ocean once. There's always an ache in my chest when I see it.

An imagined ache in the chest that isn't mine. It took me three days of focus to remember the name of the town, to taste that familiar ring to its syllables. It was by the ocean and we walked to the beach every day beneath a sky so blue it hurt my eyes. My real eyes. From the name it grew like hunger, the nagging worry about forgotten knowledge. I reach for something in my head that's no longer there. A great black pit, like someone's been digging it deeper while I wasn't looking and my whole life has fallen in. The computer offers to haul it back. I can already taste triumph. Waves of promise in my head.

Text strolls across the hovering screen. I want to sit down, out of long-forgotten habit, but there aren't any seats. Ghent doesn't need seats.

What's this? I ask.

The town you're always talking about, Ghent says. *It's in your record. I looked it up last time you got worked up about this.*

Little pictures of brick and concrete flick past. A graffiti-infested flyover and a town square tower of red with a high clock face. Cars. Their blocky image and their shiny colors stand out sharp. Wow. I'd forgotten what cars looked like. I can conjure their name, but like the rest of my life, their details are missing from my mind.

I don't recognize any of this. Are you sure this is the right place? A map at the top of some half-familiar landmass puts the town about as far from the ocean as it could be. "It isn't even by the sea. There's just a river." The flowing brown soup was hemmed in by cracked grey walls.

Yes. I don't forget things. My brain isn't broken like yours, Ghent says. He doesn't mean to be malicious.

I'm not broken. And you don't have a brain.

Then why can't you remember? I can see everything I've ever seen, so why can't you?

I don't know.

We can go back to the laboratory and have the tech give you another look over if you want.

I'm not a machine.

Back when I first woke up, my brain inside this metal case, and Ghent held back our limbs from listening to my commands. I knew, in a sudden plummeting flash, that I couldn't live like this. My memories, those few that still clung on, betrayed me.

Then as now, I'd stared at the ceiling with just one thought. I take control of our mouth.

"Please kill me."

Å

"What's the point of them if they can't remember anything?" the figure behind Ghent in the technician queue had said. "Mine just sings nursery rhymes all day. London's Burning, London's Burning… and every time I tell her it really did, she's surprised all over again. Replace them with someone new. There are many more waiting in the storage bays."

Ghent closed his eyes on the computer, so Adela could not see the thing that made her so upset, and took back control of their hands to stop the scrolling. Years of wandering the ice sheets looking for the ruins and detritus of civilization with her in his head had made him quick to act when he sensed her sadness. Humans weren't meant to exist this way. On the verge of shock. They needed someone to calm the panic and the fear, the disbelief.

Don't do that, Adela said.

What?

I want to see. Please, let me have our arms. I promise I won't try to swim again.

We're a long way from the ocean.

Please. I want to see if there's anything else.

Å

He gives in, because no matter how close we are, he still can't read my thoughts. The town continues to spin its lies. It wasn't like that. It can't have been. I remember the ocean and the beach, and the flowers in all the borders in springtime, the palm trees throwing out their fans over neat cut grass on every roundabout. I remember my home with its windows framed in green and the dappled sunlight on the kitchen worktop. From my window seat piled high with cushions I could see the winking sails of the ships fluttering in, from horizon to port, bringing unnamed treasures.

"This is wrong."

The faux-glass computer screen splinters around my fist, shards mingling with the ice below. I smash again. This vat of lies doesn't deserve to keep on blinking its tiny little light.

Someone grips our wrist. Until then, I don't realize anyone has entered the room and it stuns me. Ghent takes our hand back.

Stop, he tells me, incapable of anger. I crash against our skull, trying to force my will into our limbs. I want to make him angry, furious. I want him to bellow at me so loud it echoes round our head.

I'm sorry. I shouldn't have run the search. I thought it would help.

The other in the room lets go of our wrist. Their bland metal face is just like ours, except they have already been to the technician to have the kinks of a year's wandering on the ice smoothed out. Our nose is still a little squashed.

Glass eyes of blue light up to let us know who is speaking. Everything is designed for me. Ghent and everyone I meet. They are vessels for unpredictable and mysterious as minds who can't be trusted to exist alone. They feared I would wake, mind prisoner in a metal form, and lose myself in horror. And yet they never thought my mind would atrophy. Idiots.

"There are new arrivals," the stranger says. Ghent connects to their identity chip. Eric and Vienna. "They finished twenty more models at least this year."

"There are always new arrivals," Ghent says.

"One of them is your mother."

λ

Ghent stopped tidying the access station away and connected to the database again. As with everything else, Adela couldn't remember her mother's name, and he didn't want to press her on the matter. She would only get upset again.

This was the first time someone from Adela's sector had been removed from storage, so they'd never had to test her memory of people before.

Come on, she said. *It doesn't matter. You can connect as we walk.*

She tried to seize control of their legs, but as he tidied the computer station away, the splintered remains of the screen crunched beneath their feet. She might be right. It might make her feel better to speak to someone from before.

λ

A crowd of figures queue in the snow. They wait for the

technician's lab, or the storage bunker, or the generator battery, all hidden beneath the featureless ice. There is nothing else to see but the pylon, stretching its dishes and aerials up into the sky. If there were any more settlements out there, this may be why we haven't found them. Even if we walked right over their heads, how would we know.

Ghent sends out a low whine of a signal. A figure turns and with an awkward wave, staggers and slides across the ice. Blank face, blue lights for eyes, stylized metal hair.

"Katherine Johnson?" Ghent asks.

"Yes." Her arms jerk to her sides and her forehead tilts forward as she tries to frown with eyebrows she no longer has.

Even if I could remember anything beyond the essence of my mother, I would not recognize her in that face.

She leans nearer, glass eyes close to ours. But there's a lot of wires and circuitry between her and me. "They... he, tells me you're my son. I can't..."

Son? I reach out for the database. They've got this wrong.

Ghent throws up a block. *I already checked twice. She's your mother.*

"Will?" Her question hangs in the air, drifting like the snow. "Is that you?"

"It is," Ghent says for me.

But that isn't my name. I reach for our legs. We have to leave, stop putting the poor woman through this. She has enough to deal with. From the stilted way she walks and talks, she can't have been awake for long. She fell asleep years ago but to her it'll be like yesterday. I see it every year even though that never happened to me. I was one of the first, Ghent tells me when I forget. They made him for me when they saw what was coming, one of many worldwide ideas for surviving the global freeze. There were other solutions and theories, but we haven't found their children yet.

Not now, he says. *It was your name, before. You changed it.*

I don't remember that. *No I didn't.*

We didn't use it much. Now you are Adela. I made sure to add a note to the database.

I want to grab our hands and punch us in the face. Imagine that crinkled nose folding inwards. Ghent pretends he doesn't care, but I've watched him checking our every repaired dent and scuff.

You just let me go on thinking... But does it matter? I am Adela. Except I'm trying so hard to remember what I was before, and now I'm even less certain.

Ghent keeps on talking to my mother, explaining, but I don't listen. Then he pauses to answer my drill of demands against our skull. *You called yourself that, so I thought that's what you wanted.*

⚑

Ghent didn't understand. She saw herself as Adela, so what was the problem? A small adjustment in the database. That was nothing. But the figure in front of him fell still as he explained. Yes, this was the mother's child, and she was called Adela.

"She's confused," Denver took over. "We're still getting used to life."

"Of course." Even he and Adela had trouble with it sometimes, and it had been so much longer for them. Denver, a product of the workshops near the equator, where solar power was strongest, had only been brought online a few weeks ago.

"Perhaps we should just let them talk," Denver suggested.

Ghent agreed. He'd noticed this before. Adela did like to prattle away in their head.

⚑

"I didn't think I'd ever see you again," my mother tells me as we sit in the snow. "I thought, when they said they'd build us all bodies eventually, that they were just saying that. When I went to sleep, I remember thinking, this is it."

I want to ask about my father, because I must have had one, but it seems wrong. I wonder what my mother looked like. She looks like everyone else now. When she looks at me she sees Ghent, not Adela and not Will.

"So…" She looks to the iron sky. "Do you want me to call you Will…or Adela?" Her fingers burrow into the snow. "Not that it's a problem, either way. I don't mind. I just…"

I try to see myself as Will.

Will must have lived in a town that didn't have an ocean, or palm trees, or a neat terraced house with green-framed windows. That was just his imagined home. That story became Adela. Adela became me.

If I don't remember Will, does that mean Will is Adela, or not?

"Adela."

"So… you decided to become…" And away her eyes go again. "I'm sorry, it's just all so new."

Let's go, I tell Ghent. I can't think of anything to say.

⚑

Ghent had an idea, from his communication with the database, but he didn't tell Adela. Something dragged her down again. Something her mother had said, in that short, fragmented conversation. Adela's thoughts turned in on themselves and he didn't like to interrupt.

Katherine called after them as he walked towards the warehouse bunker. "I don't mind, really."

It's not for you to mind or not, Adela muttered to herself.

In the warehouse, a small crowd huddled around the steel-topped accession table. Two accessioners—responsible for sorting the artefacts—took notes on a tablet. Several transparent vacuum flasks sat on the table, everyone leaning close to inspect their contents.

"Where were you digging?" Ghent asked.

Someone pulled a tablet over to show him the coordinates on a map, somewhere in the northern hemisphere, several hundred miles from the base. The searchers gathered annually to re-charge, update the records and see the technicians. Unlike Ghent and Adela, who explored alone along a route assigned by the system, these surveyors had gone out as a team to tunnel through the ice beneath the site of a former city. Such sites offered unique opportunities for items to reclaim and archive. When the ice spread, those unsure of what else to do, gathered their possessions, dug deep and left them in vaults below where they estimated the burrowing ice would reach. They couldn't carry them south with the migrations, or up into space.

It seemed a lot of time and effort to expend on something they weren't ever going to come back for. He couldn't understand it.

Of course you don't. Adela reached out for their hands, attention caught by the nearest flask.

Well, they're probably dead now anyway, or in storage.

⚊

Don't say that. I reach for our mouth, but I'm not really interested in arguing. The small army of vacuum flasks calls to me. *I want to see.*

We move closer, Ghent responding to my urging so I imagine I have control of our limbs. He picks one up and we peer inside. A small light illuminates the contents, less precious than some of the other things, the accessioner informs us.

So we can take it out if we want.

I won't know what it is, I fear, and try to close our eyes. But Ghent doesn't let me. Inside the flask is an angel, with a faded lace collar and dented painted face. Responding to my imagination, Ghent raises it in the air to the height of a Christmas tree.

We had a star.

"What's that?"

Ghent processes the stilted voice without turning and identifies my mother. He relinquishes our mouth and I turn with the angel still in our hands. Her eyes, like everyone else's, stare back.

"It's a Christmas tree angel. Do you remember, we had that star and the wire broke so we had to jam it down on the top of the tree?"

"It broke?" she says. "I don't remember that."

"It snapped when I was in my teens. And then the top of the tree broke too, but we kept on using it."

Someone else moves to look at the flask in my hands. I lower it, torn between clinging on and letting someone else share the experience. They take it and raise it to their eyes.

"We had an angel," they say. "It was from my mother's mother."

"Your grandmother?" A word I hadn't used in years. It conjures a heady echo of a scent. Lilies in a vase and beeswax polish. Smooth wooden furniture glowing in the autumn sun. A phantom fist forces its way up my phantom throat.

Their head tilts. "I suppose. I never knew her though, so I never called her that."

I pick up another flask. Everyone else has gathered more intently round the table, hands clutching the forbidden, priceless things inside their tiny glass prisons.

Ghent reclaims our mouth. "Open them," he says.

The two collectors stop their tapping. "What?"

"Open them. We can't see them properly through the glass."

One accessioner scoops the flasks towards them, batting the others away as they try to skip in and steal the artefacts back. "No. Look with your eyes, like everyone else. These things are precious. If those who fled into space return, or if we find those who went south, they're going to need them. They are memories."

I want to see them, I insist, cheering on our vain attempt to claim them. If their owners had wanted these things, really wanted them, they would have taken them. They would have found a way.

"Let my daughter see them." My mother's awkward arm grips the assessor's shoulder. She's worked out how to turn up the volume on their voice.

Someone else darts round the side and steals two of the flasks. They put them at the end of the table, leaning over to try and find the switch for the light that will illuminate their contents in the dim room. But Ghent is ahead of them. He pulls the cord near the door. It flicks and bounces when he lets it go. It jars. Something from my old life. Who on Earth had designed something archaic? Accessioners and their focus on the past. It joins the old posters on the walls, the metal signage. My sculpted mouth tries to smile but can't.

"Stuff this." The figure with the flasks tosses his head. They press a button on the top of the flask and unscrew the cap. Air floods in with a hiss. Everyone stops their arguing and turns to look. Already closest, Ghent relinquishes our hands so I can take one of the flasks.

The assessor slams down the tablet. "You should all keep a hold of your human minds. That's what you're for."

I freeze, expecting Ghent to reclaim control of our hands, but he doesn't. I upend the flask. A pile of little metal cars spill out onto the table and my mother catches one as it skids off towards the floor. She puts it back, wheeling it around the others in a circle. Then her hand stops. She whips it away and reaches instead for mine. Something in my brain reacts, skipping a beat in my imagined heart. The real one keeps on beating regardless. I look at the car and it's as if something slams into our side. I glance down but there's nothing there. Blackness, recalled confusion. I don't know...

I close my eyes.

Ѫ

Ghent reached out for their hands, sensing the building anger. Every scrap leftover from Old Earth was vital to keeping its memory alive. Especially when the minds they had hoped would do that seemed to fade so quickly. But, the figures around the table moved with a new enthusiasm, their animated chatter swelling as they saw the objects from their old lives.

Do you want me to keep our eyes closed? he asked Adela. It might be easier that way.

No. I want to see.

He took the fingers.

No. I have to feel. And if we could smell, I'd do that too.

He paused for a moment, which she seemed to find funny.

Well, a moment is so much quicker for you, she said.

Your mother can smell. The technicians worked out how to do that years ago. We can go and see the technician and they might be able to...

He was so primitive, compared to these new models. But not as primitive as he'd been when they first awoke. He hadn't thought about much back then, before those years of talking to Adela. She'd made him so much more aware.

She clenched and unclenched their fingers as he gave her them back and said, *Stop trying to distract me.*

Ѫ

I open our eyes, pick up one of the little cars and hold it out in front of me.

"Do you remember?" my mother asks.

Someone else upends the other flask. A plastic device falls out and they try to turn it on but nothing happens.

"The battery is flat." The accessioner jabs at their tablet, as petulant as a robot can be. "We've been trying to work out how to charge it. It looks like…"

The figure cuts him off. "A phone."

Ghent is sending out a signal. I don't know what he's saying until everyone relinquishes command to their companions. I can tell from the way their faces linger and their hands hover, uncertain. Flasks hiss open, contents fall to the table to be turned over and over. Objects we haven't touched in many years rekindle memories, set neglected pathways sparking.

"Remember these," says the figure holding the phone in their outstretched palm, going through some reflexive motion of slipping it back and forth. "I'd forgotten. But… I never went anywhere without it. Do you remember?" He looks up. "Everyone had one?"

I didn't though. Will and Adela—they are the same—had something simpler. The memory drifts back and I don't want to seize it or interrogate it for fear it will run away.

"Do you remember?" my mother repeats.

I stare at the toy in my hand, the toy that caused my heart to skip a beat. Four wheels, windows all around. A car like every other. Like the one that gave me Ghent. I stepped off the pavement, eye on the little green man, and woke with a body that wasn't mine. There should have been pain. But they took my mind away before I felt it, and stopped me ever feeling it again. True pain. Unfettered agony as the blood rushes out and the body shuts down. I wonder what that feels like.

"I remember." I say. A city, a street, a moment.

I want to cry, and Ghent wants to let me, but he can't. No one has found a way to let us do that yet.

"futurecoffee" by Vincent Konrad

Previous Page:

A city street scene with buildings of various sizes and shapes in the background. In the foreground, there are people sitting at a street-side cafe. At a table on the left side, mid-way in the image, a woman sits alone as a male waiter takes her order. At the bottom and right of the image, a man and a woman are sitting together a table. The woman is facing the viewer, and she is asking the man sitting across from her, "How's your tea?" (the words are written in cursive). The man has his back to the viewer. He is looking down at a electronic tablet device that has the words, "HOW IS YOUR..." written in block capitals. Directly behind this couple, a man is walking down the street. This man is wearing glasses that are emitting lidar beams enabling him to "see" where he is going.

into the waters i rode down

Jack Hollis Marr

hhhhhh
??
hhhhh
well this is fucking useless isn't it
kkkkkkkkkkkkkkkkk
that's worse Romaan STOP IT
kkkkkke$_{yesn'tk}$kkkka$_{nyoukk}$kkus?
there's something now
kkkkkkkaliyekkkkkKKKKKK
fuck that hurt!
what was that
was that my name
try again
kkkkkkaliye?aliye!kkkkkk
YES I can hear it now //// I can HEAR it (guess this is hearing?)
this is fucking weird i tell you
$_{kkkk}$*Aliyeogdwe*$_{kkk}$*iditd*$_{kkkk}$*knowwhatthismeans?*

Of course I know what it fucking means. I've been working on the project as long as any of them; longer than many. I guess Romaan thinks my work didn't count because none of it's been said aloud, only input through computers. Well, screw him. He's never spoken to anyone working on this back on Earth in person either, only in text relay, but I suppose that's different, right. After all, I'm only the fallback after none of the hearing walking people's brains could adapt to the neural linkage, aren't I?

Must fucking *burn* Romaan, that I could do this and he couldn't, just cos my battered old brain's had to adjust to so much fucking adaptive tech over the decades. *Neuroplasticity.* Nice little word. I suppose it's nice to have something they're jealous of, for once. God knows several degrees don't do it, not when you're old and a woman and deaf

The hearing's secondary, of course, a side bonus of the main task: that neural linkage between my brain and an animal's. I've been working on it most of my life, this fake telepathy, trying to match the other side's advantage in this strange war.

We tried between people, but it was too overwhelming. We—lost people, in that stage.

(Saira, my dear Saira, who will never be the same; I see her each week, her in her bed and me in my chair, and she smiles and touches my hand, and doesn't speak. Leish, Persis; oh, my dead dears. I reread that poem this week, before the linkage that might have done the same to me, thinking of you. *Rock-a-bye baby, washing on the line.* The drowned dead voices asking, *How's it above?* I imagine your voices in those lines, the white bone talking: *When she smiles, is there dimples? What's the smell of parsley? I am going into the darkness of the darkness forever.* My lost darlings all, I'm so sorry, I am. I think of your sinews in the far-away earth, and how I'm not enough. I can't give you back the world, the smell of parsley, anything at all. Would you have been pleased that we succeeded, in the end?)

My Romaan was the one who worked out the audiovisual part; he's brilliant, if annoying, and being able to promote this sort of shit to civilians always does the Service good, doesn't it? Look at how helpful we are. We can even give veterans back some of the senses we cost them. Know he'll expect me to be over the moon (ha, there's an old-fashioned phrase, now) over *actually hearing* for the first time in my life. That's what I'm supposed to be excited about, isn't it? Noise, or the simulation of it, in my skull. Big deal. Bunch of hissing and clicking and the odd weirdly three-dimensional word that hurts and echoes. I'd stick with text, if it wasn't for the rest.

But. The rest. To get *down there*, and not in a clunky suit but slipping easy as fish through not-water through the strange thick air, resting light in alien animal mind, witch-riding a foreign familiar in a world no human's ever *touched*, not with skin and eyes and nose—and ears, I suppose, those too (do the otterfishcatsnake things they showed me *have* ears?)—this extraordinary modern magic that will, if it goes right, let us eavesdrop on the other and its hidden world... For that, oh God, for *that*. That's worth all the hissing and clicking inconvenience, the drilling in my skill, all the years of different aids.

And, I mean, it's war. Doing my bit for the Effort. All the shit I was meant to do, defective daughter of a military family. Daddy would be *so proud*, the old bugger. Thank fuck he's dead. Last thing I need's him being proud that his broken little girl's able to be a spy.

Them the enemy the Bad Guys the invaders (though how they're invading planets that used to be *theirs*... but you don't question that, do you, old woman? Not if you've got the sense you were born with) and worst *the aliens*. NotOfUs. The Others. Headless freaks, The Blob. Spooks, Dad called them. You'd think he'd've been less shitty, given the crap people in his own beloved military called him in his day, but I reckon there wasn't much that'd make Dad be less shitty. Whatever they are, they can move easy through that thick weird air down there, and we can't. We can protect our mining interests in vehicles and suits, missiles and lasers and bombs from space, but we can't walk among them. And we can't do what they can, use our minds as weapons, not directly. Neither of those things.

Well. *I* can, now.

The animal they bring me's as high as my knee, as long as my body lying flat. It *does* have ears, little hollow dents. I wish I could reach through the clear glass or plastic and touch it, see if those are thin scales or strange fur, if it's warm or cool against my own smooth skin. Its head is small, sharp-nosed, its legs short like a ferret's, its back supple as a cat's. Its gill-like orifices pulse gently. It looks at me through one nictating eye and then the next, turning its head like a bird. I can't remember its scientific name; we've been calling it the catsnake, and it fits.

I look for the implants but they're invisible, hidden in the scale-spike-fur. My own make my head throb, pried between the plates of my skull. I wonder if it's afraid. I can see its sides expand and deflate slowly as it breathes; maybe it's sedated. Lucky bugger.

we're going~kkkkk~**to trythelinkage h**~hhhh~**ere first**, Romaan says. The existing link, the one through the computer, is working so much better now, though I'm still adjusting to (the illusion of) actually *hearing* words in my skull. Whatever part of my brain that input stimulates *aches*, a constant weird throb. I'd rather he just used my old text relay, but he's too fucking proud of his invention. And I don't want to look *ungrateful*, do I? That doesn't look good for the cameras that've been trained on me these recent weeks, on and off, for this marvellous breakthrough: hearing to the deaf! Sight to the blind! Pick up thy bed, and walk!

This isn't being filmed, though. The Service doesn't like too many records of its little failures, and we've had too many of those in this long project. I'm very aware of that as I close my eyes, let them wire me up yet again, little clips and clamps, the vibrations that used to be my sound. I move my hands on the padded arms of my chair, feel-hear them run through me: bass throb, treble sting. Familiar and easing, beneath the godawful **kkkkkHHHkkkk**ness they've given me.

And then, the linkage.

Not much at first: sharp little zap all through me, leaving a dull ache in my back teeth, heavy sort of throb in my balls that could almost be pleasure. And then—falling. Not like falling in dreams, not like the sick whirl when you miss a step (I remember that, so clearly), but vertigo, everything spinning, no up no down and nothing to hold onto (somewhere my fingers clench, but I can't feel it, I can't *feel* it, oh god the old paralysis, please no—) and darkness and lights all mixed and through the computer feed my own *screaming* fed back to me on and on and on, ringing through me so that I batter myself against glass, supple body thrashing helplessly between panes like a sample on a slide somehow living and aware, the noise must stop the noise must *stop*—

—and this is not my body and these are not my ears that hear, this is not-i and i together, pulse of gills and beat of strange slow blood. catsnake is this you, i, i-thou, we? catsnake is frightened, and so is aliye. hush, hush. rock-a-bye. you're hurting us, we're hurting us. see, the screaming has stopped. see, there through the distorting glass, the woman in the chair. when she smiles, there's dimples. there, the slow breathing, the calming blood. i-thou-i, resting nested. nest-memory, slow weed-breathing thickness by the slow river's bank, dark hole hollow, infant scale-skin against adult fur: so we are twice mother, thou and i? so I held my baby. how soft her tiny fingers were, her soft and dented skull! so; so. we are together.

—and then we are not, and I am in my chair with everything *hurting* and my fingers tearing at the implants, Romaan shouting **kkkkkk** and the catsnake thrashing panicked in its narrow tank. I get myself free and wheel myself across to it, press my hands against the glass. There are alarms somewhere: I can feel them. The film on its eyes is flickering fast in panic. I have never touched an animal that wasn't human before—how strange it is that I still haven't, when I've been in its bloody head! I wish I could hold it to me like the baby we remembered, touch its strange pelt.

So. Hush. Rock-a-bye. The prick of a needle in my neck, putting me to sleep. Rock-a-bye, Aliye, falling into vertigo-darkness. Rock-a-bye, catsnake. Silence all.

It's months before we're ready, catsnake and me. I'm never able to make it—her?—us?—understand what it is we're doing, and I'm glad. It's its planet down there, after all, that I'm going to be creeping over in its head, when it's released, its planet that we're filleting with mining gear in the cause of Need. There are less of them now than there used to be, I'm told: rivers dammed or dried, swamps drained, and a warzone besides. I wonder what became of the kits in the nest, the thick quiet hollow, if they died or throve. There's no way to ask it. Its animal-brain works in *now* and glimpses, flashed sense-memory. We can't communicate, not properly, though I can stir or soothe it in its glass box.

What's it like to walk again, Mum? He does care so much, in his own way, doesn't he, my Romaan, though he doesn't understand a thing. Desperate to have *given* me that, like he tried to give me hearing I didn't want, had never had. To have given it *back,* as if I ever ran on four stubby legs beneath a wiggly back and tasted electricity in the air. Blinked back through my text relay: It's not so bad. It shuts him up, for a bit.

But there are always others: **You must be so happy, Aliye. Ms Parlak, it must be so liberating for you. Will you tell our viewers what it's like?** No one fucking saying: "Well done, Aliye, you and your team've fucking cracked a military and scientific problem we've been working on for a couple of lifetimes, you genius woman. How does *that* feel?" Romaan's shaking hands, accepting the awards. Saira would be furious with him, our son pushing me into the background like that. She would have understood, my Saira. She would.

I asked Romaan to turn off the noise. He didn't want to—he's been angry, the little shit—but he did it. Eventually. I suppose it hurts to have your mother reject what's meant to be a gift, even an incidental one, a side-effect. He took it better when I explained it helped me with the catsnake, that its hearing from inside is strange and muffled, the underwater booms and bangs close to what I feel through skin and bone without my ears.

It's got another sense, too, strange to me: electric zaps and tingles with nowhere to go, leaving it confused as I was in my vertigo. I've insisted they give it a bigger box, a tub of water to wallow in. It pings its electricity off the plastic sides of the tub and hums to itself constantly, a discontent whining thrum. Everyone in the lab's starting to hate it. Bet they wish *they* could turn off their hearing now. They only get peace when we're hooked up, it and me, curled together in memory-dark, sharing half-memory without words. Smell of a baby's head, taste of riverweed and strange fish, Saira's hands on my skin, sharp sweet jolt of a barbed dick inside us. I'm filling in all sorts of facts for the xenobiologists: they're the ones who really love me now. Not sure what good it does anyone, this knowledge of a dying species on a torn up world. Seem to be getting even more bitter these days, don't I? And people think old ladies're sweet.

And now. And now we're going down. My body in close orbit, catsnake's down to the surface. In the linkage still, and I'm caught in its confusion, the horrible pressure. Both of us screaming. Thick air of its tank shaking. Our bones are splitting—

—and then there is freedom, the wide soft air in which to run far and fast and then free of all the strangeness to leap and twist, dancing delighted loops under a double moon in doubled shadows, there is the river and its taste, familiar-unfamiliar home at last all full of whiskered things that swim and we are in the bottom-mud all stomach-wriggling hunting in hunger for the savour of real food after immeasurable incomprehensible long and homehomehome here an abandoned den to nest in all tail-over-nose and warm and safe **parlakparlakyouhavetomoveit** for time without measure in the slow warm dark.

parlak can you hear me. you have to move it. north-west, their camp is north-west.

in the slow. warm. dark.

parlak.

warmdarkwarmdarkwecan'thearyou

parlak. aliye.

no.

mum.

romaan? (catsnake confused: no names here.) (the kit, the kit that survived.) romaan. What?

go north-west, parlak. mum.

moving confused-obedient, body bending to the river. romaan like this? **yes mum.** deep drumming of machines. taste of metal in notwater, vibration, electricity all wrong. up out of the water, almostvoices, strange smells

there, parlak, there, we're recording. go further in.

shapes moving, vast and almost-formless. not one looks at catsnake, another animal slinking along. ones closelike to catsnake chained up, yowling protest at intrusion. pets? guards? humans've never been this close. only glimpses on screens

lightblare sudden, handshapes reaching, sirens all piercing skin and it

hurtshurtshurt **pull back pull back parlak get out they've detected our signal** and PAINPAINPAIN whiter than light all bloodsmell and *run* go go go waterseeking dive deep engines on water vibrating following. bowels voiding sudden sharpwater stink. deeper twist and flee, swamps shallow and streams thin, up and over down again twisting, catsnake-and-woman flee flee flee and there is

so

much

pain.

darkplace found, hiding now. i'm sorry, i'm sorry, i did this to you, we did, the pain, i'm sorry. this is our fault, oh god, our fault. are we dying?

our belly hurts so very much
and then

…shhhh, otherperson, rider, it tells us without words. shhhh forget, come back to riverlair safe and sleep, safenest dark and silence shhh. come back to dreams of kitsandbabes, lullaby quietsoft sleep. shh now forever silence dreams, no more machine loudshouting no more the headvoice intruding **mum** and we are back in riverdeep **mum** metaltaste slipaway silence song and home to lair and we are back in rock-a-bye memory and we are _{mum} we are we are we.

river is taste softdreaming always. remember whiskerfish crunch tasteonthetongue and home to lair, curl around. tail over nose yoursandmine, share again the memory of scaleskin and babysmell, little fingers counting lullaby sheep baabaablack and piggies gone to market. what pigssheep, otherself? and we show though we have never touched, share pictures once on screens of pink and woolly shape, otherworld wonder to us both. mothermother curled in dark, otherother nested minds together away from war

(what is war, otherself)

(hush, hisst, rock-a-bye quiet. goodbye to all that. glad I am to say it)

aliye, we have to break the linkage. that thing's dying, we have to get you out. you have to wake up. aliye.

do you remember/we remember. this is the taste of parsley, catsnake/this is the winter dreaming, otherself. we remember. we. we do. (I will.)

kkkkkk

Mum. Mum kkkou alright?

fuck off, romaan. just—fuck off/// i told you before to turn that thing off/// go away. i'm done. i quit i quit. leave me be.

Rip the connections out of the metal holes in my skull, wheel away fast. Get away, get away (deeper twist and flee through swamp and river), nails prying at the implants, ripping pain but they won't come out. I don't want to hear or walk, not again, never wanted to, that stupid side effect of war-usefulness that I was supposed to love. I can't I won't. Not part of that world ever again (sorry Daddy not sorry), not used as a warmachine instrument, soft furscale or skin body (Saira Leish Persis me) become a weapon and lost.

Another voice forced on me all **Parlak this is insubordination** and **courtmartial** and **lost her mind**. I hunch down in riverdark memory and rock, as best I can. I'm sorry. I'm sorry.

Oh, my dead dear, forgive.

Playa Song

Petra Kuppers

The hour of change. Stripes of brown, and silver, a blinding white, and a grey-blue that keeps morphing. Merl lifts her head, the cracks in the dry playa floor now a red relief embedded in her cheek. Where she touches the earth there is heat, and tingling, and on her back, the sun is beginning to scorch its own pattern into her hide. The summer dress is gone, red poppies dissolved in a moment's light, only a shriveled ring of fabric around Merl's neck left behind. She pulls it free, and throws it away. She needs to move. And she needs to find water.

The playa stretches ahead, all the way to the distant purple-hazed mountains. Merl's arms have such trouble supporting her, each handstep so painful, desert plants pricking her palms. The wheelchair lies twisted on its side, metal fused into a new sculpture. The spokes curve into the horizon, akilter, and the hub of the wheel has blossomed out with aluminum tongues. No one will sit on this chair anymore.

All around, the lightning strike has branded the ground. About four feet out, as far as her arms can drag her, Merl sees where the flash has marked its visit on earth. On this side, beneath her, sand has shifted into glass. On the other side, the ordinary salty sand keeps its wind and water patterns. The glass is getting hotter. She has to find a way to leave.

Her testing finger on the non-fused sand quickly retreats. Hot. And sticky, leaving grainy residue that will destroy even her callused palms much too quickly, long before Merl can crawl toward assistance.

Colored fracture lines in the glass hold the cracked patterns of the earth.

One finger, then two, insert themselves in one of the larger cracks. Merl applies pressure. A small explosion. With a 'ping' glass separates at a hair-line crack farther out. The rift in the glass moves a fraction. Merl lowers her face to the glass. She feels a cooler breath of air exhaling in an ozone-rich whiff.

The 'ping.' This is indeed real glass, and she can hear the scratches of her steel-toe boots as she shifts herself on the smooth surface.

She turns on her back. Her face to the sun high above, climbing steeply on its path, ready to burn the life out of her. She takes in a full breath, arranges herself in a pentagram on the glass, in the middle of the irregular circle fused into the desert.

She sings.

Sound breathes from her lips, first in small sips and hiccups, swelling as the mouth finds its moisture, hidden deep, and tissues lubricate with the swell of the sound.

She sings.

Sound escalates, vibrates, her monstrous wheelchair picking up the waves like an alien antenna, amplifying the sound.

She sings.

Sound mounts and bursts, her vocal cords stretching and deepening in exercise after exercise, running the scales. A small mouse, scurrying across the playa in search of a grain and shade, stops and twitches its whiskers.

She sings.

As the sun reaches its zenith high above, the sound is ready, bursting forth from burning lungs, superheated pressure shaping itself in a larynx that has survived so many toxic breaths already.

At the stroke of noon echoing across from the Wild West church steeple barely visible from the playa's flatness, the song zings its final crescendo, sustained, high, pitched to find impurities and the pressure lines that keep it all together.

The glass bursts.

The sound descends.

The singer falls.

The earth swallows, and belches a spring.

Water sucks its way out of deep strata, a hydraulics of pressure geysering in the wild.

The founder of the oasis swims in languid laps, and the playa blooms.

☥

18 hours before the founding of the desert spring. The red sun is setting over the playa. The founder manipulates her chair wheel out of the back seat. A snap, and the yellow frame connects to the hub. Another twist, stressful on an already weak back, and the second wheel appears, held in her brown hand. She brings the complex machinery together, and the spindle of the wheel slides into the axle without a hitch.

A satisfying click, and the chair is upright, balanced, a thing of rounded beauty on the hard-baked sand. She swings herself into it, closes the Prius's door, locks it, and wheels around.

The bands of the high desert lie in front of her: the border of the salt lakes, the alkaline waters shimmering in the evening heat, the layers of horizon and rising air. Birds swoop through the bands, knitting modern abstract art out of the pastel banding.

Merl releases her hands downward, gives a first hesitant push out into this wildness. The square blocks of the city are far behind, and this will be her realm, for the next four weeks, her artist residency, far away from it all.

She avoids looking at her car as she wheels forward—refuses to acknowledge the heavy scratches that have disfigured the shiny lacquer. The last sign of the urban unrest. Merl's mind is crawling toward peace, away from the screaming metal sounds that surrounded her when she had run the gauntlet out toward the 80 freeway entry off University. Away from the figures, bearded, some tattooed, encased in dirty Gore-Tex or bamboo fibers, who used scrap metal, bicycle chains or their own high-end car keys to mark her beloved Prius trying to make it up onto the freeway bridge, inching its way past soft flesh and destructive metal.

Berkeley was exploding—and she rode the first shockwave out of town, long before the sidewalks were ripped up, streets blockaded, the city locked down and gnarled in place. She made it. A deep breath. The air is marked by altitude and the slight sour taste of the alkali salts floating amid the dust.

Eventually, she does turn back to the scratched Prius, and, with a press of the key, the trunk opens to reveal a row of sturdy sharp-edged boxes. Whole Foods produce, her nourishment for the next four weeks. Merl's stars had shone on her, had directed her to complete her shop the day before the glint of metal began to shimmer up and down Telegraph, Shattuck and University Avenues. She had managed to snag almond butter and cans of fava beans, high-protein staples that had by now run out in all Berkeley stores.

In Lakeview, Oregon, just one hour away from her high desert residency home, she had stocked up on all perishables, yogurt, cheeses, fresh vegetables and fruit, in the dependable and slightly old-fashioned Safeway.

Merl hefts the first of the boxes out of the trunk and onto her lap. With a firm twist of her wrist, she wheels over to the cottage door, and a push of her finger opens the door to her personal retreat. Coolness and raw pine wood exhale back at her, and she crosses the threshold. On the other side of the patio, the playa lies wide and open.

⚶

24 hours before the first geysering of the desert spring. At Café Gratitude, high up Berkeley's Shattuck Avenue, Carla stiffens. She is sitting in the snug corner made between the cooling display and the bar divider, safely out of the way, not visible to anybody looking in from the street door.

Is she really safe enough? Carla can't quite parse what is going on outside, why hipsters and street citizens are on the rampage together, what the agenda is, where her own politics lie. Carla loves the Bay Area Public School, the anti-gentrification activists who make their rent by getting grants for performance art and travel the world, loves her mates at Small Press Distribution, the poets of activism and protest. So are these them, the mild graduate students, the human chain links who re-tell their stories of walking and standing with the longshoremen in Oakland's harbor, freezing the supply chains in their tracks? Or is this a different crowd, a lustier brand, swinging different kinds of chains with a jaunty air, ready to crack their Doc Martens down onto the next cockroach that tries to scuttle across the park?

Carla is bewildered, but understands that her way of grasping Berkeley's political worlds might have run its course, might have become irrelevant the moment the first bussed-in police officer's throat was cut, and a geyser of blood drenched the front window of the Himalayan restaurant down the street. The politics might have vanished an hour before this gurgling cut, alongside a wall of posters for screenings of *Fruitvale Station*, when the first five protesters found themselves astonished when another police officer's hand did not hold a nightstick, or pepper spray, but a fully loaded automatic weapon. The protesters suddenly understood the finality of the change when the officer had mowed them down, neat as a sewing machine, bullet-holes ripping apart the wooden shielding around the building site.

Carla is terrified. She had come to work this morning, has assumed that somehow, order would establish itself, that these outliers of violence would be reabsorbed into the still generally benevolent world of her youth. But no such luck. A study of post-Marxian aesthetics lays open on the bar above her head, the book still where it had been when the first stray bullet had ricocheted its way around the place. The bullet had lodged itself in a big poster, right in the curly 'g' of the "What are you grateful for?" caption. Carla isn't sure, anymore. But the time for understanding has passed. If she wants to survive, she'll have to leave this little triangle of space behind, and get out of town.

She wills her legs to help her up. She only knows of one way out. The path of least people, far away from the heaving masses of Shattuck and University. Even here, inside the corridor, she can hear the screaming, sirens, helicopters and shots down the street.

She steps out through the wooden portal, past well-trimmed evergreen bushes. The street lies empty, some posters thrown into the street all that tells of what has happened. She runs to her left, runs as fast as she can, toward Cedar Street, its mouth opening onto Shattuck just a few blocks up. She is across Telegraph, walks fast up the street, her side pressed closed to the stores that line the street. She hears a shout behind her. Unintelligible. An angry scream. She runs. The shout does not repeat, nor does the scream, and there are no running feet or roaring motors after her.

She does not let up. Finally, Cedar. She veers around the corner. The clothing store stares at her. Its window has been smashed, and a mannequin bleeds out of the opening, one hand straight, pointing upward, to the place Carla is running toward: the streets out toward Tilden Park, up and out, over the hill and into the far valleys.

At least one of her skills is working for her. With the persistence of a marathon runner, she jogs up, can smell the alluring aroma of Peet's coffee beans as she passes the original site of the chain store. The smell is stronger than usual. The door yawns open, and the windows have fallen out, too. A small heap of coffee beans has been thrown out onto the street, a curve of black brown pebbles creating a first stony beach bulwark, tenderly ringing their old home.

She pounds past, feels some of the outlier pebbles crack beneath her shoes.

The street begins to tilt upward, out of the coastal zone up toward the Berkeley hills. She's not even breathing hard yet. To her right, above a straggly community garden, she can see a smoke column: what could be burning and smoking like this at the corner or Center and University? She envisions an effigy of cars, their tires bleeding carbon dust back into the air. She imagines the Goodwill nearby, its doors wide open and its racks empty, old clothes fuelling a new Walpurgis day, warming the homeless folk who called a halt to their invisibility. She pictures the police, having switched allegiances, creating a circle of soil around the bonfire with spades looted from the last hardware stores clinging between the restaurants.

Carla does not wish to participate in whatever new communal festivities are arising out of the ashes out there. She runs on. Veers left, away from the action, and higher up the hill. She passes the rose garden.

The oily sheen of the Bay stretches out to her left. The sun is high now, glinting off the flatness before Mount Tamalpais ends the bay's reign. The smog is heavy in the air, a haze that just about erases the tops of the Golden Gate. And on the waters, about halfway out to the bridge, Carla sees a ship, and she gasps.

The supply chain is on fire. A giant tanker throws black dense smoke into the sky, a sacrifice, a burnt offering of the dying king drifting away from his people. Carla hears the distant pop of the superheated containers, their sides carving out like lilies, innards spilling into the slick-covered waters below. She imagines electronics, children's bicycles, sun glasses, all floating then sinking out of sight, and, finally, the demise of an old Ferrari that had made its way all the way from Italy, never to roar to life again, a long ship journey only to be vanquished, to drown in a deep underwater canyon.

Carla stands for a minute, gives her calves a rest. No one is around, the air is deadly still. She reaches out, snaps off a pink and white rose, and inhales.

Å

The girl is going to get away, and Jim is not ok with that. Uh-Huh. No way, little bitch. There is too much going on down University, the city is in flames, and if you get too close, you will get fucking burned. Oh yes, he is not stupid. This here, though, nice and tender, ready for the plucking, roses and all.

Jim likes roses: he remembers roses in the band tattoos emblazoned on Kevin's walls, his older brother's pad, deep down in the dungeon of their Ohio paradise. He and his brother had dragged their racing gear all over Columbus's non-existing town center, sticking it to the po-lice man, swinging in the wind. Roses, and heavy bass, and tinkering with washed-out family cars till they hang like low-riders and boomed through town.

Kevin didn't make it out of Ohio. His ass got kicked one night in a drag race, the revved up Mazda folded into a hunk of metal and plastic stuffing. And right in there, Kevin.

Jim had stood by the side of the Mazda, could see some of his spray paint patches, not quite as accomplished as Kevin's. He could see his brother's head, resting on what remained of the steering wheel. He can still remember the muscular arm across his own breast bone, Howard, one of Kevin's mates, dragging him backward, away from the car. He still hears the sound of his sneakers on the rough asphalt, half-carted away, remembers the weave in Howard's old jean jacket. He still smells the stink of hot gas one tick before he sees Kevin's hair go up around his head in a halo of fire, the head jerking upright for one final time, as if he is alive—was he alive? And then the car rocks back on its heels and yowls with the fire searing through its heart.

Jim's Keds got all scratched up, fouled by road dust, heat, and the mud by the side of the road. He still wears them, right now, long past their preppy shine and into the deeper rock-n-roll, sneaking up on little Miss Sunshine with the rose in her hand.

Carla holds the rose between thumb and forefinger, carefully, attending to her beating heart, stilling it, like her coaches have taught her. Her head snaps to the left, sensing movement. Blond dreadlock boy is coming up sideways, coming at her like a crab, scurrying across the street. Grey sweatshirt with hoodie, cigarette slim jeans, half street kid, half street cool. Not exactly threatening, not on a normal fine day, not with the flow of the city around them. But today, in the middle of riots, fancy homes up on the hill with shut faces and turned away eyes? A different story. Not an ending she wants to wait for. She inhales the rose's perfume, tosses the flower, and picks up her speed again. A few vast sprints put her well out of reach of the crab, even as he abandons all nonchalance and lunges for her.

"Bitch!" he screams, and she, normally well terrified by confrontation, bellows.

"Wanker!" A deep and satisfying vibration of her diaphragm.

⚸

22 hours to the founding of the new desert oasis. Howard drives on, unperturbed. His wheels, a gallon bottle of water next to his seat, two big bags of Doritos, and two six-packs tucked away in the cooler in the bed of the pick-up. He had left the landscaping job in Oakland's Lake Merritt Park right on the dot, at 2pm, shift change. Till then, he'd been in his usual haze, picking up and packing out garbage all morning long, ears and eyes closed to all else. But it hadn't been easy: life on the waterfront had been quite a bit more hectic than usual, what with screaming sirens and joyriders flooring and wrecking cars all about, with lots of people running, not for fun or stamina, but with fear and abandon. He'd seen someone with a TV set in his arms, obviously looted. And when he did straighten, looked toward the horizon, he had seen a plume of black smoke, from somewhere near Broadway. Huh.

On the stroke of two, he had put away his tools. There wouldn't be cash for him, he knew, and he was a bit doubtful if the city's check would come through this time. He contemplated driving over to his digs, but, his ears full of the siren's wail, he decided against it. He climbed in, hands on his steering wheel, and nosed her out and up, back streets to the road over the hill, ready to plunge down near Orinda. Time to get out.

At the turn-off to Tilden Park, he surprised himself by braking for a hitchhiker. She was good-looking, sure, but he wasn't that kind of man, and she had also looked frightened and strong. Not a bad combination. He could tell that she had run far, had seen her calf muscles bulging and the sweat outlining her arms and neck. Mousy, small woman, but steely, in her own way.

"Where to?"

"Just out of here. I just came up from Berkeley. It's dangerous out there."

"Okay. Buckle up, and here we go. Direction outta here."

They had talked just a little bit, after the first fifteen minutes saw them safely past Walnut Creek, and onto the road to the Martinez Bridge. Fifteen minutes of companionable silence, and of the concentration needed to make it past a herd of fleeing cars, keeping the pickup lined up and ready.

So here they are, rolling. The bridge, and then the turn-off to Vacaville. Past the prison exits. Howard avoids looking at the exit sign, floors the accelerator a bit. He knows people in there, a hot hell hole. He's escaping.

Carla, that's her name. She talks, after a while.

Nervous chatting, for a bit, was it this or that that started the riots, who is right, protesters, tax payers, police. Whatever. He does not give a damn, and, soon, she picks up on it, and lets it go.

"I am thinking Oregon. Up the 5, clear ride, then over at Mount Shasta."

"I haven't been there. Sounds good. We'll need liquids, I imagine, and some food."

"I have some sleeping bags and pads in the back. We'll be ok with them. And I'll stop at a Walmart once we are on the 5. Do you have some cash?"

"I have my credit card with me."

"And you got credit?"

She looks at him, uncomprehending at first. Then it dawns.

"Yes. Good limit. Unless they stop credit altogether."

"We better make it to a Walmart fast."

And they do. Out here, life looks normal. No TV set in sight, and the store is well stocked. They grab two trolleys, fill them up, food and drink and mosquito spray. Howard wishes he'd grabbed a can from his job. But that's not his way, and Carla seems undisturbed by the prices. She pays. They tank up. Onward.

Past Redding, the road thins. They are now on the 299. To their left, Mount Shasta stands solid, and protective. Howard loves riding under her: he feels the presence, and is reassured. His shoulders drop some more, and he rolls down the window, letting in the heat. His arm hooked over the door, he stretches, and the creases in his neck loosen.

"God's own country."

"Militia's own country."

"Welcome off the grid, baby."

"Shall we put the radio on?"

She is getting really nervous now, he can see her twitching in her seat.

They try, for a while, catch relatively little. NPR has a story: riots in the Bay Area, hot spot Berkeley, disturbances in SF and Oakland, short segment, little new info. They feel a bit silly, but then each remembers glimpses of what they saw: Howard, a young girl with a cut on her face, dragged behind a grown man carrying nothing but a big water bottle. Carla, the eyes of the crab by the rose garden, the sly assault.

They turn the radio off. No conversation. They drive, eyes strafing by giant trees and giant mountains, gophers daring to cross the road in a flash of fast living.

Early evening, Howard turns off the road. Pit River camp ground.

"Nice place, pretty small. Not many likely to be around. Good?"

The first words uttered in over an hour. She nods. There's a whole roadful of emotions swarming over her face as he's slowing down, and he can see that, at least. She's thinking.

He's not, not really: the rocks and the trees, and the squirrels and the sun is all he needs. But when one looks up, stuff happens. So he feels some sadness for this young woman by his side, her insides twisting in wild film strips only she can see.

He wants to tell her about stillness and just looking, but he can't find the words. All he can do is save her, bring her to the river with him, and offer quiet by the rushing water.

Å

18 hours to the geysering. Howard and Carla drive around the campground, at the bottom of the valley the Pit River, the Achuma, has cut for itself. Large trees and the constant roar of the white water fill their eyes and ears.

They are not quite alone. Two large Campervans share the grounds, and three dome tents peek out from other bays. But there is space for them, and they back the pick-up truck up one of the gravel spurs. Howard unrolls a pad and a sack for himself. Carla decides to stay in the truck bed, an arrangement that works fine for them both.

Soon, they sit by the rushing river, drinking Diet Dr. Pepper out of cans, and gnawing on peanut butter sandwiches assembled with Howard's pocket knife.

"Where are you driving to, do you know?" Carla asks

"There's a place in Oregon, high desert country, by the alkali lakes. There's a campground there, far away from people, but with reliable water. And hot springs. It'll be good."

She nods. Sounds good, as good as any. What they had heard on the radio, snatched from the waves, didn't sound good, not good at all. Too many weapons, protests, the National Army in the Bay Area, and she had heard about fires at the Lawrence Livermore National Laboratory.

Carla is exhausted. Howard is silent, though he wants to talk, wants so desperately to talk to her, to tell her, to make her see why it is becoming so important to him to keep her safe, and he turns, but he can feel her keeping her distance, he can feel that she can feel his urgency and that it makes her shrink. He retreats, turtling his neck and swiveling away. He plants his feet inches from the waterline. He eats.

The water calms him. He dozes.

His mind glides over accidents, explosions, the fiery scorch of his past. Kevin going up in a glory of fire, a Phoenix in Ohio. His arms hold Kevin's little brother close, a heart beating next to his own.

Two years later, another crash, on the turnpike. Howard's own first van lies twisted and grotesque in the far lane, a broken Mammoth, with a crushed Volvo in its mouth. There will be fire, soon, and this time, the figure in his arms is a young woman, unknown, unknowable, her face black with soot and slack with shock. She isn't blistered, has survived the whoosh of the fire drumming the sky, but her figure is strangely lax in his arms, and something is terribly wrong. Ambulances, hospital, eventually, insurance agents. All is taken care of. He has never seen her again. And now, with the smell of turpentine and smog still in his clothes, there they are, white and drifting on the river: the flowers he has trampled, floating.

Carla knows nothing of these dreams. She wants to run, to find the horizon. This glade and the river's noise enclose her, and she startles with each shiver in the bushes. She has tried a few times to ring friends in the Bay, but no call goes through. Her mobile is useless, now, her world shrunken to a peanut butter jar and the knife, to her muscles and her ability to focus. She hugs herself, hard, the sinews and long muscles of her torso warm and taunt against her skin.

"Goodbye." She whispers to her mum, her dad, her friends, after Howard has turned in for the night, has left her alone by the rushing river. She crouches, her mobile in her hand, open, lit, and creates a little raft of sticks to hold the phone in the smoother waters near the rushes. It sails off, a little lit rectangle in the falling night, bobbing from time to time. Carla can't see if it turns a corner in the river, or drowns.

Å

6 hours before the song ruptures the playa. Howard awakes, rolls out of his dreams of scorching fire, his throat aflame, screaming and caught in the folds of his sleeping bag. In a second, Carla is off the truck and by his side.

Howard keens, still half asleep, and Carla holds him, rocking him.

They sit, and rock, the world shifting beneath and above them into morning. Stars fade slowly, and a green gold glow creeps over the horizon.

The keening stops, and Carla feels Howard's muscles uncramp, relax, fall heavily toward earth. His face is blank and the eyes won't look at her. She withdraws her arms, and they sit, side by side, on the sleeping pad, looking out at the green walls around them.

Something small rotates into view, a shadow against the slowly vibrating leaves on the bushes. They both stare. Another move, an angular twist of an articulated leg, down, over, up. A small lizard, a salamander, emerges, black with yellow spots, as if bees' wax has dripped from an old alchemist's table. The salamander moves across the clearing, stays off the sharper grit that surrounds the tent site. It stops. Maybe it detects their heartbeat, or their thermal signature. Frozen in the air, only the eyes and tongue move, a small pendulum. Howard and Carla are measured, seen. The rising sun's rose sky reflects in the silvery coils of the salamander's eyes. The creature moves on, toward the sounds of the river.

It is time to pack, and get on the road again. The truck is readied in minutes. Howard and Carla step down to the river for a few minutes, their ears full with the rushing and falling of water. Then they climb in, Howard with the achy morning hitch that dropped into his bones so many years ago, that night in the van, breathing petrol fumes into a woman's life; Carla, nimble, holding onto the overhead struts of the truck as she swings herself into place. Next stop, past the green and blue, into the banded lands: Oregon's alkali lakes. Behind them, far behind, the skies begin to change.

⚴

An hour after the emergence. The founder arcs her back, her legs a sea anemone beneath her, beside her, floating white in the blue. She has tried to crawl onto the land, but the new lake's edges are sculpted glass, bulbous forms with sharp edges. Merl does not want to cut unknowingly into unfeeling flesh. The water is warm, thermal, but not scalding or unpleasant. It is drinkable, too, tastes delicious and health-giving, with an edge of metal. The mineral content makes her float easily, and she watches hair and limbs entwine around her, delighting in sensual rolls and curves, her strong arms carving furrows through the water.

Merl sings, to herself, not the keening of the rupture, but a pleasant vocalization, old melodies and newer harmonics melding on her tongue. The sun is high above her, and she can no longer hear the church bells, or any sounds. Only the water lapping at the glass rim.

Later, change.

Two heads appear above her. Merl is nearly transparent now, her tissues swelled and full with the desert water. The heads talk. She tries to focus her thoughts to decode the sounds. And raises a hand, a greeting, a blessing, an invitation. The heads withdraw. Merl sings.

Later still. A new sight. A raft is lowered into her lake. Antlers and sticks make a filigree nest, old amazon book box air cushions provide lift, and, in the raft, jars of peanut butter, white bread, and packets of beef jerky stand in neat rows, surrounded by nutritional bars and small sealable containers with toilet paper tissue. Merl sings to it.

Larger sounds. A wave. One being has jumped in, and she is no longer alone. After a while, the second. The beings are naked, like her, brown sinuous shapes darting around her. She does not wish to stop singing, and there is nothing to say.

They all touch, and drift. The sky changes color above them now, pearlescent shades bow to a deep red, then a white flash. The air moves. They float.

"Flux" by Pandalion Death

Previous Page:
A person with curly hair stands with their back facing the viewer. They are wearing striped pajamas and slippers. The person is standing in front of a large pane of glass that looks out on to a cityscape of buildings. The image of the buildings to the right and left of the person is sharp and clear. The space that directly surrounds the person is all clouded, leaving the image of the buildings in front of them blurred and indistinguishable.

Puppetry

A.C. Buchanan

In the bunk room, I pick shrapnel out of the puckered skin around my knee.

"Med can assist," comes the voice in my ear. "Topical anaesthetic available."

No thank you, I think back. *I'd like to do this myself.*

"Agreed."

The sheets are pale blue, smooth and clean, and I'm about to splatter them with blood. Too late now. This is a minor wound, and I'm quite capable of seeing to it myself, of instructing my hands in the delicate motions to repair it, quite capable of not fainting under the pain of each extraction.

By the time it is finished, I feel like vomiting. The only other in the room, Lance Corporal Cannan, a convicted murderer, is asleep, so I could probably get away with it, but instead I swallow painfully, pour half a bottle of antiseptic over the wound, and bandage myself up.

I'll be back on the front lines shortly. Six years to go. Six years of war.

We fight good, honest, ethical wars these days. I've seen film from a previous era, on Earth or its closest planets, of drones striking the innocent, cities in ruins. The Harken-Achanli treaty put paid to that. We know, though we don't like to admit it, that humans are the weaker of the three known races. When our governments see how quickly all their worlds can be taken over or obliterated by aliens many times more advanced than us, they have to pay more than lip-service to not killing civilians.

So everyone on the battlefield is, at least nominally, a volunteer. We've *chosen* to fight Cerule over this strip of dusty land or, a few hundred miles away, New Catalonia over water supply. Most have been found guilty in a court of law of a sufficiently heinous crime that this is their only chance of freedom. Others have fled a hostile nation or planet, and are paying the price of citizenship. And some of us have other reasons, like me.

The bell sounds and there is a hiss in my ear which signifies external command kicking in. I'm pulled from my bunk, my arm moves to straighten my trousers and I'm standing, perfectly arched back, against my bunk. Cannan has leapt down from hers, and other soldiers file in, in various states of tidiness. I look out at the 32 perfectly made beds. Mine is a disaster. Blood and antiseptic are dripping down my leg. Waves of childhood shame wash over me. "Elevated heart rate," the voice in my ear confirms.

Thanks! I think back, probably unwisely. *Never would have noticed that.*

I try to not hold anything against the Sergeant who enters this room, the sound of his boots on the grey glass corridors making me shudder. I know exactly what's happening, that the voice in his ear is informing his every word. Computers are good at this kind of interaction.

"Tanner."

"Yes Ser."

"Is your bunk made correctly?"

"No Ser."

"Do you have an excuse for this?"

"I was injured and I..."

"Do you have an excuse for this?"

"No Ser. No excuse Ser."

Like I said, computers are good at this type of interaction. The external command drops off, and all but three of us file out. Cannan gives me a sympathetic nod as she leaves. Not sympathetic as in "poor you" but closer to "we both know they're a pile of shit". I think my way through each fast motion, while behind me I can hear Private Joben shaking out his bedsheets as if raising a sail to catch an imaginary wind.

Being able to make my bed like this, a skill afforded to me by the wires and implants running through my body, is still a novelty, and one I'm not entirely sure I'm comfortable with. As a child, my ability to move was unpredictable. It was like, I said once, having message scramblers along my nervous system. Anything could become scrambled in any way. *Move your left foot forward one step* might emerge as just that, but it could also result in me putting my right foot atop my left and falling facedown in the dust. Chairs and exosuits, which allowed me to choose from pre-selected sequences of movements, none designed to injure me, helped. My body still didn't do what I wanted much of the time, but what it did at least translated into typical patterns like "moving forward".

The command system, wires made of organic material implanted throughout my body, was, I told people, what would make me normal. It's true, I can make near every movement anyone else can. I can climb rockfaces, I can dance. What I don't tell them is that none of it comes automatically. That I have to plan each motion in my brain. That just as internal command augments rather than replaces their abilities, so it has done mine. That motion still requires conscious thought, draining mental effort, in a way they'll never understand.

They think I'm cured. Right now, I want them to keep thinking that.

I pull the sheets off the bed and refit them. I'll be back on the front lines tomorrow; I need to make the most of today. The blasts that shake the building even back here don't make me jump any more, but the thought of being back in the thick of it sends a cold shudder through my skin like a wave.

After our attempts are finally approved, Joben and I make our way to the mess hall where there's cold hi-carb, hi-protein food waiting for us. I don't care anymore; it's gone within seconds. After collecting my equipment from servicing, I steal time to compose a message to my family.

I hope you are all well. Things carry on here much the same, and as usually you'll know more about the progress of the wars than I do out here. I have sustained a minor—minor! don't worry!—injury but it's healing well. I'm now past my second year of service. Six years to go. That desk job at central office is very appealing right now. I know you are worried, but I also know you understand what a difference this can make to my life. Your support means everything; I know that with persistence I'll have the life I always dreamed of, be the person I always knew I was supposed to be.

I tell myself that part of being an adult is distancing yourself from your parents, finding your own beliefs. But it doesn't stop me feeling that each time I tell them something like this, it's driving a wedge between us that will never be healed.

Janny, good luck with your exams. Remember, no one will care about them in a year or two (and yes, I can see mum shaking her head in disgust I've told you that. Sorry, ma, but it's the truth!).

All my love to all of you,

Merie

Private Merie Jae Tanner 59FFRK920 Platoon 867

Unclassified Personal Communication

Before the sun rises in its murky, turquoise haze, we are en route to the front, clinging to the side of buggies, pulling on noise insulators one handed as the sound of plasma fire grows louder. Nausea grows in me, and not for the first time I wonder if I could leap down into the blue-grey dust and run and run and run.

Of course, I can't. That's the whole point of this setup.

Once, back on Earth, wars were driven by fervour and patriotism. Young men—it was mostly men then, I'm told—stood firm in the face of danger, their conviction that they were in the right outweighing the determination of the body to save itself. They clambered out of trenches into direct fire, kept walking as mines picked off one then another.

That's what they tell us, anyway. And that our generation is a fickle one, our society selfish and materialistic. We probably all believe that this strip of land is ours by right; no doubt some of us even believe that's worth fighting for. But I don't know anyone who believes it strongly enough that when it comes to it, when there's plasma fire in front of you about to burn open your chest or blow off your face, that instinct won't kick in and tell you to run the hell away.

I pull on my eye shields as the flashes grow brighter. Did I mention oxygen's increasing again? That sure makes warfare fun.

So these days, they make it so we can't run away. We've all signed up to this, of course, so they can fulfil treaty requirements that we're not forced into anything. But once we leap down from these buggies, we're switched to external command. The command system moves our bodies, not us. No matter how much everything in us is signalling otherwise, even if we consciously try and override it, our bodies are not our own. And so we stay and so we fight.

I turn my head and give weak smiles to Cannan, in front of me, and Joben behind. Our eyes say it's okay, that we'll make it through this. It doesn't matter that the odds are that, if we do, they'll get us some other time. Both of them have been here a while, and we're all still alive and intend to stay that way. Survive all eight of these terrifying, ugly years.

That's the mark everyone's aiming for. Eight years and our term of service is up and we are free. Eight years and the felons have their records erased and are allowed back into society. Eight years and we get a nice resettlement grant and a desk job at Central Office if we so desire. Eight years and external command falls forever silent. Eight years and I get the life I used to dream of.

But for now there's only the blue dust, the plasma guns in our hands, and the flashes of fire. The buggy slows as it turns and we leap down, one after another, into the dust, and as soon as our boots hit the ground the command switches over, we're pulled instantly to standing and we run to make way for others jumping to the ground behind us. The dust coats our eye shields and then falls away, our hands draw our guns as we're tugged into formation. Our footsteps drum out a continuous rhythm in what I still think of as low gravity; fast and unpausing, over mounds and debris, never stopping, fanning out into a series of lines approaching the front, taking cover between rows of defences built on previous shifts.

We fire and we return fire, make repeated assaults, form new formations. We edge forwards and gain small slivers of territory only to lose them again, try not to look around us and see those who have been felled. Stims are pumped in until I no longer feel awake, only alert. The cooling system in my armour turns my sweat into a layer of cold.

When night falls, the fighting dies down. It's more force of habit that anything else; it's not like we couldn't illuminate the whole battlefield if we chose to. But night is a time for shattered sleep and surprise assaults. Watch shifts are assigned and we fall back to makeshift shelters and dust-dug trenches. I use a wet wipe to try and scrape the worst of the dust from my arms, take off my outer armour and lie tightly squeezed in, in a line of soldiers.

I don't think I'll ever like this dust again, I think as I try and force myself to sleep. In childhood it was a welcome cushion from my many falls, my dust-covered clothes and face treated as endearing. In adulthood I learned to appreciate it as a natural feature of the planet, a pre-human beauty, sacred in its own right. But now it is bound with blood and exhaustion, death and burning flesh…

"Induced sleep offered," comes the voice in my ear.

Accept, I think back gratefully, and it comes instantly.

There are no attacks that night, though my sleep is disturbed by the anticipation of them. By the time a blue glow has begun to seep through the edges of the shelter, we are pulled to our feet, all armour on, spreading out into formation once again. My muscles ache already and it will be a while before another shift takes over, unless I get injured again.

It's tempting sometimes.

I couldn't do it. Emotionally maybe, physically I couldn't. So I just do what I need to do. I fight.

Our armour has sensors that help us avoid fire, and it's heavy today. I'm pulled to the left and right, falling down in the dust. I think the same thing has happened when Joben, a metre or two to my right, falls backwards, except he doesn't get up. I look frantically around for a medic. No one.

Permission to tend wounded, I think.

"Medic will tend wounded. Keep fighting." My hand squeezes the trigger and lets out another burst of fire, the plasma bright even through my eye shields.

No fucking medics here. Do you see a medic? Permission to tend the fucking wounded NOW!

I realise I'm not just thinking but shouting, though I'm not sure anyone can hear me over the din.

"Approved." The voice sounds resigned, though of course I'm just imagining that. I run, turn him gently, knowing that his armour will protect his neck. His legs are torn and bloody, his face swollen, flesh pulsing through the spaces in his facial armour.

"Okay. Just move with me. We'll get you out of here." My mouth is dry.

"It's almost my anniversary date," he says, his mouth foaming with saliva, obscuring the words.

"How many years?" I ask, laying him down gently and surveying his injuries. Anything to keep him talking. The smell of singed flesh hits unexpectedly.

"Eight."

Shiite. I leap up and look away, biting down hard on my lip, aware that I should be reacting calmly, that I'm not helping, that this isn't about me…

"Why would you say that? What's wrong with you? You've just doomed yourself. That's how it always goes."

"We're not in the movies," he rasps. "I'll be okay."

Oddly, he is, though it's many weeks before I hear news. His right leg is unsalvageable, but the prosthetics are good, and though the internal damage is significant it is also survivable. Eight years. He's out of here. I'm not so lucky. The fire keeps picking us off. Two days after Joben's injury, they pick off Private Halsew. Her face is black with plasma burns as I see her carted away. She's less lucky than Joben. And here I want to rest and sob, but my body is forced to move, forced to stay.

And so this is how I try to survive my eight years out here in the dust, bullets and limbs flying in the lowered gravity.

⚔

It was in my early teens that the gravity began to decrease. A space station was launched into orbit around the sun, a spinning disk just visible at sunrise, a joint project between humans and Elaayans, deploying technology we had only used once before, and never on a populated planet. From it launched a wormhole into the centre of our world, sucking in molten rock and firing it into the sun. I remember the seismic waves of that era, the feeling of being constantly on edge, never sure if a rumbling was going to grow louder or roll longer, never sure when the next one would strike, dusty and uncertain days.

And I remember the celebrations too, the giant lit-up meter outside the council chambers, its goal—just under ten m/s^2—the gravity of Earth, a world none of us were likely to ever see. I remember how people—even respectable people, officials and business people—would leap through the air, testing the new force, whooping in jubilation. For a while, it was comforting; the world seemed alien to them too, never quite doing what they'd expect. As much as they celebrated the change, they also struggled, using too much force or too little. I once saw a man attempt to leap onto a transport, exert too much power and bash his head on the upper doorframe.

I shouldn't have laughed, but I did. And perhaps it is moments like this that define the future: a fourteen year old girl in a clunky exosuit and a messy ponytail, standing by the side of the road laughing at this world turned upside down.

My delight was shortlived. Though the decreased gravity ultimately made things easier for most, it took me much longer to acclimatise. Even now, now the gravity has adjusted and wormholes formed in several more planets in turn, it suits me less well. The heavy pull on my body grounded me, drawing out and stabilizing my movements. Once the gravity decreased, I may have fallen lighter but I fell more. My carefully and exhaustingly practiced motions needed to be relearned. I felt as if not just society, but the literal physical world had turned on me, slammed doors in front of my face.

Oh sure, there was a fair heap of teenage melodrama amidst my rage, but there was also bitterness and hurt. I was learning just how invisible and insignificant I could be and would continue to be.

In my seventeenth year they melted ice to flood the Sahelan Basin, water gushing into the dust, murky and then settling. We were transported out there to watch from a high vantage point as it flowed, held back behind ropes. We had not seen a body of water like it before, and even in our cynical teens we could not help but be impressed.

But at night it haunted me. I dreamed I had been left on the floor of the basin when the evac sounded, my suit drained of power, scrabbling in the sand trying to stand, and the waves washing over me and over me until I was tugged beneath them, sinking and thrashing and pulled to the bottom.

I mentioned them to a classmate once, laughing at myself even as I didn't find it funny. And that was how I found myself in an upper floor room, technically a bedroom of someone's apartment but not furnished as such; rather, there was a bench around three walls and cushions on the floor. I, using a chair again at this point, took up a position in one corner, jutting out awkwardly into the room, trying not to block out too much seating. Exposed, out of place.

Someone pulled up a projection. It was a familiar sight—not this particular clip, which I hadn't seen before—but the type of action it showed was one which had permeated our lives. This time, though, everyone in the room watched intently, their faces pained and serious, as crafts swept across a planet's surface, releasing algae and nitrogen bundles which dropped like bombs onto the rocky surface.

"Harapana, third planet in the Karlwe system just two weeks ago," said a tall woman rising from a cushion, her dark hair branching out in the artificial light as if by static. "Far from slowing, the pace of terraforming is increasing dramatically. The terms of the latest treaty mean humans are allowed to get away with... basically whatever the fuck we want provided we don't make the planet uninhabitable for either of the other two known sentient species. Note the word *make*. If it's already uninhabitable, we have free rein."

The image of the shuttle, now extinguished, remained unshakeably in my head as she spoke. Something had been woken in me, the ability to see through the propaganda to a growing destruction. Later, as brownies were passed around, she came up to me. "I'm Lu," she said, extending her hand. I missed, ending up grasping her sleeve. I knew instantly we'd become friends.

For two years, neglecting my studies, I worked on semi-underground anti-terraforming campaigns. Behind the scenes stuff: publicity and propaganda, logistics, organising supplies for groups in other areas and on other planets. Images of unspoilt planets filled me with an emotional intensity like I had never before known, and the absolutes, the enormities—how many billions of years it had been left alone, how completely it was gone forever—overwhelmed me.

We achieved minor victories; slight changes in protocols, designation of reserve areas. But the terraforming continued regardless, one uninhabited planet after another slowly turned into approximations of a world we'd never see. When we spoke about it, it was a moral question, a belief that each planet had almost an intrinsic right to be left alone. But for me there was something else. I wanted there to be worlds different to this one, worlds that might be more welcoming.

It was in the early hours of morning when I heard Lu and Kass—a stalwart of the movement who we not entirely jokingly referred to as our resident scientist—talking outside, in hushed but forceful tones. I'd been working through the night in our makeshift offices, my fingers greasy with the food I used to keep myself awake. The conversation I heard changed everything.

I heard snatches, knowing I shouldn't be listening but unable to help myself. "We have to do this. What we're doing from the outside just isn't working. We need to be on the inside."

"It's eight years... eight years of war," Lu responded.

"Well someone's got to do it... it's our only chance."

"Let's say you did. Let's say this isn't completely fucking stupid. They'd suspect you straight away. Or are you planning to get yourself sent to prison as well?"

"I could do it," I said, forcing my voice not to shake. They both swung round. "They'd believe me if I volunteered."

Kass reacted instantly, his hand flying to my shoulder. I stumbled. "No. You can't do that."

I raised my hand, adrenalin hitting, not yet understanding the enormity of my proposal. "You said someone's got to. Well I'm the obvious choice. My motivations would make sense. I don't need citizenship or exoneration, but those aren't the only things they're offering. You get internal command. They don't remove the system when you're discharged, just hand it over to you. Most people, it increases their physical capacity a little, they slow less as they age, but for me... it would give me a typical level of motor control. Make me normal, is what I'll say. Now *that* would convince them."

The authorities, when it came to it, did actually need some convincing, but they were also short of soldiers. Something about how they all kept dying. So I handed myself over to them under the observation of an appointed lawyer. In surgery I was numbed but awake so I could test the command. Recovery time in the accelerated chamber was six weeks. I had no right to change my mind. In those weeks I wondered how much I really believed in what I was doing, but I had to believe in something.

My custom armour was pre-fitted, deep purple to correspond with my rank. It made me feel unexpectedly vulnerable. I was sent to training and then to war, on a narrow strip of land two nations had been fighting over, on and off, since before I was born.

⚔

We're transported back, eventually, only external command keeping our grip tight enough to hold us on the buggies, a mess of exhaustion and blood and singed dust. I've lost track, now, of how many times I've been to the front. Our armour is supposed to be a microsystem, temperature and humidity controlled, but each time my skin is red and raw, my breasts aching from the compression, my feet swollen and painful.

I sleep fitfully, uninduced. I wonder, again, how I can stick out my eight years but I really, literally have no choice. After a spate of suicides, they added a script that senses self-destructive actions, kicks in external command.

It's all quite ironic really. I spent most of my life being told how I needed to *foster my independence*. The first major choice I made, going against everything I had been taught and requiring me to lie to my family, involved sacrificing it.

I find I'm sobbing, near silently. Though everyone has the option of turning on white noise in their ears—and they usually do—I still feel self-conscious in this crowded bunkroom. *External command*, I think, *paralyse tear ducts*.

I wonder how closely they monitor this type of thing, and how many people have to use functions like that. Whether I'm unusually weak, or if everyone thinks the same.

I stare at the plastic slats of the bunk above me, just able to make out their lines in the dimmed light. There's a rustling in my field of hearing and then a voice crackles through. Not the one I'm used to.

"Merie. Merie are you there? Stay quiet. I can't talk long."

Unwisely, I sit bolt upright. Someone a couple of bunks away stirs in response to the sound, but thankfully returns to sleep. I lie back down, carefully. *Kass?*

"We don't have long. Things have escalated. They've caught infiltrators on Baltica and Zagros. Explosion in New Chicago. Two dead. Terraforming shuttles destroyed. They say we did it."

Did we?

"Awaiting confirmation. But we're all in danger. Many governments are taking activists into custody. If we lose our leaders, we lose the battle. And Lu…"

What about Lu? Panic is coursing through my veins. I'm not offered a tranq. Kass must have overridden the systems.

"Lu's missing. We have to act now. Risks are high but we have no choice."

It's odd, because I'm being told the cause I believe in above all else is about to be crushed. That friends are missing or in prison. That I'm facing life imprisonment, if they stick to the law—and worse if they don't. And then my first thought is that there will be no more six years. I won't return to the front.

If they lock me away, I don't think I'll try and seek redemption out here. Not that they'd let me.

"Merie are you listening to me? You're not our only infiltrator. Cannan was recruited in prison… there was a risk of… we needed to increase the odds someone would make it through."

I feel a dull pain in my chest. I'd have made the same calculation, but it hurts knowing it was made about me.

"We need an army behind us. Merie, you need to take control of external command."

⚔

My external command remains off. I'm aware of it even when in monitoring mode, and after two years it feels uncomfortably silent.

Today is, I tell myself, a death or freedom day. A change the universe or be forgotten day. It feels more like a I got fuck all sleep and really need a break right now type of day.

But these things are sent to try us, as my grandmother would say, or choices have consequences, to quote one of the posters in the mess hall. I dress quietly, leave the room. I don't have a plan.

There are few guards around the complex. We can be roused from our beds and at full combat capacity in seconds should an attack come from outside, and external command can sense if we're anywhere we shouldn't and control us. It's a while down the glass corridor before I come to a guard.

"Nightmares," I say. "I don't want sleep, just to be alone for a bit." I'm taking a risk; it'll be sheer luck as to whether I receive empathy or get told to harden the fuck up. A soldier's own experience can push them either way. But tonight, I'm lucky.

I take a right at the end of the corridor and then break into a run. I hope my guess about which bunkroom Cannan's in is correct.

"Heading back to bed," I say to the next guard I come across. They'll have changed shifts half an hour ago so we won't know from sight which room I'm in. At lease I hope not.

I wake Cannan with a hand over her mouth, pushing three fingers into her arm, hoping she understands because I can't take the risk of waking anyone. Three fingers for the three tyrannies, of terran sea, terran land and terran sky.

She carefully eases herself out of bed, fully clothed, and pulls me into one of the adjoining washrooms. We whisper amongst rows of sinks and showers, and I can only hope no one's listening in.

"I've been waiting for you. What are we doing?"

"Kass says we need to take control of external command, send troops to support them."

"And how do we do that?"

My mouth is dry. I'm thinking on my feet, blood pressure building up in my face until it's burning. "I think we'd have to localise it first. I don't think other bases can be controlled from here, so it would be best to shut it off entirely. If we need to, we can use the soldiers to take over other bases and bring them under our control."

"Before they told me tonight," she whispers, "I never would have picked you as one of us."

I ignore her. "I've no idea how the whole thing works though. I didn't expect to even have to think about this until... well, six years from now." I can almost see those six years melting away in front of me.

"I've done a bit of research. We'll go for the long-range antenna first. Let's get out of here."

Cannan takes a bar from her trousers and levers the window from the wall. She's much more prepared than I am; I'm in hastily thrown on clothes and only half awake. We drop ourselves down into dust, run crouched to the antenna.

Cannan takes a pair of wire cutters from her other leg. I frown at the wires leading up the skeletal transmission column. Point at two. Part knowledge, mostly instinct. This isn't a bomb, I tell myself, but that's not enough to quell the panic. Nothing happens. She looks at me and I shrug. I suppose we just won't know if it has been successful until the end.

I hear noise behind us, swing round. Private Brinshe has followed us from the bunkroom.

In a second Cannan is holding a gun to his throat. He's a weedy kid, in his twenties but looks barely eighteen, a refugee from a failed planet, citizenshipless with nowhere to go. We joined as part of the same cohort, trained together. Cannan's still not taking any chances.

"It's real easy," I hear her saying. "We're gonna stop the terraforming and you're gonna shut up and die. Actually dead people are pretty quiet so I suppose it's the same thing."

I stifle a laugh. I'm not sure how much of Cannan's style is an act, but the absurdity is pretty close to funny right now. Or would be, if our lives weren't hanging in the balance.

"You're... anti-terraforming. What about her?"

Cannan raises her eyebrows in despair. Brinshe looks at me in shock. "You... did this to infiltrate? I thought you were doing it so you could walk."

I laugh, bitterly, the ground feeling illogically unstable beneath me. "You think my life was so terrible that I'd spend eight years getting shot at just to make it a little easier."

"I... no... I..."

I smile, more kindly that I feel. "Oh whatever. It wouldn't have worked hadn't so many people thought like you. That I was just this tragic girl who would do anything for a miracle cure, and no one even considering that I might have beliefs or goals, that I would die for something other than myself. And for the record my life was pretty great, difficult, sure, but..."

I'm getting teary. Longing for a life I left behind, a life which so many people thought wasn't even worth living. I'm too generous to articulate to Brinshe what I know he believes. That he saw my journey not as one to gain a better quality of technology, but one of salvation.

"Are you going to help me or not?" I say, swallowing my pain. I ignore the fact that Cannan's giving him no choice. I need him truly on side.

His face is empty. Stunned by all his perceptions of me falling apart, perhaps, or more likely realising the danger we're in. Recognition shows eventually, though uneasily. "Ok. Don't see much other chance of me getting out of this. What do I do?"

We move to the command centre. There won't be many guards here, because external command knows who should and should not be here. Cannan says that when Kass switched hers off he gave her a reactivate key and a false identity. It won't last long, she says, maybe five minutes, before they figure it out. And she can't be certain if it will work.

I watch as the glass walls slide open before her. For all that this is a hastily constructed base on a constantly changing border, they've put some effort into this. I move hastily, barely waiting until Cannan's false identity has overridden the security of the system to start dragging at the screen, trying to work out how this all fits together… and how I can change it.

The noise comes before I realise it, and then it's all upon us. A guard is approaching, weapon drawn, Cannan spins and then she falls. He's approaching, I know it's over, and then he falls, burning flesh blocking up the air. Brinshe stands still as if frozen, his weapon still drawn.

They'll know within seconds, now he's dead. I can't do anything but keep frantically going—I'm part way there, and then the whole system falls into place. Paralyse. Everyone on the base motionless.

I finally breathe.

I'm there, and the power awaiting me seems surreal. Merie Tanner, the kid people dismissed because she "couldn't even control her own body", now with the ability to move armies. A puppet master, of sorts, thousands of bodies at my command, moving exactly how I command. If only they could see me now. Perhaps they *will* see me now.

Perhaps I'd make a good evil genius, cackling away at my controls. The image provides a brief moment of levity amidst the smell of burned flesh. And then I'm back to being me, me in circumstances I would never have thought possible.

I turn, finally, make eye contact with Brinshe and he lowers his weapon slowly.

"You're going to turn them against the government," he says. It's not really a question. I hesitate. I think that's what Kass has planned; to send them all back to the capital. But I'm not sure I can force anyone to fight my war. Not after what I've seen.

I look at the screen, find what I'm looking for. The news projection splutters then comes to life, a blond woman reading the latest updates.

...will not give in to terrorists. In a move to show that the pace of terraforming is unhindered, the Interplanetary Authority has named the tenth planet to benefit from gravitational reduction as Zagros. Yesterday scientific development centres outside the Zagros city of New Chicago were rocked by explosions believed to have been carried out by anti-terraforming extremists. In a statement, IPA Convenor Jameel Elangue praised the Zagrosian authorities for their quick response and apprehension of suspects and said he hoped the gravitational adjustment would send a message to the people of Zagros that they will not be abandoned or disadvantaged by...

I switch it off. Another image. The ring of the station hanging in space, somewhere between us and the sun which I can see the first glow of through the glass roof. I turn to look at Brinshe.

"They're already against the government," I say.

My voice sounds shaky as I project it to every immobilised soldier on the base. "The International... the International Government and the IPA have thought for too long that everything is theirs. That our lives are theirs to put on the battleground. That our bodies are theirs to control. That every planet is theirs to mold in the likeness of a faraway world. It's time to stand up. I will do no harm to any of you, but I call for volunteers to undertake a mission against a power that has gone too far. There are risks, but there is also hope."

There is silence. My heart is beating furiously and every part of me aches.

Just silence.

Perhaps we've lost.

And then symbols flicker up in projection and I hear the unmistakable sound of boots clinking against the corridors, see, finally, the volunteers arrive.

I use the systems to track the nearest shuttle, do a quick assessment of skills. Three with piloting ability is luckier than I could imagine, even though most of the control will be done from the ground. We take a buggy the few miles to a shuttle, leaving behind a base in wakeful sleep, and I laugh as the dust blows up into my face—an anxious laugh born of sleep deprivation, but a laugh nonetheless.

As the shuttle takes off, I breathe. "Kass, are you there? Kass, respond please, respond."

Å

I think Kass's response was along the lines of "what the fuck have you done?" He was waiting on troops to back them up in the city, but instead, invisible to the naked eye, there were flashes in the sky two days later. A station left disarmed and empty, a waste of metal floating above us.

"I couldn't send them to another war," I said later. "I couldn't." He said he understood, but he may just have been saying that, because what good would an argument do now.

Gravity adjustments were halted, perhaps forever. The IPA would have a hard time convincing the races responsible for much of the technology to work with us again, given how irresponsible humans had been with it this time. Opinion turned more in favour of us than it did against us. Bowing to popular pressure, new treaties were negotiated. A partial victory in a long, long war.

But for those of us at the heart of the whole episode, we're still terrorists. There's no safe place for us here.

I walk slowly to my shuttle, sit cramped between two others. It'll be a long trip and I know only our first port of call and not my final destination. In my luggage are parts that will replace elements of my internal command system as they wear out. It's useful for now, worth maintaining. But as the bars come down to hold us in place for take-off, I'm dreaming of a world where I won't even want it, that somewhere amidst the millions of undiscovered, untouched worlds, there's one I was born for.

Lyric

A.F. Sanchez

"I found seven thousand one hundred and seven images that resemble the hologram," Lyric says.

"Fields?"

"Mythology, popular culture."

"Okay, Lyric. Stand by."

You stare at Lyric's top search results, fascinated by the variety of the Animal's incarnations, but the resemblances don't matter as much as the Animal itself. The design is not original, crafted instead to resonate with collective fantasies of a hybrid creature: a reptile's slitted eyes and forked tongue, a wildcat's dripping fangs, wide leather wings that unfurl in the black night, scales that glisten down its spine all the way to the tip of a prehensile tail. Its legs are goat-like, but too long and too thin, tapering down into hooves that might clip-clop on stone.

If you happen to meet this creature after sunset, on one of the poorly lit streets that infest your hometown, it is not the strangeness of its visage that will terrify you. You will not even see it coming. Instead, you will hear it approach, in the thickness of silence: the beating of wings which you will mistake for a blistering wind, and right behind you, so soft that you can pretend not to hear it, the ring of hooves on the pavement. You won't even notice the odor of blood and rotting meat, not until you turn around and face the terrible gaping mouth.

But you do not encounter it outside. You come face to face with it in the airconditioned safety of your work cubicle where you have accessed the company catalog. You maneuver the hologram every which way to examine the Animal's details. Fully grown! The typical Cosmetic Companion™ is bioengineered to only the size of a human child, programmed for elite lifestyles of sunshine and softness. Yet this item's wingspan and too-thin goat legs only prove that whoever commissioned it had intended to push the limits of the experimental series. Is its lifespan longer or shorter than the regular series? Does it have more awareness of what it is than the others?

"Lyric, keywords."

The app searches the catalog and selects what it deems the most syntactically important phrases from the product description. "Currently available, heavily damaged, discount," Lyric announces, simultaneously flashing the phrases on your gadget screen. A discount due to damage—add to that your employee discount and you're good to go.

Your supervisor Rae is conveniently out of town for a seminar. You send her the link to the image anyway, hoping that she is too busy right now to video-yell at you.

⚐

Your father, once:

"A woman in my old support group, she had an older brother who was pretty severe. Nonverbal, delayed, wore diapers well into adulthood. Bit her a couple of times, once on the arm, the second on the shoulder hard enough to need stitches. He had to be restrained on more than one occasion because of violent moods—one time, he took a knife from the kitchen and woke up their mother with it. When I heard the story, I kept thinking, he must have been in some kind of pain, his brain must have overloaded with who knows what stimuli. The woman telling the story, she was just so angry and sad. I mean, when they were kids, the other children simply called her older brother crazy, and they both had to live with that.

"But I wondered what her older brother felt, and I started wondering what feelings my own child had, and was I being selfish for prioritizing my own emotions and opinions about the matter, and in the end I thought what the hell, be angry with me for my selfishness or don't, as long as the day comes that my kid begins to understand what I'm saying, and begins to say things back."

⚐

The first time you saw Rae—young, slender, fair and foreign—you thought of hummingbirds from your old picture books: delicate, frenetic apparitions among flowers. Not that there was anything remotely flowery about your first meeting. It was at your hometown's municipal hall, made unbearable that day by a rare international job fair that filled the lobby with tech booths, crowds, and the smells of sweat and desperation. At the entrance, private security turned away applicants who couldn't comply with the dress code, like three of your neighbors, including a young woman who excelled at programming but couldn't tolerate footwear other than rubber slippers.

Rae already worked in the marketing department of the local office of Cosmetic Animals International, but on that day she was volunteering at the consultants' booth. You waited in line with your mother and the families of two of her friends. When it was your turn at the booth, you focused on Rae's friendly smile. The results of the exam saddened you but didn't surprise: you had above average scores for memory retention and spatial relations, but failed the other sections because you didn't follow instructions.

"Your language impairment really gets in the way," Rae remarked.

You glanced at your mother who looked like she was about to cry, and one of the phrases that you have learned to use easily throughout the years falls from your mouth: "It's okay."

Rae nodded her head quickly. "My niece is the same. I had to bring her with me when the company branched out here, and I've seen firsthand the challenges in a culture where only English is used in school and local languages are used everywhere else. Lyric can help, you know?"

At the time Lyric was a relatively new language app that targeted non-English-speaking clients, but your mother had heard good things about Lyric from one or two other members of her support group—it's just that no one in your circle of non-virtual acquaintances had the means to purchase it. Lyric required a specific brand of handheld device and monthly fees that your household budgets couldn't accommodate.

Rae listened to your mother explain the general situation in the country, which is that the national government didn't seem like it had ever heard of disability benefits, and the particular situation in your finances, which is that massive debts have resulted from years of various therapies and private special schools . "That sucks," Rae says. "Maybe we can do something about this. I'll make a few calls to our hiring department, all right?" Then she placed her hands on yours, and only then did you realize that you had been flapping them again.

For several months after you joined Rae's department as an assistant layout artist—a position she created specifically for you—you wondered if she had hired and trained you simply out of charity. That suspicion faded into irrelevance when your mother died, and suddenly Rae was all you had.

Å

Up close, or as close as the company regulations allow, the Animal looks even more impossible, but your disbelief is subdued by the nature of the damage that necessitated the multiple discounts. Between it and you is a fiberglass wall and the iron bars of a cage. Through the bars you glimpse one hoof—the other is nowhere to be found, the spindly goat leg ending instead in filthy bandages at the ankle. You don't see its wings, either. You can't even see if it's still alive, not until it shifts its weight, moving a little in the light to reveal its silhouette.

What you do see in the shadows of the cage for which the Animal is too small are the lines of a human form. The torso is thin but with graceful slope, the arms limp but wiry, the neck, chin, mouth, nose all grotesquely human.

The eyes are not. They terrify you so much that your hands flap upward to block the view—an old habit you revert to in the presence of something that overwhelms.

But really, it's impossible to look away.

The releasing officer is so bored that he does not care about your choice. He reveals that the Animal is set to be euthanized anyway, thanks to the wealthy collectors that commissioned it and then backed out despite having paid fully for the experiment. He is nonetheless obligated to suggest the smaller yet more expensive bestsellers, like the baby-faced Winged Song-Monkey Wanda or the miniature Deer-Centaur Darius or Palpatine the Platypus, all guaranteed Cosmetic Companions™, experts at greetings, small talk, moral support, even therapeutic functions. He informs you that the Animal you're choosing doesn't even have a brand name. "It doesn't even speak," he says.

You didn't catch that detail in the catalog. Rae really won't like this.

You sneak another glance at the caged monster. It has turned its attention down to its injured leg, licking the fur slowly above the amputated foot. You want to ask the officer if he knows how the scientists made the monster adult-sized, how difficult it probably was to grow it, what made it a failure, how it lost its left foot, why it was going to be euthanized. You start inputting keywords in your device so that Lyric can help you form the questions, but when the officer starts asking who your supervisor is, you reach out for the employee-purchase forms, the delivery forms and the disclaimer forms, signing your name everywhere the sleepy officer tells you to.

Å

Your mother, once:

"You might remember the eyes of a snake, like the enormous python that you saw at that zoo we went to when you were a child, the thick one that the wranglers draped across our laps so that the three of us could take a souvenir photo. You were so terrified of the python's head that you covered your eyes and howled nonstop from a dozen yards away until the photo was taken without you.

"Or you might remember the eyes of the cat your father adopted for you, because your doctor had suggested that having a pet might help you adjust better to new sensory experiences. A dog was out of the question, since barking of any sort hit your ears like a boxer's gloves. The cat was an almost fully grown tabby, and I held her in my arms almost as often as I held you. It was soft and warm and furry, and you fed it and even tried conversing with it—it meowed at you and you babbled phrases back—but once, it sat on your lap and gazed at your face for a long time, and it unnerved you so much that you never let it sit on your lap again."

☖

The online community you belong to have a name for people like that releasing officer, and even for your late parents, Rae, and most of your co-workers. NT, they're called. You're not sure exactly what makes someone NT—people who don't quite get you, maybe? Who either don't have much patience for you, or worry too much about you? A lot of your virtual acquaintances post lengthy essays that not even Lyric can help you understand, but there's also a good number of image-based posts, and in these threads you participate regularly, linking photos and videos you enjoy, and even the occasional painting you manage to finish.

Riding home on the company's service transport, you have just latched onto the transport's network to surf image threads when Rae attempts to video-call again. Travel time these days takes a couple of hours because of the heavy traffic further worsened by the recent accidental derailing of one of the metro trains. Lyric highlights keywords in the news sites so that you can understand the gist: "Poor maintenance, diverted funds," says Lyric. The transport crawls onto the expressway as you finally decide to accept the call.

"Hi, Rae."

Rae's lovely face is red with emotion. "Why haven't you been answering my calls?"

Why-questions are the hardest to answer any given day, but not as hard as it is this moment. On the one hand you have missed your morning sessions with her, missed how patiently she waited for your sentences to unfold, how skillfully she feigned interest in the random videos of your favorite animals or favorite singers or favorite cooking shows just so you can get it all out of your system and focus on the day's work. On the other hand...

Finally you say, "Afraid."

"Afraid? Of what?"

"Rae."

She catches her breath at this, and then calms down. "Fine, I won't be angry. I just wanted to tell you that you shouldn't get that item. It's a waste of your money. Do not buy it, understand?"

"Why?" you ask. Lyric corrects you: "Why not?"

"It's marked as damaged! That means it's a failure, that it didn't turn out the way it was supposed to. And it's almost as big as an adult human—how would you be able to control it?"

Lyric identifies the keywords you have been looking for, and you ask Rae, "What was it supposed to be?"

"A menagerie resident, according to the details you sent me. But if it's damaged and now for sale at a discount, that means the original clients didn't want them anymore, and how badly must it have turned out to be discarded? These Animals are so expensive to make, especially the experimental ones." She widens her eyes at you—her virtual way of holding your hands. "Look, the point is, it wasn't designed to speak or interact like the other items were, so what good is it to you? You need something else. Something like my niece's parrot. Or the cat types—but not the dogs because they still bark and I know you hate the sound. But something you can hug and talk to and bring to family reunions. You understand? Or better yet, wait for me, I'll be back in a few days."

With effort you avert your eyes. "Sorry. Didn't wait." When she doesn't reply, you repeat, still without looking at the screen, "Sorry, Rae."

You raise your head to meet her gaze, and it is a stony one, the kind that tells you she is trying very hard not to explode. She says, "You are already so bad with money and then you do this."

When your mother died, the only person you could bother about it was Rae. You knocked on the door of her office and showed her the papers your mother had left behind: a life insurance policy, pre-paid funeral arrangements, the deed to the tiny rowhouse that was all she could afford for you and her to live in after having paid off your deceased father's hospital bills. Rae stared at you with those big bright eyes of hers and then wrapped her arms around you tightly. Because you could not explain the immensity of your grief, you spent the next twenty minutes quietly breathing in her perfume as you wept.

You want to remember it now, that scent. "Sorry, Rae."

"You know you got a bad deal, right?" She sighs. "Fine. I'm not mad. I'll see you once I get back."

For the rest of the ride you gaze out the transport. Traffic becomes slightly lighter as you go past one of the most exclusive villages in the metro. Among several ads being projected near the entrance is one for Cosmetic Companions™ featuring the most expensive item in the regular series: *Dragon Dagger—A Cosmetic Companion™ by Cosmetic Animals International. We engineer the perfect pet for your perfect lifestyle.*

You take a picture of it, and after cross-referencing with the company catalog Lyric declares, "The animal base is no dragon, which is a fictional creature, but a rare gliding lizard once populous in woodland areas of Southeast Asia." In the ad, a mountain climber stretches his limbs up a wall of rock; perched on a ledge just above him to the right is the draco-child, a beautiful, intense look on its scaly face, the leathery membrane stretching from its ribs lighting up like gold and ruby in the late afternoon sun.

You think of your own Animal's wings, of how impossible they are.

⚼

Lyric:

"The keywords you have entered are 'I' and 'damaged', question mark.

"Do you want to ask, *Am I damaged?*

"Do you want to ask, *Have I damaged?*

'Damaged', adjective: *defaced, mutilated, mangled, impaired, injured, disfigured*. Latin *damnum,* meaning *loss* or *hurt.*"

⚼

The delivery men bring the Animal to your house in its narrow cage. The releasing officer comes to oversee the transfer, and before the men remove the cage cover, he plays a holographic presentation enumerating do's and don'ts. Do switch on the electric field around the cage to keep the Animal from reaching past the bars. Don't forget to hold the taser baton at all times within sight of this experimental Animal because it doesn't respond to verbal commands. Do give the right dosage for sedatives when necessary. Do not starve the animal so that it can live to its maximum lifespan of—

Lyric highlights the keywords, and you pause the presentation. "Three years?" The typical Cosmetic Companion™ is good for five to six years before termination is required.

"Less," replies the officer, honest as usual. "You never know with these trial items."

"Foot," you say, remembering the missing hoof. "It's missing. What happened?"

"Oh, the original client needed it less mobile, fast. The drugs took too long to work."

Your heart sinks. "Wings?"

"Technically still there."

They give you an enormous starter pack of specially formulated meals to feed it; you'll have to buy more at the company store to get an employee discount when the supply runs out. They hand you a data stick containing the official Cosmetic Companions™ manual. Finally they show you how to use the baton. It's heavy in your hand as you grip it to trigger the switch. The men remove the cage cover to reveal the crouching Animal, and your hand flaps anxiously, waving the baton. A tiny streak of blue lightning crackles across the tip. You almost drop it to cover your ears, and you notice the cautious way that the Animal raises its head toward you, listening and watching. Its pupils dilate, its veined human hands and jagged fingernails scrabble quietly on the cage floor.

Truly up close, without the shield of fiberglass, the Animal's stench is a cloud so dense you can choke and drown in air.

It is with great difficulty that you convince the delivery personnel to give it a bath before they leave. "Have to see," you tell them awkwardly, trying to explain that they need to teach you the exact steps in bathing the creature without having to reveal that you didn't even learn how to take a proper bath by yourself until you were a teenager, and only thanks to the step-by-step graphics that your parents had to make for you.

They laugh at your apparent lack of common sense as they open the cage and lock a harness-type leash around the Animal's neck and shoulders. It starts to struggle when it realizes that it is being led out of the cage. The baton crackles with blue lightning and it heaves itself up on its hands and leg, hobbling slowly so as not to put weight on the amputated hoof.

You watch as they yank the leash to make the monster move faster. It falls forward on its injured leg with a whimper, the sound simultaneously high-pitched and cavernous. One of the men throws a sack onto the Animal's head. Suddenly its wings vault out—what's left of them—and claws like hunting knives spring from the metacarpals barely a moment before another man strikes the creature with the baton.

"That was close!" The releasing officer laughs in relief as the Animal crumples to the floor. "Didn't know those claws had grown back!"

The men struggle to secure a muzzle around its mouth and to tie its wings. When the seizure subsides, the men drag the beast across the bedroom floor and into the bathroom where they hose it down with soap and cold water. You watch the soap and water drench its fur and run down its scales and around the tattered leather curled tightly on its back and down a tense leathery tail. You do not look at its eyes, nor do you watch them replace the dirty bandages on the amputated hoof. You move away to do something irrelevant, like search for an old quilt that you can put in the cage.

They warn you against untying its wings until you have filed a request for a Cosmetic Companion Vet to clip its claws for you. They switch on the cage's electric field before you can find the perfect quilt, so after they leave you switch off the field and push in your old comforter, summer-yellow despite the years.

The Animal doesn't move, stays down with its face to the floor, so you reach out and brush aside its damp hair (deep and black) to unlock the muzzle. Just as carefully, you untie the knots from its wings.

A flash of leather, luminous black. Your right arm feels the impact—a slicing heat near your elbow, another at the forearm—but the iron bars catch most of it. There is surprisingly little blood, and the cut flesh begin to throb only when you stop staring at the gashes.

The Animal retreats into its cage, and you sit there looking at the hunched form as you staunch your wounds with the bright yellow quilt.

Å

Your father, confessing:

"I told the group that your mother and I were thinking of having a second child so that you wouldn't grow up alone, and that woman with the brother, she said no, we shouldn't, it wouldn't be fair to the new kid. I don't know why, but for some reason we believed her. At that time it was so easy for us to believe what everyone else said, because we didn't know enough not to.

"So we had only you and I didn't want you to grow up. I wanted you to be Peter Pan, Alice in Wonderland, a happy child who was content looking at pictures of animals and listening to music and people's voices. That woman whose brother pulled a knife on their mother, the problem was that he had grown up, he had gotten too big to control. And that's the scarier problem, right? Who controls, whom to control."

Å

It is not at all like Pirate Parrot Polly. Polly is the Cosmetic Companion™ that Rae bought her niece some time ago. Meeting them was one of the recommendations from the company-mandated mediation and counseling you had to go through as a result of an incident that took place not three months after your mother died. The incident involved the layout artist to whom you were an assistant; he had given you an earful about a row of data you had encoded erroneously in the new holograms, and you responded with what Rae called a meltdown. In fact what you suffered was an inexplicable rage at the piles of words that your co-worker had dumped on you, and what you actually threw at him was an ancient stapler.

The first framed photo you noticed in Rae's living room was an old blown up one of herself and her sister taken back when she wasn't quite herself yet: that is, when she was still the younger brother of

Jenny's deceased mom. Brother and sister had the same happy smiles. All the other pictures included little Jenny—baby Jenny with her mother, Jenny and Aunt Rae at a talent show in a special school, Jenny and Polly in a playground. In person, Pirate Parrot Polly seemed unreal even as it squeezed past your knees to run away from Jenny.

Polly was about the height of a toddler—the standard size of a Cosmetic Companion™—but without the clumsiness. It rushed around Rae's apartment playing tag with her niece, tickling her with the fingers on its wings, and cheating by flying to its perch well out of the little girl's reach.

"Polly, come down!"

"Arrr, you come up and catch me!" squawked the parrot. It looked like a mascot in a kids' show with its bright green bird-head and its feathery human child-body, which had on a tacky blue jumpsuit.

"Okay, Polly, up, up," said the girl, standing on a chair.

Pirate Parrot Polly unclenched the talons of its feet and flapped down to the girl, giving her a hug. "It's okay, Jenny, I am here."

Rae was beaming as she turned to you and said, "You know what? You should consider getting your own Cosmetic Companion™. Polly has helped Jenny so much with her speech, her gross motor skills, her sensory processing disorder…"

You stared at the perfection of her lips, nodding as she talked so that she wouldn't notice how hard you were clenching your fists to stop them from blocking Polly from your line of sight. The thoughts in your head then weren't in words, of course, but had you been able to articulate them, they would've come out as, *Why would anyone want a Cosmetic Animal? Pirate Parrot Polly is scary as hell.*

But Jenny looked so happy with her chatty bird friend. Your parents would have bought you one, too, debts be damned, had the Animals already existed in the country a decade ago. And it's likely that you would have been happy too, and you might have even grown comfortable with words—*It's okay, I am here*—but that is an alternate reality that you have no access to, and therefore to fixate on it is futile. The reality that has become yours is one where you exist just outside the realm of language, but the validation of your existence lies within it, and you feel like you must always keep fitting yourself in it somewhere. Sometimes you want to talk to Rae about language—how expansive and liberating it is, and also how limiting. Language is a culture that both includes and discriminates. But images aren't as confining as words, and the way images are manipulated is only as dangerous as words are manipulated, and the point is just that you are tired of having to change just so you can speak the same language as everyone else.

In that apartment, watching Jenny and Polly play, you were seized with a frustration that was impossible to explain. "Rae," you called out, and Rae glanced up from knotting her little niece's hair.

I am here, you wanted to say. Instead you told her that you were hungry, so you and Rae and Jenny shared a reheated pizza while Polly ate vitamin birdseed.

⚨

"Owners of Cosmetic Companions™ are mandated by law to feed their Animals only their special meals. Their food has to remain different from humans', and Cosmetic Animals International cannot be held liable for any Animal behavior resulting from deviating from the law.

"Animal-food only," Lyric rephrases. "No people-food." It repeats this for you each time you run the data from the Cosmetic Companions™ manual. It's a provision in one of the contracts that you signed. You run the manual through Lyric several more times anyway, because your Animal has refused its specially formulated meals for two days, and you still don't know how to get it to eat. It sits in its cage hardly moving when you're around, which is fine; you have not been so foolish as to come too near again. You know it must be weak by now, but when its food arrives it hardly even raises its head. You scour the Cosmetic Companions™ forums but none of the participants own one from the experimental series, and none of the regular types have ever had appetite issues. Obsessed with this problem—and the wounds on your arm, which are at least healing well enough—you have not left home at all, not even to work.

On the third day that the Animal refuses to eat, though, you decide that you need to go outside.

One of your neighbors has just arrived from work. He is just about to open his front door when he sees you walk past, and suddenly he is upon you, regaling you about trains. He talks about trains all the time— he's why you knew about the derailing that worsened the traffic—but you don't really understand much of what he says even as Lyric tries to translate. He talks too fast and you listen too slow. You do know that he is older than you, that he is very good at math, and that he keeps track of how much he has saved each month because he wants to go to Japan someday so he can see the old bullet trains up close. You and him are the only ones in the rowhouse complex who have stable jobs. You don't know yet where you want to go someday.

When he finally disappears into his house, the sunlight has turned golden from the afternoon clouds and the rush hour smog. Even the pavement seems to glow. There is one fracture that you follow, and by the time you raise your head, the sun is lowering itself below the skyline, and you have wandered far beyond your street's transport stop and ended up near the highway. In the distance, perched on the wall at the entrance of the most exclusive village in the metro, is the holographic Dragon Dagger—Cosmetic Companion™ in all its scaly splendor.

Thanks to Lyric, as always, you find your way back home, to where your Animal still won't touch its food.

That night, it prowls into your dream. It unfurls its great wings. At certain angles their unfathomable blackness yields into the red-gold of Dragon Dagger's scales, and at others into the emerald sheen of Pirate Parrot Polly's feathers. Where they are torn, the night begins.

One hoof is still gone, but with the tattered wings stretched out the Animal can still stand, towering, hovering, over the landscape of a disintegrating world: glaciers, magma, swamps opening up like overripe fruit, mountains falling apart and catching the stars. In the starlit destruction you wonder—in the dream—if the monster can do, and become, anything it desires.

Å

Your mother, confessing:

"When you were very young you needed to get rid of almost half a dozen baby teeth, your dentist would strap you really tight to the chair and ask your father and me to weigh your arms and legs down even more so that you wouldn't be able to fight. Of course, you fought all the more. As you grew older, we had more choices—restraints or sedatives.

"It was the same when we had the doctors put a tracker in you. Harmless procedure but you were screaming like crazy. We decided to get you one after I almost lost you in a mall. One moment you were beside me as I was rummaging through the discount bins, and the next you were gone. I combed through every rack of clothing in that huge store hoping you were still, all the while fighting to keep my panic down. I was about to ask the manager to send out the mall bots in case strangers were leaving with you, when one of the sales clerks found you in a changing cubicle. You were dancing in front of the full-length mirror, slowly, studying your hands and arms as you stretched and folded them in time with a melody only you can hear."

Å

Lyric plays their voices for you and translates, highlighting keywords, flashing visual cues to help you get a better sense of meaning and intent. You've listened to the recordings so often that you've half memorized the words. You've even shared excerpts with a few members of your online community, and the verdict has been that it's all "NT stuff. Nothing special."

Which is irrelevant, of course, because while you can't quite understand how it was for your parents, the voices you've captured are theirs, and that alone gives them value.

The recording of your father's voice is the oldest, taken during his last days before you even started using Lyric. The recording of your mother's was made a couple of months before her heart attack. They are the voices of the dead but they are important to you.

You would have wanted to record Rae's voice as well, but in your regular morning sessions she deliberately plays the role of listener so that you are forced to be the speaker. Even in the few other times that you were together outside of work—meeting Jenny and Polly, eating lunch in the canteen, intervening on your behalf after the meltdown—she talked only about Jenny or your work. Never about her and you.

The day she returns from her seminar and visits you is hardly the opportunity you've been waiting for, though. She has learned that you haven't been to work; you find it impossible to meet her stony glare. You decide immediately that you will not roll up your sleeves to show her the bandaged gashes on your forearms. The two of you are quiet as you show her the Animal sulking in its cage; she is decidedly unimpressed, especially when you tell her that it has not eaten since it was delivered here almost a week ago.

In the living room, she goes over your copy of the purchase forms and contract, sighing occasionally at their irreversibility. "The only time it will stop being yours before the designated three-year lifespan is after you've decided to terminate it early," she tells you. "Either way, payment will be deducted from your salary for the next six years—long after it's dead. Did you understand that when you signed your money away?"

"Money," you say, and Lyric suggests the appropriate syntax, "Money did not matter."

You read the disagreement in her face, but what else can you say? How can two people who think so differently begin to understand each other?

Rae leans back in her seat and stares at you. "Can I ask you something? Why were you so dead set on that specific Animal?"

Why, why, why—the hardest question of them all. She waits for you as you prompt Lyric to help you answer it in a way that she might understand.

"Temple Grandin, cattle, humane," Lyric says. Its search yields a quotation about how a person who thinks in words can even imagine that cattle have feelings. You read it aloud for Rae, but she doesn't know the name, and doesn't make the connection.

"Is it because you liked how different it was from the other items in the company catalog?" she asks, her brow furrowed in an earnest attempt to guess what it is that you were thinking. "Or because you thought it would have something extraordinary about it other than its physical strangeness? Or did you pity it for being so damaged?"

You start to flap your hands, and hurriedly she clasps them in hers. "Relax and breathe," she reminds you, her touch soft and kind, but your hands extricate themselves from her grasp nonetheless.

"All right, I'll let you be," she says, a smile of resignation crossing her face. "But only because I still have jet lag. I'll see you at work on Monday, okay?"

"Okay."

"I hope you get it to eat. I'm surprised it's still alive."

You remain seated in the living room for some time after Rae leaves. You let yourself think of hummingbirds, lovely apparitions of which you've only seen pictures and videos. You wonder if hummingbirds are real.

When dinnertime comes, you approach the Animal's cage with two sets of meals. One is yours, chicken and rice. You switch off the electric field so that you can eat in peace two feet away from the iron bars. It can continue to ignore its food, but if it wanted to, it can reach out and take either rice or chicken from your plate. The Animal is lying on its side, immobile from hunger, and its nose twitches as it watches you polish off your food. But it still doesn't touch it's own meal.

"What do you like?" you ask loudly. Its ears twitch at the sound of your voice. You glance at the device in your hand, where Lyric is on standby, and suddenly you think of your father's sincere inflections, your mother's soothing tone. Flustered, you stammer out, "To eat. Eat. What to eat?"

It catches a whiff of your excitement, raising its head a little, nose twitching endlessly. "Eat chicken?" you ask, jumping up to get what remaining meat you can find. Some defrosted shreds of chicken left. You grab a few and push it into the cage gap.

The Animal moves across the floor and uses one hand to pick up the meat. It sniffs it, licks it, nibbles, bites. It reaches for another scrap, and then one wing extends too, clutching another piece of chicken. The flesh in its claws reminds you of your own, and you press down on your wounds, as if to pacify them.

"Don't be afraid," you tell yourself aloud, and the Animal's ears

twitch again, flexing almost imperceptibly towards you.
   It is what it is.
   Maybe you can coax it to live.

"High Handed" by Jane Baker

Previous Page:

The setting is of a busy market place on an alien planet. In the background of the image, there are two suns in the sky, a small flying spaceship, and odd looking buildings and plants. In the middle of the image, a woman, who is wearing a visor and a loosely-draped robe, has her back to the viewer. She is interacting with a small child who is apparently trying to purchase some spotted fruits. In the foreground of the image is the back of the seller woman's stall where there are two other children. In the centre of the image, there is an alien child in a dress, holding a stuffed toy, who has eyes on long antenna-like stems. One of her eyes is looking backwards at the seller, and the other eye is watching the human child next to her. On the left bottom side of the image, there is a human child, who has long hair, is wearing only shorts (no shoes or shirt), and has a prosthetic right arm. This child is standing on their tiptoes, holding their detached right prosthetic arm in their left hand in order to reach a high cage on top of wooden crates that contains a small animal.

Courting the Silent Sun

Rachael K. Jones

Renee and Ismael can never agree about the lights. He wants them off when they make love so the glorious sweep of Renee's skin under his fingers become his whole world. But if he reaches for the switch, she swipes at the dragonfly that rests behind his ear. It peels off easily beneath damp fingers, fluttering clockwork wings and eyes that glow like windows in burning houses. She could crush it if she tried. It is well-made, resistant to water and pressure, sweat and oils from skin and hair, but delicate, full of tiny coiled machines which give him the gift of tongues. She flings it into the air, and it flies, circles the room, and lands again on his ear. Without it, his world plunges back into the watery depths of his childhood, to the time when he lived by eyes and touch and taste alone. When it returns, Renee brushes it off again.

That's not fair, Ismael signs, more playful than angry, because Renee is all magnificent dark curves and soft potbelly and hard obsidian eyes.

When you are with me, Husband, you will live in my world only. Besides, I want to look at you. I am going to do something very wicked. Her gaze is predatory, her teeth hungry on his earlobe, and the lights stay on.

They have made a pact to make love every day they are in space, all thirty days to the war in Vega, because who knows when they will ever get the chance again. Each day, weight reduces as the ship's computer dials down the artificial gravity until it is gone, power diverted to the FTL drive. Halfway through the journey, the process will reverse.

Day one: full gravity. Missionary position on the thin mattress on the floor.

Day five: three quarters gravity. Lateral position, Ismael on top but not crushing Renee. His weight reminds her of an old girlfriend, the smell of strawberry shampoo on the pillow at night.

Day ten: one quarter gravity. He presses her bare back against the chilly triple-thick window that overlooks the void, Renee's hand resting lightly on Ismael's clavicle to buoy herself up against him. It feels like flying.

Day fifteen: zero G. Top or bottom lose all meaning—just hot, damp limbs tumbling round and round each other, a new center of gravity.

Renee has always had her own orbital force. He remembers her from across the bar, all the pilot wannabes vying for her attention, Renee the Ace, the hotshot, the one who could fly circles around all of them. Renee ignoring them. Bored. Swizzling her half-finished beer higher and higher up the side of the glass until it almost boiled over, but didn't. She never spilled a drop.

Renee ordered the chaos. She missed nothing. She commanded a room like a guardian goddess, which was also how she watched the void.

Å

Everyone has an opinion on what Vega should be, who should use it. Some call it a human heritage site. This is what they tell children during astronomy lessons when they pick out that distant star and say, Look! That is the Promised Land, where you can be anything you want. Where you can take a whole island for a private kingdom. Where you will find room for all of your dreams.

Others see economic opportunity, that Earth's great mining vessels might touch down in those distant oceans and fall deep into the rock below, which are streaked through with gold and rare minerals.

Others see a nature preserve. No human should go there at all. The colonies should be dismantled, all traces of settling removed. Vega is no place for a new imperialism.

The Vegans themselves, descended in centuries past from the first colonists, have no such debate. They learned to live in the thin atmosphere and adapt to the new flu strains. They have graveyards for the dead and days of remembrance unobserved on Earth. They pray to gods that never looked upon Sol, and their language is estranged. Now all diplomats must wear the dragonflies to understand them.

It has been ten years since they murdered the last diplomat and returned her mummified tongue in her shuttle, flung carelessly on a long trajectory back home.

Å

In the mess hall, Ismael can always feel the other passengers staring. *They are jealous because we are so in love*, Renee signs.

No, it's because you intimidate them. Ismael is closer to the mark, but he cheats with his dragonfly. Renee doesn't point this out. Instead, she draws him into a long kiss in front of everyone, her tongue probing and lingering in his mouth, uncaring of their stares. Her whole life she has felt them watching her, and Ismael knows she likes it that way.

They always wait until their backs are turned to gossip. Hearing people are like that. They hold their words like drinks in long-stemmed glasses, offered and snatched back after one sip.

I've got to report to Navigation, she signs when he finally gasps and breaks the kiss. *Meet you at our room in three hours.*

In the hallway outside their room, a hearing woman stops Ismael. He remembers her from boarding day.

"I'm Lacy. We're staying next door." She extends her hand. "Me and my husband Ivan."

Ismael, he signs, and the sensors in his gloves signal the dragonfly, which buzzes and speaks the words for her benefit with a perfect accent. He is self-conscious about his voice. He never fully eliminated the traces of his Deafness in his speech, not after all these years.

"Your language is so beautiful," Lacy notes with a patronizing smile that Ismael knows too well. Renee would hate this woman. "How do you say hello in sign language?"

He wants to say *you just wave, you dumbass,* but that wouldn't be politic, and Ismael prides himself on his diplomacy.

As a gift to Renee, he teaches the hearing woman how to say *Nice to meet you,* except he bypasses the autotranslator and makes it *Nice to fuck you*—only a single finger's difference. He almost feels bad about it, until she adds:

"One more thing. I don't know if you realize this, because of how you are—" a slight emphasis, a dismissive twirl of the hand—"but the walls are thin, and sound carries more than you think." She raises an eyebrow significantly, and Ismael hates her for it, but gives her his sweetest aw-shucks Deaf boy smile.

Thanks for telling me, he says. *I'll try to keep that in mind.*

⚛

The Perseus is a military-class warship transporter. There are thirty-six jets tucked in each hangar, each with their own nuclear payload. Renee's jet is the fastest, but only because she is. There are no parachutes aboard. Their landing gear is not tooled to land on an alien world like Vega. There are no radios tuned for communication with the Vegan way stations on the planet's surface, and there are no programs like the one that runs Ismael's dragonfly that can speak their tongue.

They recruited Renee because she is the best. They recruited Renee because she was the top of her class, a decorated hero. They recruited Renee because she has no children to complicate matters, only Ismael. They recruited Renee because the moment the mission was announced, even before she spoke with Ismael, she drove to Central Command, flooring the gas the whole way, and volunteered.

An unspoken truth: Ismael has come with his wife in order to say goodbye.

⚔

Ismael and Renee have marked the passage of the years with notches on the world's bedposts. They like fucking in the strangest places they can manage. It has become their tradition.

On their third date they made love in the space flight training simulator after Renee gave Ismael a behind-the-scenes tour of the training facility: Ismael in the pilot's seat and Renee straddling him, her head bumping up against the controls in the ceiling, gray-socked feet ramming the thrusters. The simulated spacecraft wrecked from orbit, and they scored a 36%, high marks in speed but low in accuracy.

Marry me, Ismael signed twenty seconds after climax, still gasping for breath, but her eyes were rolled upwards, fixed and concentrating hard on the ceiling, so he wasn't sure if her answering *yes* against his back was a response to her question, or something else.

After that, they entered into a tacit game of one-upmanship. There have been Mile-High Clubs and Seventy-Mile High Clubs. There have been close calls at their parents' houses, and at the grocery store. Once they did each other in the closet of an elementary school where Renee had been invited to speak for Career Day. They apologized profusely when the school nurse walked in on them. After her speech, they went back and fucked each other again, taking care to lock the door.

It took all of this before Renee finally convinced Ismael to take off the dragonfly for the first time. It scared him. It still scares him. But with her there to anchor him, it was okay.

⚔

Public Law 170-112—alternately called the *Universal Newborn Implant Act,* or the *Deaf Genocide,* depending on your political affiliation—establishes the right of all newborns to receive a neural implant shortly after birth. If it can access the cranial nerves early on, neuroplasticity will ensure a lifetime of easy access to the brain, should any sort of ailment require it. Paired with the right accessories, it can correct visual problems, take over functions lost in a stroke, or bypass the cochlea to stimulate the auditory nerve directly, should a child be born deaf.

It is this last thing that shattered the Deaf community in two: those who saw wisdom in the law, and those who saw a future without name-signs and visual storytellers. At Gallaudet University, at Deaf Mecca, they argued, and as dragonflies alit behind thousands of tiny ears, some took to the sea rather than allow it to happen to their children.

No one even tried to defend us, Renee once said on the subject, hands trembling in anger. *The hearing-people don't believe there was anything wrong with what they did.* She signed *hearing-people* the derogatory way, high up on the forehead, face mocking. *They could have left us alone.*

Clashes like these are the faults that form mountain ranges. Revolutions arise from smaller disagreements than this.

⚐

Ismael has nightmares where his dragonfly falls from his head, its little legs crooked around its body, its lights snuffed out. With it goes his voice. There is no sound in a vacuum.

An unspoken truth: Ismael is terrified of the void.

Ever since Renee volunteered for the mission, though, his nightmares have changed. There is a mountain range, and from one side, the dragonflies rise in the night like embers in the wind, cross the ridge, and fall like bullets upon the Deaf children below.

In these dreams he catches one in his fingers and tosses it in the air again. It circles, rises, and returns over the ridge.

⚐

You've been pranking the neighbors, I see. Renee giggles and turns the door latch hard behind her so the seal catches.

She deserved it. You'll like her. Ismael is already zipped into the double sleeping bag hooked to the wall so he won't careen into the ceiling during the night. It's supposed to be two one-person sleeping bags, but when the gravity got too low for blankets and sheets, they opened them flat, placed the nylon faces together, and zipped them into one.

Ismael stows his book into the wall locker and kisses her lightly, chastely. Renee is already peeling off her flight suit and working the zipper down the sleeping bag.

Nice to see you, he says.

Nice to fuck you, she answers, rolling her eyes, lolling her tongue.

Ismael cuts his eyes toward the shared wall. *They said we're being too loud.*

Renee's grin is wicked, feline as she shimmies his shirt off and lets it float free into the cabin. *Let's show them how much louder we can be.* She swats off the dragonfly, and it takes flight.

⚐

Ismael's game is code-matching dialects. He loves the unenforced boundaries of languages, the shifting vowels and consonants creeping from palate to teeth to lips, how there comes a point of demarcation where meaning shifts.

It reminds him of genetic drift. A bear and its mate cross a mountain ridge. Many generations later, two distant relations meet. If they are still one species, they can mate. If they have changed, if they are lost in translation, they will clash as strangers.

Why not give the hearing people the benefit of a doubt, Renee? he says after one of her angry monologues. It is day seventeen since launch, and they are drinking coffee in the mess hall.

The time for conversation is over. They lost their chance to call us their own when they tried to exterminate us. Her heat is palpable; even the hearing people have stopped pretending not to stare. *There can be no conversation between two people when one doesn't think the other is human. But maybe they're right. Maybe we have moved beyond humanity. Maybe it's time we just... left.*

This argument has come around and around since they first met.

They have the implant too, Ismael points out. *It's not a concession, Renee. It's... a bridge.*

Well, it only goes one way, then. I've never once seen them make the effort to speak to me in my own language.

Oh, that's not true. Plenty of hearing people try to learn sign. Ismael feels a pang of guilt for the bad-faith lesson to the neighbor woman.

But they don't sign well. Just as a hobby. A condescension.

You're being a little unfair. They're trying. It's hard to learn to sign when you've only ever spoken, Ismael points out. *Just like it's hard to lipread.*

Stop defending them.

You never used your implant, You don't know what it's like. It's useful.

Renee's fingers brush the scar behind her ear, a numb white line in the crease, practically invisible. *No one had the right to modify our bodies without our say-so.*

It only works if you get it young. They wanted us to have the most options.

They could have given you signing. Your signing is sloppy now.

Sorry. But he grins, because he knows she finds the sloppiness charming.

Renee rises, draws him to his feet, folds him into her arms, inhales the sweaty musk of his skin. Then she holds him at arm's length. *Ismael. Listen. What kind of marriage would ours be, if we were not free to leave? It makes the staying matter. That's what the hearing people don't understand.* Her keen pilot's eye glances upon the bright star of Vega out the panoramic viewing port. *At least, not the ones on this ship.*

⚓

On the eighteenth day of the voyage, their ship has reached hailing distance of Vega, and Ismael works in shifts with the other diplomats, trying to make contact. In a closet-sized room off the bridge, he sets his dragonfly to communicate with the broadcaster and calls out into the void for someone to answer him.

No one has heard from the Vegans since they sent back the diplomat's tongue with the declaration ceding their humanity. No one knows what to make of the declaration. It may or may not be true. They closed their ports to trade, cut off all communication. Satellites showed earthen mounds raised over the cities, the residents gone below. Then the satellite feeds went dark, too.

There is a script the diplomats all agreed upon. It drones on repeat, identifying the ship, demanding the Vegans respond to their mother-world, that they end their rebellion and enter negotiations. But when Ismael is on duty, he takes the program offline and speaks for himself. Mainly he tells stories, bright exciting tales sketched in the air, moving through time and space. There once was a sailor on a long voyage. There once was a woman who flew to the Moon. There once were two bears who crossed a mountain range, and when their descendants returned, it was a homecoming. Family long lost, but never forgotten.

If they would only answer, Ismael thinks he could change Renee's mind. But nobody answers.

⚓

Tell me, he begs while making love. *Tell me why you volunteered.*

Renee smiles, slit-eyed, and slides down his chest to nuzzle his belly. *I am a wicked woman. I am going to do something very wicked.* Her head slides lower.

The dragonfly alights on his ear and crawls down the rounded pinna to its customary spot in the crease. At once the soundscape bathes his brain: Renee's ragged gasps, and his answering moans, the distant, droning hum of the engines, voices murmuring through the thin metal panels, and the neighbors pounding on the wall. *Keep it down, would you,* says the woman next door. Ismael flinches, loses concentration, reaches to pull Renee close to his chest.

When she raises her head, her eye flick straight to the dragonfly. She angles him off with an elbow. *Oh, for fuck's sake. You never listen when you wear that thing.*

I do too, he tries to say, but Renee has already cut him off, rolled away, closed her eyes, gone where his hands can't reach her.

Tell me why you volunteered, he signs again to himself, in the dark. Then, clearing his throat: "Tell me."

Λ

He knows. He knows he is going to lose her when they get to Vega. It hits him while the pre-recorded message drones in the little room: he will have to be the bridge. If he can make her love them, this long descent into the void will stop, maybe even reverse.

He waits until they are in the middle of it together, sweat sticking skin to skin. He draws her into a long kiss and holds her there. It isn't hard to find the dragonfly, peel it from behind his ear. He caresses Renee's pinna, feels the little button-sized bump of her implant, and presses the dragonfly there firmly, holding it in place so it won't zip back to its proper spot.

Renee's eyes snap open, wide and terrified. Her lips pull back against the kiss. Her teeth snap shut like a falling gate. She tries to claw at her head, but Ismael pins her arms down. Silenced, she struggles more, now kicking and biting at him, jabbing at all his soft, naked places.

"It's okay," he tries, but she plants a foot in his stomach and forces him away. The dragonfly takes off, circles, and lands behind his ear, and when it does, he realizes she's sobbing.

What the hell was that, Ismael? She signs compact and small, near the center of her body. Her arms and knees curl tight to her middle as she floats away from him.

Oh, it was nothing to be scared of, Love. It was just the dragonfly. He reaches for her, but she shudders away from him.

You knew. You knew I didn't want that.

I just wanted you to understand.

Understand what?

It's not so bad. They're not so bad. I don't want you to do... what you're planning.

Renee rubs tears and sweat from her face, and draws a blanket around her. *And just what am I planning, Ismael?*

Maybe he got it wrong. Maybe he has been wrong this whole time. *I don't know. I think... I just don't want to lose you.*

Renee grabs a free-floating strap on the sleeping bag and tugs her way closer, and he thinks she has forgiven him until she starts working the double-zipped sleeping bag apart. *Well, you're doing a lousy job of that.*

Λ

Day twenty: one quarter gravity. Renee is asleep by the time he gets back from the broadcast station. At least, she pretends to be. In the night, confused by gravity's return, he rolls off the bed and hits the floor in slow motion.

Day twenty five: three quarters gravity. The weight feels like wearing too many clothes. Stuffy. Uncomfortable. Renee waves him off when he reaches for her. *We should rest for the arrival.* The truth is, neither sleeps much.

Day thirty: full gravity. Feeling time slipping away from him, Ismael tries to draw her close when she comes to bed that night.

You're crushing me, Renee says, and shoves him off.

Are we okay?

Of course, she answers, but she turns her back on him and goes to sleep on their last night together.

Å

The morning before the mission, Vega looms outside their porthole window, green and white against the black of space. Renee rises very early and dresses in her dark green flight suit before the breakfast call. Stirred by her absence, Ismael snaps awake just in time to see the door swinging shut behind her.

She never told him she had to report for duty today. They were supposed to spend it together, alone, in case it was their last.

Quickly Ismael pulls on dirty sweats and steals after her down the back corridors of the ship, passing only a few tired-eyed lookouts on their way to their bunks, before arriving in the darkened hangar where all the gleaming jets stand ready for tomorrow's fall into the void. Renee is struggling to load a missile into her jet's cargo hold when his reflection shimmers on the painted metal.

Her lips pull sideways, caught between a frown and gentle grin. *You followed me. You figured it out.*

Ismael searches the deep earth-brown of her eyes, hazards a guess. *You're deserting.*

She rests the missile sideways on the floor. *You make it sound like a bad thing. I call it "stopping a war."*

But Renee, you know what they did to their last diplomat.

Renee shrugs, opens the hatch. *They can take my tongue if they want. I'm not using it.*

What makes you think they'll listen to you? No one on the planet will even respond to our signals.

But you're wrong about that. You should know by now what they've been telling us. Renee pauses to rub behind her ear, looking straight through Ismael like he doesn't exist at all. *They want to be left alone.*

The missiles, then?

She squats down and runs a hand along the missile's silver length. *Can't bomb the colonies without bombs.*

And the Vegans? What if they use them against us?

I guess we'll just have to see whether they're still human or not. But they deserve the chance to decide on their terms.

Ismael's throat tightens. He realizes he cannot make her stay. *Oh, Renee.* He traces her name-sign down her cheek with soft, sad fingers. *Please. Please don't leave me without your forgiveness. I am so, so sorry, Love.* Tears wet his cheeks.

She buries her fingers in his beard and tugs it toward her, kisses him deep, and it feels like a real kiss for the first time since their fight. Ismael's shoulders shake with deep, wracking sobs. When he pulls back, her raking fingers lift away the dragonfly. It buzzes against the cage of her hand, its glowing red eyes set on his ear.

Now you will be in the Deaf world only, until we're together again, she tells him.

In the sudden silence left by the dragonfly, Ismael feels unbalanced, like the void waits just behind his heels. She has cut out his tongue. He leans into Renee's gravity all at once, giving himself into her hands. *I love you.*

I love you, too.

Will you help me load the rest of these? she asks, nodding toward the cargo hold half-full of missiles.

Okay, I will.

In his last glimpse of Renee, she signs *Nice to fuck you* through the tinted glass of the cockpit. Her face is lost beneath her helmet, and her fingers clumsy in thick gloves. He thinks he sees the dragonfly shimmer against the glass, free and loose and frantic to get back to him, but perhaps he only imagines it.

Out the big viewing port, the jet falls into the void like a racing silver dragonfly. It circles once and flies toward the planet in slow motion.

Ismael shuts his eyes. He feels the void rush in all around him, wrapping close like it cradles his Renee. He imagines Vega. Mountain ranges dividing up continents. A civilization long estranged, a city split in two, a tongue divided and unintelligible. A dream of dragonflies pelting through the air, warheads gripped in their tiny little legs, traversing the great mountain peaks. But one dragonfly lifts into the air from Renee's fingertips. It flies high, circles, and zooms back again.

Tell me why you volunteered.

I am going to do something very wicked.

On the bridge, people have marked Renee's desertion, but Ismael slips by without notice in the bustle. He forces himself to walk—not run—to the broadcasting room, where he takes the prerecorded message offline. *Once there was a woman who left, and came home again,* he signs to the planet. Then, just in case, he says it again using his voice, and puts both messages on auto-broadcast. Maybe someday she will try the dragonfly again. Maybe she will signal from Vega. Maybe he will go to her next week on his own shuttle, on a newly invigorated diplomatic mission of peace. Or maybe the armistice will last forever, and no one will cross that mountain range again.

Across the widening distance, the dragonfly calls out for him, pressing to return, its signal locked forever to the numb spot behind his ear. There will be a reconciliation against the fire and ash, against the silence in the void. But someday, they will be together again. He has not forgotten their pact.

And Vega would be an interesting place to make love.

The dragonfly lifts, circles, and does not land.

"Everyday Future" by Tostoini

Previous Page:
The style of this image is abstract. There is a star map at the top of the image. In the centre of the image, a woman is sitting a table that has a steaming mug on it. The floor space around the woman has a repeating geometric tile design. The woman is looking down at a tablet. At the bottom of the image, there is an electronic device on the floor that is fabricating the wireframe outlines of the woman's legs from her knees down.

In Open Air

David Jón Fuller

Soraiya Courchene wasn't sure she'd heard Rotational Captain Genevieve Makwa correctly; but it sounded, as the captain peered at her monitor and held her chin thoughtfully, that she'd said, "Well, here's something new."

In four generations aboard, even in the one-thousand-odd days of that that they'd been orbiting the planet, that wasn't an expression you heard every day. It was the sort of thing reserved for events such as seeing the sun set in open air—something Soraiya would have dearly loved, but knew she would probably not live long enough for.

Soraiya turned to face the captain. She liked her; Captain Makwa usually remembered to look right at her when speaking, and she always welcomed her to the bridge with an old Anishinaabe compliment: "You're so fat!" Which, coming from the captain with her big smile and dark eyes, never sounded like the whispers from some of the other crew that fluttered at the edge of what Soraiya could hear and couldn't; and of course the whispers were meant to prick at her hearing loss as well as her weight. Soraiya, at 60, was long since sick of it. Most of the rotational command crew respected her ability to read the old data files, crusted in archaic monolingual constructions rather than in the current blend of the language they shared more with every new generation. But there were always some who thought it was a waste of time to study anything Prelaunch.

Soraiya cleared her throat. The air on the bridge was more stale than usual and it made her want to cough, but she made the sound mainly to get the captain's attention. Captain Makwa looked up and faced her. Soraiya noticed that she hadn't been looking at the blue/red/white whorls of the planet below, but rather the sensor array they used for tracking meteorites. "It's moving," said the captain.

Soraiya's heart started to pound. "Evasive?" she asked, her fingers itching to engage the thrusters, which hadn't been used since they'd manoeuvred into geosynchronous. A thousand-odd days ago.

The captain might have grinned if it were only a matter of positioning their massive hollowed-out asteroid out of the way to avoid a collision. Captain Makwa sometimes cackled at the thought of something so dangerous, but not this time. "No," she said thoughtfully. "I think it's coming to look for us."

She patched over the data stream to Soraiya's monitor. There it was: not just a tracking signal showing a tiny object headed straight for them, slowly, but a hail. Soraiya recognized the Mandarin text immediately, and the English, somewhat; the third was written in Cyrillic characters, but she had not studied Prelaunch Ukrainian much. The Mandarin had many unfamiliar phonetic characters, and the English dialect before her was very odd.

"What do you think?" asked the captain. Meaning, *Do we wake the rest of the command crew two hours early for this? And is it worth alerting all 435 people aboard?*

"The ID isn't one of the other generation ships," said Soraiya, stalling, afraid of what the rest of the hail signified. "They're saying they're here to check on our 'progress'." Soraiya felt her throat tighten as she spoke; she knew that meant she was talking more quietly, so she forced herself to speak up, which always meant she ended up shouting. No use cursing the loss of her hearing aids; they'd been repurposed into a stethoscope when she was thirty-two, and not all the headsets on the bridge still worked. She called up a sidebar display to check some of their oldest records, and the Prelaunch dating system. She swallowed. "It says they left Earth 28 days ago."

Captain Makwa sucked on her teeth. Soraiya always thought that made her look older than her 46 years. "They got here faster than light. I'd say that was new."

Λ

Things might have been simpler if the captain's rotational duty hadn't ended before the new ship got close enough to dock. For the first time in two generations, the ship might have to halt its gravity-simulating rotation to allow the FTL craft from Earth to couple. The entire population of the asteroid they all called Home was abuzz.

Soraiya spent her off hours with friends chatting by one of the crowded observation decks, huge transparent panels beneath their feet allowing them to watch the planet as it passed by like clockwork. The population of the ship, renamed Home generations ago, had (eventually) unanimously agreed the planet they had journeyed so long to explore should be called They Are To Be Respected. The deep blues of seawater sworled into the white of clouds, the crimson and indigo vegetation seeming like swaths from a painter's brush this far out. The planet rose and set while they watched. Before the hail from the Earth craft Soraiya had enjoyed the spark and argument of discussions over ecosystems, flora and fauna, the wonder of the smells their molecular scanners had detected at ground level and clumsily replicated in their labs. Like most aboard Home, Soraiya couldn't bear the thought of intruding on the planet's surface. The early days of Home's journey, they had grown up learning, were filled with the incomplete attitude that you had to take what you needed and if you didn't have enough, take more or take from someone else. That had worked, somewhat, as they were still mining the asteroid they travelled in for resources to sustain the journey; but when their ancestors (some of them) had begun fighting over them, there had been trouble. Murder. Strife. And, briefly, worse. But they had eventually changed their attitude, adopted a way of life that allowed them to survive in the frigid emptiness of space, and sometimes it took generations to see the best decision. Theirs was not the only way to do it, perhaps; but then they were the only generation ship that had been able to complete the journey.

They would not rush a human visit to the surface of They Are To Be Respected. Even their satellites stayed at a high enough orbit that (they hoped) indigenous life would never see them. That was, of course, at total odds with the Prelaunch goals, which Soraiya now found herself poring over, wondering less *how* the FTL craft had made the journey than *why*.

And while she was a firm believer in leaving They Are To Be Respected untouched and unsettled while they undertook a long study of it—how much of that was bound up in simply not wanting to leave Home, for all of them?—she felt more than curiosity to walk in its wildly coloured forests, rather than the clean but manufactured halls of Home, and to feel on her face the wash of sea spray in the wind, not just the comfortable, stale climate they depended on.

Now the conversations raged over what the new arrivals would look like, why they talked so differently, what news they had from Earth. The younger generation was most excited by this last part. The middle-aged and older, like Soraiya, had suddenly eager audiences for stories handed down. But in her few moments alone Soraiya stared out at They Are To Be Respected and wondered whether their practices of studying the planet from afar for the next generation were about to change.

Soraiya's rotation was staggered from the captain's, the better to transition from one command crew to the next, and she was relieved to note Dr. Mak's shift did as well. She trusted his judgment, given his experience with their sporadic epidemics. But the new captain for this 40-day shift was Kenneth Rodriguez, one of the growing number of the younger generation who didn't hold with leaving the planet below untouched while they studied it. He didn't go so far as to suggest colonizing it, not yet, that was too radical a notion; but many felt a pull from They Are To Be Respected that went beyond mere gravity. Rodriguez's fervour to meet with the new arrivals seemed to go beyond simple curiosity, she thought.

"Can you make sense of what they're saying?" he barked at her in front of the rest of the bridge, assuming she just needed higher volume to understand him. You could tell someone a hundred times that wasn't how your hearing loss worked; that you could hear quiet and loud sounds just fine, in fact very well—it was hearing anything against conversational hubbub of more than four people at once, or the white noise of their forced air system sometimes, that was impossible.

She put up a hand to signal for him to wait—and for everyone else to shut up. They almost never did, so she'd probably end up shouting. The signal from the FTL craft was strong, the words reasonably clear; it was the pronunciation and dialect that sounded foreign. It reminded her of the rigid simplicity of the old English text from early Postlaunch times, without the added Xhosa, Anishinaabe, Kirundi and Spanish metaphors and constructions they all took for granted now. It was like watching one of the uncorrupted old movies, but without subtitles. So she relied more on the automatic transcription of the incoming messages on her screen. "They're asking permission to dock."

"Do they need us to stop rotation?"

She sent the question to them, in Chinese. They'd long since adopted the non-strictly-phonetic characters of the Mandarin script aboard Home, adapting it to new idioms to accommodate 70 languages. As a writing system it was far better than Prelaunch English, and it had taken nearly a generation to replace all the signage and labelling they'd Launched with.

The monitors flashed with the reply back, in Mandarin, something like *Our ships must be at rest for us to dock*. Soraiya wondered if their pilots lacked the skill or their craft the fuel to do it otherwise. Now that it was up close, they could all see the FTL vessel was barely bigger than one of their unused dropships. How had these people crossed so much space so quickly in a craft like that? She knew the engineers aboard Home were burning to know. But she seemed to be one of the few worried about what these people wanted from them.

"Very well then," said Captain Rodriguez. "Let's prepare for zero-G."

The signal went throughout Home, and everyone who was awake—which was all except the newborns and young children, given the excitement over seeing people from Earth—scurried to carry out emergency measures rarely used. Loose items were stowed; sick bay patients and the infirm were assisted to secure beds and chairs; children corralled; and many just grabbed on to bolted-down handrails, unable to tear themselves away from the newsfeed from the bridge.

In twenty minutes they were ready and Home's thrusters slowed its rotation until they lost all sensation of weight; the following three hours as the FTL craft manoeuvred, coupled, and achieved hard seal seemed to last forever and yet take no time at all.

Once the Home technicians gave the thumbs-up on the lock between the two craft, the captain asked Soraiya to let the new arrivals know they would be beginning rotation again. Soraiya did; there was a long pause before the other crew responded, in the affirmative. As Home resumed rotation, the pull of gravity returned. Soraiya wondered, fleetingly, if this were how it felt to enter a planet's atmosphere and feel its welcoming strength. She knew it wasn't; but the desire to feel it put a lump in her throat.

Captain Rodriguez now turned to Dr. Mak. "How long?"

"Depends on what they're carrying," came the doctor's answer. "Could be a few days, could be weeks. We may have to figure out how to feed them while they're quarantined, given the size of their ship."

Soraiya eased her grip on the armrests of her workstation. Why had she been clenching them? She breathed out slowly. Now the newcomers were here and would be dealing with the captain directly, her part in this was likely done.

⚸

For the first few days, she was right about that. The captain took linguists when he went to meet with the strangers separated by the airlock, since they could barely understand the versions of English and Mandarin the visitors spoke. And scanning them for disease, despite their apparent protestations they were "clean" (was that really what they were saying?) proved difficult, as the equipment Dr. Mak used for this had never been fitted to the airlock before, and the process took much longer than it should have. "Probably not taking long enough," the doctor confided to her in her bunk room after the third day of quarantine. "But everyone wants to welcome them aboard. And they keep asking for our research."

At that Soraiya's stomach went cold. She offered him more tea. "Why do you think that is?"

He shrugged. "They seem in a great hurry."

So, it seemed, was Captain Rodriguez. He called her to a meeting on the fourth day of quarantine when she had been rereading the last signals they'd received from the four other generation ships. The one that had been ahead of them, the three behind them, each separated by hundreds of days of travel. For safety, the Prelaunch thinking had been; but while the ships did not then share in the same disasters on the journey by being too close, it meant they were nearly powerless to come to another ship's aid when communication ceased. She thought perhaps there would be something in those communiqués that would shed light on this new arrival; but if there was, she was missing it.

Captain Rodriguez asked her to join him at the airlock. She had to tear her eyes away from the faces she saw through the porthole on the door. There were three people she could see there, from the shoulders up, in white and grey uniforms. A man and a woman glanced at her when she looked in on them. The other seemed to be a man with his back to the portal, communicating with the other ship.

One of Home's linguists, Enrique Hoffman, was with the captain. "Officer Courchene," he said with a nod. "I'm having trouble making out what they're saying, and I'd be interested to hear your thoughts."

She smiled. "What do you think they are saying?"

"They keep asking about fuel, I think, in addition to some other things about food and questions about us."

"Captain, if you would be so kind as to type a message to them?" she said.

"Right." He sent a text in Mandarin to the people in the airlock.

The man who'd been facing away from them turned as the woman alerted him to Captain Rodriguez's message. He began addressing the P.A. link in the airlock, and his voice came through clearly on the Home side. She ignored the sound, the decibel level falling within the range she could barely hear, what most people used for a conversational tone. Instead she read the stranger's lips through the porthole. The accent and constructions were odd, but that wasn't the problem. Listening to his pronunciations were what seemed to be causing Hoffman trouble. The shape of the stranger's consonants were sharper, and his distorted vowels muted, however, when you watched the words he shaped. Soraiya had been reading lips to help her carry on a conversation since before she could read, with or without her long-since recycled hearing aids.

Making out what the man on the other side was saying still wasn't easy. "It's like a mix of Prelaunch English and Portuguese," she said. "He does want to fuel his ship, they've used up more than they expected and he wants to know... how much of, of certain elements we've found on They Are To Be Respected."

"Of course," said Captain Rodriguez. Soraiya tore her eyes from the stranger's face and looked at the rotational captain's. His bearing was upright, he seemed almost to vibrate in his well-worn uniform, and while his mouth was set his eyes shone. "They think we have begun to colonize the planet. Perhaps they think we are merely an outpost."

Soraiya nodded. She hadn't seen any words to that effect from the visitor but she felt the captain had guessed correctly.

"How long did Dr. Mak say the quarantine should last?"

"Twenty-one days," said Hoffman. "He wanted to be able to scan for—"

"Let's see if we can shorten that."

Soraiya's eyes widened. "Sir, what about the risk?"

"I feel the risk to them may be greater. Their life support may depend on that fuel, and I'm not sure we have what they need on Home."

There was more to the captain's words than he was saying. But she realized, he also knew she was watching him.

♟

When the quarantine was ended five days early the newcomers were welcomed into a celebration the likes of which had not been seen aboard Home for a generation. The eight strangers were treated to a feast of all the foods Home could muster; and their stores of rice, dried fruit, nuts, legumes, bread, chicken, pork, and precious spices, even salt, were opened. Two of them, a man with ruddy skin and short, space-black hair and a handlebar moustache, and a woman with brown-black hair, light brown skin and freckles, seemed somehow different from the other six, four men and two women. Soraiya noticed the six seemed to defer to the man and woman, and let them speak for the group more often than not. How long did these people serve as rotational captains, she wondered? If the journey from Earth had been so short, how would such behaviour become the norm? She wanted to ask Past Captain Makwa about it, but she was sitting too far away.

In the raucous gathering with a view to the observation deck, everyone sat on mats and shared plates and bowls with the newcomers, who clearly seemed at turns amused, awed, surprised, and confused, as They Are To Be Respected rose and set.

Soraiya could not hear anything against the conversation all around her; and the spikes of laughter or whoops of excitement hit right in the high-decibel, high-pitch range she heard quite well, and they seemed to erupt out of nowhere, to her; and the sound hurt.

The Earth captain had many questions for Captain Rodriguez, and Soraiya noticed him asking something about meeting in private, away from the noise. She couldn't hear the rotational captain's response, and only caught the nod of his head; his face was directed at the stranger's. But a few minutes later, both stood as if to go get something to drink. But after they got to the edge of the huge room, they kept walking.

Soraiya managed to catch Past Captain Makwa's eye, receiving a big smile in return, which faded when Soraiya stood and seemed unwilling to speak. She didn't want to draw attention to herself, it was bad enough feeling like she was missing everything said by people when she wasn't watching them. But then she noticed two of the other visitors had left their mats, and another was carefully rising and working his way through the crowd. The remaining four, including the woman who seemed to be a co-captain, remained, laughing and trying to speak with the inhabitants of Home.

Makwa and Soraiya moved to the exit and once in the hallway, closed the door.

"You seem worried," said Makwa.

Soraiya nodded. "I think the visitors want something from They Are to Be Respected."

"Fuel, eh? I don't know what their ship runs on but I hear they were asking for our data from the molecular scanners."

"Do any of our dropships still work?" A practice drill was one thing, but Soraiya had never thought about whether it would actually be possible to use one of the vehicles.

Makwa sucked her teeth. "One, for sure. When I was younger my dad worked on the modifications they made, before we got here. There might be a couple, but a lot of them had parts he'd said we needed to add thrusters to maintain orbit."

"I think we should take a look."

"Should I call someone?" Soraiya knew that meant alerting Home's authorities. But then Captain Rodriguez would receive the feed as well. And she didn't want to look foolish. Doubt gnawed at her.

Makwa put a hand on her shoulder. "Let's go for a walk, eh? Just see."

Soraiya nodded.

Together they followed the labyrinthine hallways that lined the outer shell of Home, leading to the dropship bays. Only one had not been abandoned and repurposed for farming. And as soon as they got there, they found the door locked.

Soraiya tried her passcode; her clearance as current command crew was high enough to override.

As the door slid open, two of the strangers noticed them and leapt at them. Soraiya pushed Makwa back and blocked the entrance. They seized her and dragged her through. The door closed and Past Captain Makwa was left outside. Soraiya knew she had clearance to open the door as well; but she hoped her friend would instead sound the alarm and bring help.

The man and woman who gripped her arms roughly didn't give her time to worry about that, instead hauling her through to the hangar, where she beheld a terrible sight. Captain Rodriguez lay splayed on the floor, eyes staring at some unseen corner of the room. Unfamiliar packs of equipment with the same logo as the Earth people's uniforms lay nearby.

"What did you do?" she shouted, pulling against her captors.

The leader of the others put his hands up in a placating gesture—though the expression on his face was hard—and gestured to Captain Rodriguez as he spoke. She couldn't fathom some of the words and expressions he used, but one of them seemed to mean "asleep for a time."

Soraiya was about to retort when the shipwide klaxon blared. She winced at the sudden noise and strained to cover her ears. The two strangers pulled her to the open hatch of the dropship. The captain raised a circular device that glowed violet at its periphery and shouted above the sound of the alarm, indicating Captain Rodriguez again. What would his crew do to the inhabitants of Home, she wondered? Surely Makwa had gotten word to the rest of the crew in time?

The captain signalled to the two holding her and they dragged her aboard the dropship in its launch blister. A fourth person was already at its helm, trying to understand the ancient controls. The captain tapped at the insignia on Soraiya's uniform and then at the pilot's seat. She set her jaw. They all trained on the ship's system, once every 365 days. So while the old writing and displays seemed odd, she knew the routine and they were reasonably sure the ship would still work.

She shook her head.

The captain nodded curtly to one of her captors, who released her arm roughly and disappeared out of the craft. A moment later he returned, dragging Captain Rodriguez's body. The crewman put his hand on the helpless man's throat and squeezed, then looked to his captain. The Earth captain turned back to Soraiya and stared at her.

What had Rodriguez hoped to do? Show off the dropship? Take them to the surface, against everything they had practised since arriving—take nothing, send only drones to the planet, leave as much untouched as possible? So they had meant to continue for at least a generation, until they began to understand more about They Are To Be Respected. But some burned with curiosity to go down themselves. Soraiya felt that same wild hope flare up as she struggled to decide what to do, how to save the captain without compromising what Home was here to do.

There was no other way. "All right!" she shouted, tugging herself to the pilot's seat but keeping her eyes on the captain's face. After a long few seconds, he looked to his crewman and gave an order; the man released Captain Rodriguez's throat.

He gave a order to one of his companions and the man wrote a message in Mandarin on his communicator and showed it to her: *We need elements from the planet to make*—and here there was a new character Soraiya had never seen—*for fuel. Is this ship in proper working order? If it has been sabotaged, you will be held responsible.* The threat was clear.

She replied via the communicator: *The dropship is in perfect working order.*

The captain nodded curtly. Two of his crew went to retrieve the equipment they had brought to the hangar.

⚡

Soraiya felt her ears burn as she sat, for the first time in her life taking control of the dropship knowing it was not a drill—the first person on Home, ever, to do so—and her heart thumped deep in her chest. She was really doing it. She was going down to the planet. She prayed this was the right thing to do. It was reckless. But they would kill Captain Rodriguez if she didn't. But she was so, so curious. But they didn't know enough, yet, about the planet.

She clasped the seat harness with shaking hands. "Secure crew!" she shouted, as per routine, and flicked the dropship's systems to life.

Normally a Home crew oversaw the opening of the launch blister doors, but that could be done remotely from the dropship under emergency protocols. She knew the contingencies.

She pulled a headset on as the captain and the others strapped themselves in. She delayed opening the exterior doors, her hand hovering above the controls and watching the Earth captain, until he secured Captain Rodriguez as well. Then she engaged, ignoring the amplified chatter in her headset from the Earth woman who had elected to be copilot. The outer doors slid open, as they had with every routine practice. Soraiya felt the same thrill she always did, that there was nothing but the emptiness of space beyond. She shook her head and instead of miming the movements over the controls, she placed her hands on the grips and set the dropship free. Out they tumbled, gently spiralling away from Home, the gravity falling away rom their bodies.

It took her longer than during the drills to snap the manouevring thrusters to life. She doublechecked all the systems. Yes, Past Captain Makwa was right. There had been some changes, even to this ship. She breathed a sigh of relief. Perhaps this was the only right thing, or perhaps the best of bad choices she could make.

The Earth copilot had given up asking her questions through the headset. Soraiya saw a message from the woman flash on her screen in Mandarin. *Can you land this and get us back to our ship.*

Soraiya glanced at the copilot, whose cheeks were flat and glistened with nervous sweat. What was she afraid of? Her captain? Death? Or was it something they'd left behind on Earth? Soraiya replied, *The ship is in perfect working order.*

The descent was unlike anything she had ever experienced. The copilot was an able assistant, given she was still trying to adapt to the archaic interfaces and controls, but since there was no time to type out their communication with each other she and Soraiya were essentially acting alone. The vibrating roar of atmosphere against the armoured hull felt like an interminable grind of stone on stone, as if They Are To Be Respected meant to crush them for their intrusion. Soraiya whispered a brief prayer. *Do what you must. I will protect you.*

She could not spare a look away from her console to see whether Captain Rodriguez was all right, but she hoped he was. She hoped the rest of the inhabitants of Home were, as well.

⚓

The harder part, of course, was landing.

The purple-pink of the landscape, the white froth of clouds, and deep blue of the oceans rushed up to greet them frighteningly fast, and Soraiya deployed the chutes at the appropriate altitude, noting the prevailing wind at this part of the southern hemisphere matched what their satellites and scanners had indicated. As their speed decreased and the atmosphere pushed them around, she panicked. The air was so thick; it wasn't like manouevring an exovehicle around Home at all. Keep calm, she told herself even as her knuckles whitened and the sweat on her palms made her grip on the controls slip. *Your people did not survive generations in space for you to die like this.*

The impossibly high branches of pink and red trees reached up as if to grab them. The copilot yelled something through the headset until Soraiya tore it off. "Let me do this!" she shouted back. The dropship yawed as Soraiya guided what was left in the thrusters toward an opening in the forest, a deep purple swath of grass or moss. She hoped it was soft.

THUNK the craft landed with an impact that threw them against the webbing of their harnesses.

Then it was quiet.

Soraiya blinked and unbuckled herself. The Earth captain was already free of his harness and barred the way out. He barked something at her; the way her ears were ringing from the concussion of their landing, she read his lips instead. Something about suits. Protection. She shook her head. "It's fine. We already know we can breathe down here." With difficulty, according to their estimates and rigorous simulations.

He pulled out the circular weapon as his crew unbuckled themselves and stood. Captain Rodriguez remained in his seat but he blinked and raised his head. He grimaced as if suffering a migraine. "What—"

The Earth captain spat out another order, gesturing for Soraiya to open the door and holding his weapon ready. Trembling, she nodded. Part of her—a large part—wished he would kill her with it, so it would not be she who defiled They Are To Be Respected. But that was an evasion. She had brought them down here. She could have deliberately scuttled the dropship by fumbling the atmo entry, burned them all up before getting anywhere near the surface. Part of her hungered to step outside, and see it, breathe it, drink it in. She revelled in the pull of real gravity—they had recalibrated the rotation aboard Home upon arrival, to match what a person would feel on They Are To Be Respected, so that the younger generations would grow up ready when they decided to make planetfall. As it was, Soraiya's joints gave her some grief. But she would take the first steps on the planet. It was more than she had ever dared dream. It felt wrong. But thrilling.

The Earth captain spoke sharply again, to her and then to his companions. They picked up packs of equipment they had brought with them.

Soraiya stepped into the small airlock and secured it. Then she opened the outer door.

The warm wind sworled in around her, playing with her hair. It was unlike the blasting air currents in the long hallways and curved corridors aboard Home; it was so random and fresh and wild. She hesitated for a moment. *I am still aboard the dropship*, she thought. That was both an excuse to stay and an impetus to leave. She stepped out and down onto the surface.

The red vegetation was a dizzying variety of tall red and purple stalks, with leaflike petals adoring the tops, the breeze whistling through them at a high enough pitch Soraiya heard it well. *What other sounds are there here?* she wondered, aching for the first time in thousands of days for her hearing aids.

She began to sneeze at something in the air, even as she marvelled at the touch of sunlight on her face. The Earth captain and his crew marched out of the dropship. Captain Rodriguez stumbled down the ramp after them. They began unpacking equipment and their captain directed them to different points of the clearing. As they took readings and called to each other on what they found, Soraiya helped Captain Rodriguez stay on his feet.

"They, they said they needed to fuel their craft to return to Earth. I said we didn't have any of what they asked for not already tied to life support." He blinked and sneezed as well. "Of course, there is plenty on They Are To Be Respected."

They left much unspoken about his motives. Soraiya's stomach was still in knots over what they had done, what they were doing right now, the sight of the Earth people already plotting and marking and measuring.

"This dropship, it's the same as the other ones?" he asked.

Soraiya nodded. "Only difference is that it was able to get us down here." She wondered what the Earth captain's reaction would be, when they told him.

He marched over to them, holding out a communicator. It showed a message from Past Captain Makwa. "Earth crew have taken control of bridge. Demand safe return of Earth captain and fuel, then they will leave."

"No one will leave," said Soraiya to the Earth captain.

He said something, the sharp confusion clear on his face.

Soraiya gestured for the communicator, and after a moment he handed it to her. She wrote a message in Mandarin, hoping he would understand. "Our dropships are meant only to bring down, not to launch back up. We needed their thrusters for Home. And we decided that we would only land on They Are To Be Respected when They, and we, were ready. If your crew wishes to come down here, they will have to build a new dropship."

She passed it back to him. He read it. She sneezed again, several times. Her eyes had begun to feel sticky from whatever was in the air. The Earth people didn't seem to be as bothered by it.

The Earth captain's face went darker as he read. Then he began shouting at her. He threw the communicator down and grabbed the front of her handed-down uniform, shaking her. Captain Rodriguez pulled one of his arms away. "What did you think?" he shouted at him, as Soraiya covered her ears. "That we would let you just come and take things away?"

The other Earth people were running to intervene, she couldn't tell if they were shouting at her or their captain.

But she didn't care. She stood on the surface of They Are To Be Respected. They had rations to last seven days. Beyond that, who knew? Soraiya knew some of the information Home had collected in its hundreds of days of study from orbit might bear fruit, so to speak. But she suspected they would not have enough time to learn. That might suit the Earth people, she thought darkly; they seemed to like to get things over with so quickly.

The Earth captain was pulled away from her by his crew, one of whom was shouting at him and the others demanding answers or explanations from her and Captain Rodriguez. Through the snot and sneezing and tears clogging her nose and eyes, Soraiya smiled. She would finally see the sun set in open air.

Afterword

Derek Newman-Stille

Accessible Space... the Final Frontier?

We constantly hear metaphors of disability used to describe the "problems" with the world around us: in our **crippling** economy, when we hear that our politicians are **blind** to the issues, how our interests are **lame**, how people turn a **deaf** ear to the real issues. Our media perpetually shows us tropes of disability: the self-loathing cripple, the cure narrative that solves everything, how people with disabilities just need to really try hard to not be disabled and they will become "normal" people...

Our society is perpetually creating fictions about disability, fantasies that serve its purpose, but at least Science Fiction, Fantasy, and Horror are clear about the fact that they are creating fictions when they deal with disability.

This is not to say that our speculative genres are free of culpability. They, like other media, are constantly reinforcing tropes that limit disability, that constrain it within a stereotypical box that marks disabled bodies as tokenistic. Science Fiction is all too inclined to find a medical cure for disabilities. Apocalyptic fiction tends to evoke the horror of the end of humanity by first showing it twisted in the form of disabled bodies. Horror relies too keenly on the idea of body horror and the disgust evoked by the thought of disability or the sight of disfigurement. Fantasy is all to inclined toward the magic cure and tends to delight in perfect, archetypal bodies.

As people with disabilities, we often look into the world and see these archetypes reflected back to us—the world telling us that our bodies are horrors, our erasure from the future since it is a "better place," or fantasies where we can be made able-bodied with a flick of a wand with the assumption that all of us want to be able-bodied. Even our fictions erase us, contain us, and seek to expel us out of this world. So, it is beautiful when a collection like this comes along that plays with the idea that we, the disabled, are out of this world and takes us to other worlds, to futures that consider our bodies, and, most importantly, into fiction that doesn't limit us to genre tropes.

It is too easy for most literature to project its fictions onto the disabled body. We expect it. The rest of our society lauds it (particularly when they can give an award to an able-bodied actor for playing disabled, or to an able-bodied author to really capture the suffering of the disabled protagonist). Our bodies become a site where authors can explore so many of the themes that they enjoy: the quest for a solution, the plot of "overcoming," the character with a past that haunts them and that is etched onto their body,

We, the disabled, have always appeared in fiction, but always pushed into roles as the wise mentor for the able-bodied hero, the cautionary tale for the youthful character, the self-loathing cripple who becomes a villain because he or she wants to be able-bodied. We have always been put into narrative positions that support the protagonist, and I suppose this is why I am so excited about *Accessing the Future*, because it centres the disabled body. It puts us in the role of the heroes and it gives us the depth and breadth of experience that our lives create.

Many of us have spent our lives looking for ourselves in our fiction, projecting ourselves into the pages of our fantastic literature with the hopes of finding a resonance, but have so often been met with disappointment as our roles in that literature are constrained by our bodies, pushing us to the margins and inking over our complexity. Many of us have spent our lives asking: *Where is the braille on that space ship? Why don't they try signing to that alien—is the whole universe really so dependent on hearing and verbal speech? Did the architecture of that space station take into account any diverse mobility concerns? Maybe someone who is not quite so neurotypical could better get into the mind of that entity?*

It is time for us to CRIP the light fantastic, write ourselves into the perception of the future, to push the boundaries of expectations about our bodies, and to shift the way that disability is imagined.

Accessing the Future is so exciting because it imagines new ways to think about access and it invites those of us with disabilities into a generally inaccessible space (whether it be "space" as in "place" or "space" as in "the final frontier"), the writing of our own bodies, our own identities, and our own futures. The range of disabilities invites an awareness of bodily and cognitive diversity and portrays disability as something that is not limiting, but rather expansive, opening up a whole range of new imaginative possibilities and ways of being. These narrators are not meant to be *inspirational* as so many disabled heroes are portrayed in popular ableist media, but are rather *human* and full of the same flaws and complexities of any other character. Not only does this collection play with a range of disabilities, but it explores the intersection of identities, whether between gender and disability, race and disability, or sexual orientation and disability.

While a character's disability does not define them in the stories in this collection, it does permit them nuanced ways of understanding the world. From a character with spina bifida (Nicolette Barischoff's "Pirate Songs") who discovers how societies find convenient ways to hide their social undesirables and hide them away from public view (an issue that perpetually faces those of us with disabilities as our society seeks to erase disability from public perception) to a character with LD (learning disabilties) discovering that societies will use people with disabilities to test technology before marketing it to neurotypicals as enhancement (Sarah Pinsker's "Pay Attention"), to exploring how the neuroplasticity of disability allows us to better explore possibilities that are unthought of by the neurotypical able-bodied mind (Jack Hollis Marr's "into the waters i rode down"), the disabilities of these characters invite new ways of exploring the world.

Technology is not portrayed in these stories as it is in so many scifi stories by non-disabled people as a "cure all," but is instead in a nuanced relationship to disability. It is questioned, interrogated, and ends up in a space of question, which is as it should be. Our technology should be open to imaginative possibilities and questions. Characters in this collection question whether their essential self is the self that predates technology, or the integrated self that incorporates tech ("Pay Attention"; Louise Hughes' "Losing Touch"). They explore the possibility that technology is an invasive and inadequate way of interacting with others. They question the limits of the fleshy body and our relationship to health care, which has always been problematic. They invite questions about the visibility of our bodies and the use of biometric technology (Samantha Rich's "Screens"; Margaret Killjoy's "Invisible People"). They question pharmaceuticals and our engagement with them and the meaning we can take from our use of pharmaceuticals (Kate O'Connor's "Better to Have Loved"). They explore which technologies are available to us and under what conditions (Toby McNutt's "Morphic Resonance"; David Jon Fuller's "In the Open Air"; Joyce Chng's "The Lessons of the Moon"; Rachel Jones' "Courting the Silent Sun")… and, of course, which technologies are not available to us due to price, restricted use, and limited access. They ask what types of technologies question the limits of what we define as "human" and how far we can push these limits. These are not easy questions, nor do the authors provide simple answers, but rather open up more ways of questioning our engagement with our technology and the ways that it can extend our experience of the world. Technology doesn't become the traditional sci fi fix all, but is instead engaged in a complicated relationship with disability.

These stories explore the tropes that are written onto disabled bodies and disrupt them—playing with the reader's expectation of reading about characters who are vulnerable because of their disabilities, want to be cured, or want social support... and then subverting these expectations, turning them on their heads and disrupting the tropes that have been taken as norms in our society.

Whether battling rogue droids (Sara Patterson's "A Sense All its Own"), negotiating with space pirates ("Pirate Songs"), being fitted with surveillance devices (Samantha Rich's "Screens" and A.C. Buchanan's "Puppetry"), engaging in telepathy or other forms of communication with alien or other non-human beings ("into the waters i rode down"; A.F. Sanchez's "Lyric"), exploring war ("Puppetry") and other types of civil unrest (Petra Kuppers's "Playa Song"; "Courting the Silent Sun"), the stories in *Accessing the Future* create those ramps, braille instructions, sign languages, and neuro-diverse environments for us to engage in a future rich with potential for disability. The future just got more exciting by providing us with an accessible space (the final frontier).

Contributors

Kathryn Allan splits her time between running Academic Editing Canada and pursuing independent scholarship. Her writing appears in both academic and popular venues, and she is editor of *Disability in Science Fiction* (Palgrave Macmillan 2013). She writes about representations of disability, SF, and living with chronic illness on her blog and Twitter as Bleeding Chrome.

☖

Fabian Alvarado is an illustrator, sculptor, designer, scriptwriter... born in the Republic of Glassdavoldovia a long time ago. He has been drawing, painting and sculpting since he was 5 years old, actually he hasn't been able to get any great achievements in any way and he keeps dreaming something impossible.

☖

Djibril al-Ayad is the *nom de guerre* of a historian, futurist, writer and editor of *The Future Fire*, magazine of social-political speculative fiction. His interests span science, religion and magic; education and public engagement; diversity, inclusivity and political awareness in the arts.

☖

L.E. Badillo is a creator whose work includes cover art, interior illustrations, independent comic books and short stories. L.E. Badillo's latest projects and whereabouts can be followed at elbad.net, @elBadArt on Twitter and at elbad.deviantart.com. L.E. Badillo is a member of the HWA.

☖

Jane Baker is a freelance illustrator, longer-suffering wife of a writer, and mother of two far-too-energetic sons. This is her second publication. She likes working on her future garden or hiding in her office to draw or play video games. You can see more of her art at arleea.com.

☖

Nicolette Barischoff was born with spastic cerebral palsy, which has only made her more awesome. Her first story was published in *Long Hidden: Speculative Fiction From the Margins of History*. This is her second. She is very aware of how cool it is to be launching her career with two such kick-ass anthologies. She can be reached via Twitter at @NBarischoff.

☖

A.C. Buchanan lives near Wellington, Aotearoa New Zealand. Their recent MA thesis examined blindness in Wells's "The Country of the Blind" and Wyndham's *The Day of the Triffids* and their fiction has been published in a number of venues, including the 2012 Futurefire.net anthology *Outlaw Bodies*. Their website is at www.acbuchanan.org.

☖

Born in Singapore but a global citizen, **Joyce Chng** writes mainly science fiction and YA fiction. She likes steampunk and tales of transformation/transfiguration. Her fiction has appeared in *Crossed Genres, The Apex Book of World SF II, We See A Different Frontier* and *Luna Station Quarterly*. Her website/blog can be found at A Wolf's Tale (awolfstale.wordpress.com) and she tweets too: @jolantru.

☖

Comebab is an Italian artist in the Art and Science field. A former researcher in chemistry for cultural heritage, and ex-intern in digital humanities at King's College London, she studied painting at the Academy of Fine Arts of Venice. Her works are strongly influenced by stained glass imagery. Find them at comebab.it.

☖

Pandalion Death is an illustrator and pattern-maker rumoured to be as mysterious as the dark side of the moon. Fortunately, you can get to know her better at @pandaliondeath and pandaliondeath.tumblr.com.

☖

David Jón Fuller is a Winnipeg writer and editor, but has also lived in Edmonton, AB, and Reykjavík, Iceland. His work has been published in *Long Hidden: Speculative Fiction From the Margins of History*; *Tesseracts 17*; *Kneeling in the Silver Light: Stories From the Great War*; and *Tesseracts 18: Wrestling With Gods*.

☖

Louise Hughes is an ancient history graduate and time traveller. When she isn't exploring the past with a cup of tea and a knitting project, she writes speculative fiction to travel that little bit further. Her stories have appeared in *Strange Horizons* and *Daily Science Fiction*.

☖

Rachael K. Jones grew up across Europe and North America, learned six languages, mostly forgot them, and now writes from her secret hideout in Athens, Georgia. Her work has appeared in many venues, including *Crossed Genres*, *Strange Horizons*, and *PodCastle*. She is a SFWA member, editor, and a secret android.

⚔

Robin E. Kaplan splits her time between picture books, comics, and genre illustration, and sells her work online and at comic cons as The Gorgonist. She is dedicated to showing diversity in sci-fi & fantasy. Her weekly fantasy web comic, *Ushala at World's End*, can be found at ushalacomic.com.

⚔

Rachel Keslensky writes, draws, and transforms coffee into the cyberpunk graphic novel series *Last Res0rt*, featuring a feline alien vampire and her adventures on a deadly, galaxy-spanning reality TV program, available to read online at lastres0rt.com. Her artwork has also been featured at multiple hacker conferences.

⚔

Margaret Killjoy is a nomadic author and editor who is, as of this writing, based in the Pacific Northwest. Margaret's most recent book is *A Country of Ghosts*, an anarchist utopian novel published by Combustion Books in 2014. Margaret blogs at birdsbeforethestorm.net.

⚔

Vincent Konrad is a cartoonist, illustrator, and writer from Aotearoa. He is also a punk, a dandy, and a bore. His work can be found online by looking for it.

⚔

Petra Kuppers teaches at the University of Michigan and in Goddard College's low-residency MFA in Interdisciplinary Arts. Beyond her academic credits and a book of poetry (*Cripple Poetics: A Love Story*, Homofactus Press, 2008), she has published short stories in British and US journals like *Visionary Tongue*, *Festival Writer*, *Wordgathering*, *Quietus*, *Cambrensis* and beyond.

⚔

Jack Hollis Marr (also published as Jack H. Marr) writes speculative fiction and poetry for adults and teens. His work often tackles issues of gender, sexuality and disability, interlaced with mythic and folkloric themes and rural life past and present.

Ⳟ

Toby MacNutt is a dis/abled, nonbinary queer/trans dancer, choreographer, textile artist, and now author. In hir day job, ze works on arts integration and universal access in secondary and post-secondary teaching environments. This is hir first professional publication. Find hir online at TobyMacNutt.com.

Ⳟ

Derek Newman-Stille is a PhD student researching the representation of disability in Canadian speculative fiction. He is the creator of the Aurora Award-winning website Speculating Canada and runs a show on Trent Radio. Derek has been a juror for the Sunburst Awards, runs the Peterborough branch of the cross-Canada author reading series *ChiSeries*, and has published on Canadian SF in fora such as *Quill and Quire*, *Mosaic* and *The Canadian Fantastic in Focus*.

Ⳟ

Kate O'Connor was born in Virginia in 1982. She now lives and works in the New York area. In between telling stories, she flies airplanes, digs up artifacts, and manages a kennel full of Airedales. Kate has been writing science fiction and fantasy since 2011.

Ⳟ

Sara Patterson was born legally blind but has never let bad eyesight stop her imagination. Aside from writing, Sara spends her free time listening to audiobooks, playing *The Sims*, and hanging out with her two mischievous ferrets.

Ⳟ

Sarah Pinsker is the author of the novelette "In Joy, Knowing the Abyss Behind," winner of the 2014 Sturgeon Award and 2013 Nebula finalist. Her fiction has appeared in *Asimov's*, *Strange Horizons*, *Fantasy & Science Fiction*, and *Lightspeed*, and in several anthologies. Find her online at sarahpinsker.com and twitter.com/sarahpinsker.

Ⳟ

Samantha Rich is a fan of speculative fiction, chocolate-based foods, textual analysis, and history. She lives in the mid-Atlantic with a (bossy) cat and a (nervous) dog.

Ⳟ

Anna Felicia Sanchez is a fiction writer, assistant professor at the University of the Philippines, and parent to a special child with whom she shares an obsession with animals. Sanchez's speculative fiction has appeared in the local anthologies *Nine Supernatural Stories*, *Pinoy Amazing Adventures*, and *Tales of Enchantment and Fantasy*.

☖

Tostoini says: "I studied to be an anthropologist though I always wanted to be an illustrator. Born in Sardinia, living in Milan, missing the sea all the time. My proper name is Roberta Ragona but it's easier to find me as Tostoini. I draw for magazines, ebooks, advertising, websites, exhibitions and also for fun."

☖

JoSelle Vanderhooft is a freelance writer and editor. When not editing, she's putting together anthologies, one of which—*Steam-Powered: Lesbian Steampunk Stories*—was a finalist for the 2012 Lambda Literary Award. Her first novel, *Ebenezer*, was also a finalist for the 2014 Rainbow Reader Award. She lives in Florida.